THE VINEYARD INN

MELODY ARCHER

"This book is the first book in a women's fiction romance series. It holds a tinge of suspense and there is a series long mystery that definitely piqued my interest.

My mind is buzzing with possibilities for the mystery(s) aspect. Our setting is an island town with a group of sisters who all have previous connections and old flames.
I enjoyed the second chance aspect of this romance.

Our characters were sweet and we definitely felt their pains over the past. The author did a good job of creating a whole town and world with all of the characters and their descriptions.

A unique aspect was the inclusion of a newspaper and

having some articles written out within. They added an interesting dynamic to the whole experience.

I'm looking forward to reading more of this series and both seeing how these characters develop and sussing out some nefarious actions, both present and past."
~Michaela

I hadn't read this author before and I'm hooked. Can't wait for book 2 to come out.
Thank you Melody for a trip to Martha's Vineyard, I visited there back in the 90's." ~ Amazon Reader

WANT TO READ MORE SWEET AND CLEAN ROMANCE?

Eliza and Daniel Stevenson's Christmas love story is waiting for you to read and enjoy!

Simply, paste the web address below into your browser window to get your copy of this Free Clean Romance.:)

Go here: **https://memorablefictionbooks.com/pages/ pb-free-book**

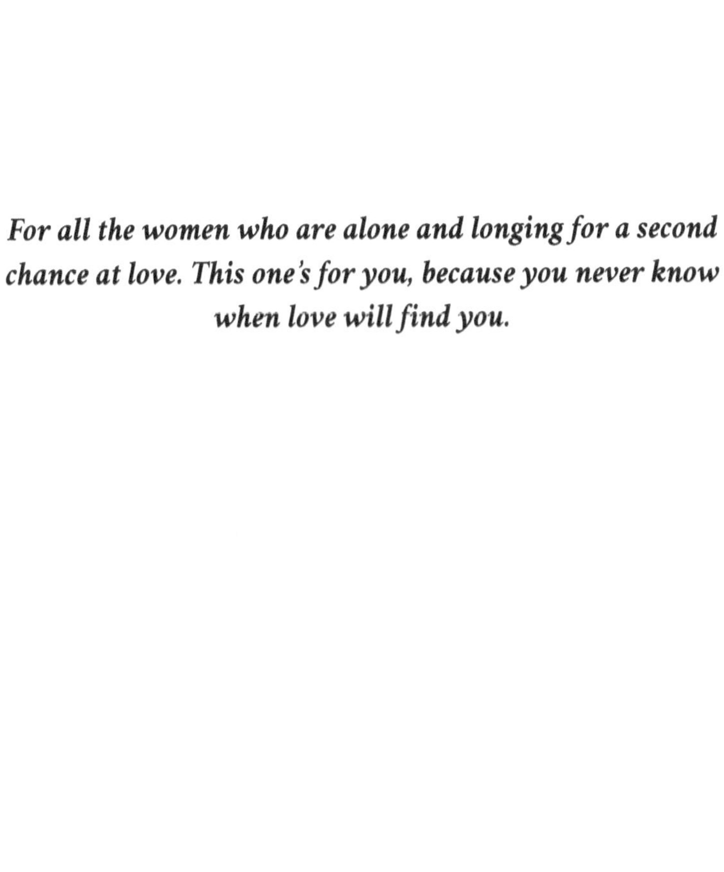

For all the women who are alone and longing for a second chance at love. This one's for you, because you never know when love will find you.

PROLOGUE

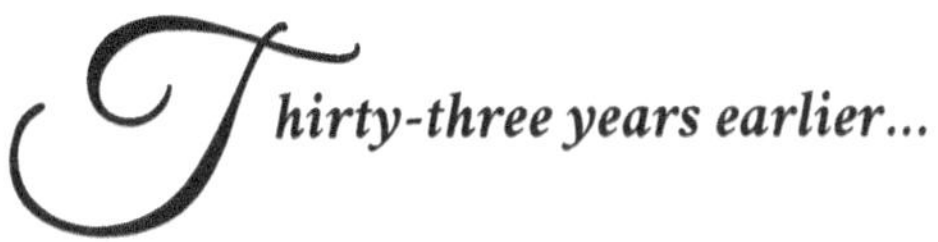 *hirty-three years earlier...*

JONATHAN SPOTTED the girl playing in the sand near the water's edge as soon as he arrived at the beach.

Her long, reddish-brown braid fell over one thin shoulder as she scooped up another bucket of sand to finish building her sandcastle.

She looked to be around twelve years old, close to his own age.

As he stood on the gentle slope just above the beach, he watched other children playing in the water and chasing the ball running through the sand.

His dog pulled on the leash at the loud sounds of laughter from the children.

"Buck, sit." Jonathan spoke to the brown lab who rubbed up against his leg.

At his command, the dog sat on his haunches.

"Good boy." Jonathan rubbed the fur behind his ears, satisfied that the past few months of dog training had resulted in quick obedience.

A warmth filled his belly to have his faithful companion at his side.

Any given day was better when his dog was nearby. He had rescued the lab almost a year ago. He'd been laying in a ditch on the roadside, wounded.

Mother had said if he promised to take care of the dog, Jonathan could keep him. They brought the furry creature home, and Jonathan dedicated himself to taking care of his new pet until he was well.

The dog's teeth stuck out a little. So, Jonathan called him Buck. Ever since they first met, he and his dog were good friends. Trust, loyalty and compassion had been important to their budding relationship.

Those were some of the character traits Jonathan hadn't experienced a lot of in his young life.

Getting to know people had been hard for him because he found it difficult to trust others.

It was the reason he hadn't wanted to come to Mrs. Stafford's cottage today. But his mother insisted. She said it was important for him and his sisters to meet other children who lived on Martha's Vineyard.

Jonathan's mom explained that he and his sisters needed to make new friends now that their family had moved to Martha's Vineyard.

The last place they lived, he and his sisters were too scared that the neighbors would uncover their family's shameful secret.

He rubbed the faded purple bruise on his arm, remembering. There were reasons he avoided any close friendships.

He didn't expect to make friends here on the island either. But it didn't mean his heart didn't hope for it.

A handful of girls, who also looked to be around twelve or thirteen years of age, sank down on the sand to talk with the girl.

Soon, the delightful sound of giggles and girlish chatter filled the air.

Peels of happiness filled the atmosphere around him like a warm, yet unfamiliar, blanket.

A deep yearning erupted from somewhere inside his belly.

He wanted that happiness. He wanted to laugh again. He wanted to hear the sounds of joy coming from his mom and sisters once more.

The sights and sounds on the beach today were reminders of what was missing in his life.

People were drawn to this girl, and he couldn't help but notice. She was happy and carefree, enjoying creating the sandcastle.

Drawn by her joy, he took a step forward, then stopped. Insecurity and fear bubbled up inside him.

He didn't know how to speak to girls, except for his sisters and mother. Talking to girls intimidated him.

Yet, he longed to meet the sandcastle girl.

For the first time ever, he was willing to do something — anything — to push past his fear of speaking to girls.

He wanted to push through his fears so he could meet the beautiful girl with the long, reddish-brown braid.

Sounds of tourists chatting while walking down the beach drew his attention. Most of the people stopped by an old-style house that had been turned into a shop.

He noticed two older women talking to the tourists who stopped by. As the women talked with people, their hands were busy making home-made cold drinks and chocolate coated candy.

Folks walked away with big smiles on their faces, tasting the sugar-filled treats.

He noticed further along the beach was a stand where there were beach balls and other water equipment.

It wasn't long before the beach filled with teenagers, tossing the ball back and forth.

There were about six or seven guys and gals who threw the ball back and forth, creating their own fun game.

Suddenly, one guy missed his turn to catch the ball. It flew in the girl's direction.

The teenager backed up — half running, half walking — when he tripped. His tall, gangly body landed on top of the girl's finished sandcastle.

It lay there on the beach, crushed into dust.

The boy scurried to his feet, picked up the ball, and ran back to his friends.

But someone destroyed the girl's sand project.

Tears ran down her cheeks as she stared at the ruins. The girl remained motionless and silent.

Jonathan's belly tightened in pain. The beautiful face that moments ago was lit up with happiness — now drooped with sadness.

Without thinking, he hurried down the hill, his dog running by his side.

The moment he reached her side, he stopped.

Anger rose inside him when he looked down at the crumbled pieces of the girl's perfect sandcastle.

The girl's tears kindled a familiar protective instinct.

Jonathan decided he would do whatever it took to fix what had brought heartache for the girl.

"S--sorry about y—your sandcastle," he stuttered as his cheeks heated with embarrassment.

Surprised to see him standing there, her eyes widened.

Wiping her wet cheeks against her t-shirt, she replied in a raw voice, "It was the best sandcastle I've ever made."

Jonathan sank to his knees on the soft sand.

He didn't know what to say, so for a moment, he stayed silent. But the pain lingering in her green eyes reached out to him.

"S—sorry it's ruined." When she didn't say anything, he introduced himself, "I'm Jonathan."

"Elizabeth. But everyone calls me Lizzie."

Lizzie. It was the perfect name for a pretty girl. "Lizzie, I will h—help fix your s-s—sandcastle."

Her eyes widened, and she whispered, "You will?"

He nodded, his jaw clamped in determination, willing to do everything he could to help her.

Restless, the dog stirred beside him.

"Buck, sit," Jonathan commanded. At once, his obedient dog walked over to the girl sitting on his haunches beside her.

Jonathan gathered the sand from the broken sandcastle.

"Your dog is so nice, Jonathan." She reached out to touch Buck's fur. His dog leaned in to receive more of her gentle touch.

Unexpectedly, he licked the tears from her cheek.

From his sisters, he'd learned first-hand how good his dog was at bringing cheer to people who were sad.

"Th—thanks." He glanced over to see her wrap her arms around Buck's neck. He would need to give his dog a treat later for bringing comfort to Lizzie.

Jonathan turned back to the sandcastle he was working on building.

Looking around, he noticed the girl had a pail and two carving tools she used to make her sandcastle.

He was determined to make Lizzie the best sandcastle ever.

With all his heart, Jonathan wanted to bring that warm smile back to her beautiful face once more.

"I'll get more water." He reached for the bucket and ran to the ocean, dipping it in quickly to fill it up.

Returning, he saw she watched him with big eyes.

His lips formed a small smile as he looked at her.

Without speaking, he knelt on the sand and began to draw a line in the sand to outline where they would build the large sandcastle.

He began to pile the sand higher, forming it into a large base. After he formed holes in the sand, he poured water inside the holes so the sand would be wet and easier to pack down.

Then he pushed down on the base of the sandcastle, hoping to make the foundation strong.

"I can help." Lizzie began to push down on the sand, following his example.

Jonathan was pleased when he saw a glimmer of joy return to those green eyes. The light in her eyes made him eager to finish rebuilding what had been broken. He began to add more sand and water until the base of the sandcastle was one foot high.

Every once in a while, Jonathan ran to get more water so he could pack down the sand. Soon, he had the castle built. Lizzie helped him carve out rounded towers and pillars at the top of their sandcastle.

"Wow. This is a really great sandcastle." Lizzie's smile widened as she stared at the structure they built together.

"That's because we b—built it together." Jonathan sat back, eyeing the finished project with pleasure.

Turning to look at the girl, his heart swelled with happiness. The brightness in her green eyes made his heart race.

Lizzie sent him a happy smile.

He was about to say something when he heard someone call his name.

"Jonathan, there you are. I've been looking for you." Mary Beth, his oldest sister, walked towards him. Sue Ann, his other sister, followed at her heels.

"You found me." Jonathan turned to his brown-haired sister, who hurried towards him. "What's up?"

"Mother says it's time for us to go. She wants to be home before Dad gets back." Mary Beth stopped when she reached him. Her eyes widened as she looked at what they had made.

"You've been busy. Who's your friend?"

Jonathan smiled. "This is Lizzie. These are my sisters, Mary Beth and Sue Ann."

Lizzie smiled widely. "It's nice to meet you both. Your brother helped rebuild my sandcastle. I love it."

"It looks really nice," Sue Ann commented, but was interrupted by her older sister.

"Jonathan." His sister's firm tone got his attention. "Mom said to hurry. She doesn't want us to be late getting home." Mary Beth's words were hurried.

Jonathan's body tensed.

He knew his mother was afraid that his father would come home drunk. Worse, his mom was afraid if she wasn't home that her husband could stagger drunkenly to the neighbors on either side of them. This would cause worse problems for their family.

It had happened before.

Jonathan jumped to his feet.

It was urgent they return home now.

His hurried words tumbled over each other. "I've gotta go. Nice to meet you, Lizzie."

Buck ran to his side. Jonathan reached down and grabbed his dog's leash.

He turned to go, when Lizzie's soft voice spoke up.

"I'm grateful to you for rebuilding my sandcastle, Jonathan. That was a lot of fun!" Lizzie called after him.

Jonathan turned to watch her for a moment.

His heart somersaulted at her words. She thought the sandcastle was one of the best gifts she'd been given. And he had been the one to give it to her.

His heart swelled with satisfaction and pleasure.

"I'm glad."

Lizzie whispered, "I hope to see you again soon, Jonathan."

He nodded, his heart lurching in agreement. "I do too."

Turning to leave, he turned back, his eyes lingering on her face. The smile she sent him made his heart glow.

He waved, then reluctantly followed his sisters to where his mother waited.

All the way home, his mind swirled with thoughts of the beautiful sandcastle girl.

His new friend Lizzie.

She was the one person who had accepted him right away, in spite of his stuttered words and shyness.

Her presence gave him joy.

Jonathan decided he was going to do whatever it took to see her again.

He couldn't shake the feeling that somehow the sandcastle girl would be someone important in his life for years to come.

CHAPTER ONE

 *izzie*

Elizabeth Stafford Wentworth gripped the recent bank statement with shaky hands.

Two weeks ago, her husband of twenty-six years unexpectedly passed away.

The hospital staff confirmed that he'd suffered a heart attack.

Doctor Jones said he was convinced her husband's death had been caused by the high blood pressure Gray had developed over the last few years.

Stress had been a constant factor in her husband's Boston law office and that carried over into their home life.

She mourned Gray's loss together with their three college-age children.

Lizzie was grateful for family and friends that had gathered around in support.

Every day, she was thankful for her three children. They had been a big help to her during this difficult time.

However, now that the funeral was over, everyone had returned home.

Her children also went back to their busy lives.

Will, her oldest son, had returned to his new job at the law firm in Boston. He'd just graduated from Harvard with a degree in law, following in his father's footsteps.

Annie had just completed her degree in design. She'd been working with a design and marketing firm located in Boston.

Her boyfriend Christopher was almost ready to complete his journeyman exam as a house builder. He worked with his dad's company, working long hours six days a week.

From the look on Chris's face when they were together, he seemed to be getting serious about her daughter.

Jake, her youngest son, had chosen to apprentice with a journeyman carpenter in the area for the last couple of years.

There was always a smile on her son's face as he worked to form a new design with wood.

Jake was like Lizzie's grandfather in that way. When William Stafford hadn't been on his boat, he had been building something. It was the reason her grandmother's house had so many pieces of handcrafted furniture.

A heaviness centered in her chest rose as she remembered losing her parents during her childhood on Martha's Vineyard.

Now her children had lost their dad too.

Lizzie was determined to be there for them.

Yet, even with all the support she had around her, she felt all alone now.

Lizzie was afraid of what lay ahead.

Staring down at the statements in front of her, she quickly noticed that most of the money Gray spent went to pay bills at expensive hotels, restaurants and casinos.

With half fear and half dread, she looked a little closer at the papers in her hands.

Had she mixed up the details?

Searching through the documents again, she read through each statement a third time. The final outcome was still the same.

The stark truth stared back at her in black and white.

Almost all their money was gone.

Only a small amount remained in their bank accounts, which her husband had said were doing well enough only two months ago.

Lizzie sucked in a quick breath at this unexpected revelation.

At this moment, she needed to face the worst truth of all.

Her late husband — the same man whom Lizzie thought she knew inside and out — had kept a terrible secret from her.

Alcohol caused her late husband to spin out of control. The result was that their money was almost gone.

She set the papers down on the table quickly, swallowing back raw emotions, trying desperately to hold her feelings in check.

Lizzie sucked in a quick breath.

Anger flooded her.

His addiction ended up dwindling their finances. Wreaking havoc on the lives of her and their three children.

A nauseating sinking of despair filled her belly. She wrapped herself in a cocoon of anguish.

An acute sense of loss, misery, and heartache filled her.

How could Grayson have allowed this problem to continue? He must have known a financial loss like this would ruin their family.

Lizzie struggled to make sense of the mixed emotions that burned in her belly.

Anger, fear, and a feeling of betrayal at how her husband had secretly brought their family to the brink of ruin.

The bank statement she had in front of her showed there had been regular monthly withdrawals starting two years ago. Her husband had set up the bank account ten years ago.

But she remembered three years ago, Gray had begun acting somewhat strange.

At the time she thought it was simply restlessness.

Now, looking back with twenty-twenty hindsight, she could recall that his actions were more like a man desperate to recover something he'd lost.

In the past three years, there had been more times when her husband came home after midnight than all the years of their marriage combined.

His moods were sporadic, too. Early in their marriage, he was never quick to anger. But something had begun to change in him about three years ago, and since then, the littlest things could set him off.

Gray had taken to drinking more until, finally, he craved five or six glasses of alcohol every night.

When he was drunk, Gray became more irrational and unreasonable. She noticed the spending and gambling began when he started drinking heavily.

She tried to talk to him about what was going on, but her husband would either change the subject or tell Lizzie that he didn't want to talk about it.

Sadly, it had taken until today — shortly after the death of her husband — to finally uncover the truth.

It was the necessity of paying for funeral expenses that forced her to check their joint bank account. Shock numbed her at the sight of how meager their finances really were.

By her estimate, she had enough money to live on for two months if she was careful.

Her husband's debts would need to be paid off from the sale of the house.

Picking up her cup of coffee with a shaky hand, she took a sip.

She only had a short time left to make some desperately needed changes in her life.

Where would she live? Where would she get a job? Who would hire her?

The only work she was good at was that of being a wife and mom. Gray had wanted her to stay home with the children, and to be available to attend his firm's charity banquets, and to host people in their home.

Hosting and cooking, that's all she was good at.

She had no other real skills. She didn't have a college degree or years of experience working outside the home.

Turning to look out the kitchen window, tears rolled down her cheeks as memories surrounded her once again of her dead husband.

Gray Wentworth had swept her off her feet when she had been working as a waitress. He had been in college for his last year of law school when they met.

Against his parent's wishes, he had successfully wooed her. His mother wanted her son to marry a girl from the upper-class society of the Wentworth's acquaintances.

Her new mother-in-law was angry at her son for choosing her. Lizzie remembered Mrs. Wentworth's harsh criticism the first time Gray took her to visit his parents.

She had accidentally spilled tea on a new dress her husband bought her.

"Clumsy girl." Mrs. Wentworth shook her head in disgust. *"I can see my son chose to marry you for your beauty. But your pretty face doesn't make up for the many attributes you lack — like having the refinement of the well-bred ladies from our social circle."*

She wasn't good enough for their son.

Lizzie had struggled with feeling worthy much of her life.

Past failures and mistakes surged through her at that moment.

Memories haunted her from the night when her parents died in the boating accident.

That stormy night, she had failed her father.

Too many times she'd failed. Self-blame and a sense of unworthiness had been her constant companions for all these years.

Self-doubt, unworthiness and a fear of failure had tormented her for so many years, she didn't know how to feel any differently.

When Gray chose her, a poor working girl, Lizzie had been so happy. She felt like she belonged again.

It wasn't long before she fell in love.

Lizzie married him the following year.

Their three children had been born within the first five years of their marriage. Together as a couple, they decided Lizzie would stay at home with the children until they were old enough to go to school.

Gray told her that his law practice was doing so well, that she didn't need to work outside the home. They even bought a lovely home in the Boston suburbs.

She happily took care of the children. She cooked, organized and hosted many events over the years to help further her husband's career.

When their three children were in high school, her husband had set up a retirement account for the two of them.

He had also set up another account where he made monthly deposits. Her husband said that money was for vacations and any extras.

When her husband told her that she didn't need to worry about money, she believed him. He explained that he had set things up so that the bills would be paid automatically each month.

So Lizzie hadn't worried about the bills.

Everything was fine… until the day her husband died.

Then suddenly, her life wasn't fine at all.

Now she knew the truth.

Her life was in shambles.

Not only was her husband gone, but their money was almost gone, too.

Gray's secret drinking and gambling addiction would be sure to ruin her and their children unless she made some serious changes… fast.

Oh, she had known about the harmless bets Gray made with his friends over football games or at racing events throughout the years.

She assumed her husband only gambled occasionally.

But the reality was more sobering.

He had been addicted to alcohol and had irrationally spent their money.

The money in their joint accounts was almost nonexistent.

The fact that she now needed to pay off Gray's massive debts was overwhelming and distressing.

Lizzie hoped the house would sell quickly.

She decided to sell items from their house so she would have much needed cash in hand.

Lizzie needed to be extremely frugal now. Only necessary bills and weekly groceries would be included on her list from now on.

Anything else would be considered an unnecessary expense.

All those extras were things she used to take for granted — like going on a yearly vacation with their family and visiting her grandmother on Martha's Vine-yard — those were expenses of the past.

Those family times held some of the best memories for her. But now she was forced to put a stop to them while she figured out her next steps.

She would need to apply for jobs soon. It would be especially difficult after not working in the real world for over two decades.

Nobody would want to hire a forty-five-year-old woman.

However, she'd been given no choice but to try.

After twenty-six years of marriage, her world had suddenly been tilted upside down.

With a shaky hand, she set down her steaming cup of coffee on the table and stood to her feet.

Wiping a stray tear from her cheek, she walked toward the fridge.

She rubbed her forehead with a trembling hand and looked inside.

How would she be able to find a way out of this situation? It seemed hopeless to her.

She needed to cook. The act of putting ingredients together always calmed her and gave her clarity.

Lizzie spotted a few ripe avocados. She decided to make her favorite guacamole. She put them in a bowl and peeled them and then began to mash them with a fork.

Next, she diced a sweet onion into tiny pieces and tossed it into the bowl. Then she cut the fresh cilantro from her small herb garden and diced it up. Adding lime juice, salt, and pepper, she stirred the ingredients together until smooth and creamy.

Opening a bag of tortilla chips, she dipped one into the guacamole.

Yum.

Smiling, she grabbed another tortilla chip and dipped it in, savoring the flavor on her tongue.

A loud knock on the door startled her.

Lizzie quickly washed her hands and hurried to open the door.

A rush of warmth flooded her belly when she saw her best friend's smiling face.

She waved her hand, gesturing for her friend to come inside. "Tess, this is a nice surprise.'

Tess handed Lizzie one of her favorite specialty coffees she'd picked up at the local coffee shop.

"I took a chance, thinking you might want a friend to talk with today." Tess opened the large French doors that opened to the large backyard.

Lizzie followed her friend outside, joining her on the outdoor patio.

One Mother's Day a few years ago, Grayson had bought her a two-seater wooden swing set that she simply adored.

"I'll bring the tortilla chips and guacamole dip."

"You made my favorite dip? Oh, my goodness. I love being friends with an amazing cook." Tess grinned from ear to ear.

Lizzie carried the bowl of dip, which she had set on a plate, and placed the chips so they circled the dip.

The two of them sat down together and looked out at the spring flowers in the backyard nibbling on their snack.

Spring was in the air and the tulips were beginning to bloom in her backyard.

Turning to her best friend, she sighed and smiled softly.

"I'm glad you stopped by Tess." Lizzie swallowed back emotion that threatened to spill over. "But I'm not very good company, I'm afraid."

"I'm sorry. I am here for you, for whatever you need." Tears pricked the back of Lizzie's eyes at Tess's compassion and true friendship.

Biting her lip, she forced her emotions under control. Shaking her head, she said, "It's not just the fact that Grayson died, it's more than that."

"I did notice the dark circles under your eyes, a telltale sign that you've been losing sleep. Want to tell me what happened, Lizzie?"

Lizzie toyed with the coffee cup, unsure of how to tell her best friend.

"I was going through my financial statements today and was shocked to learn that my husband had an addiction to gambling." She sighed heavily, still reeling from the truth. "Now, I'm afraid I have a huge debt and hardly any money left in our bank account."

Tess reached over and squeezed her hand. "That's an awful thing to find out, right after your husband's passing."

Lizzie nodded. "It is. I feel angry, betrayed, and fearful of the future."

Tess just sat beside her, listening to her vent. In moments like this, a listening ear was exactly what she needed.

"Why didn't Gray talk to me about what was going on?" Lizzie sighed heavily.

Tess sat beside her, deep in thought, as she listened.

Lizzie's voice was hoarse with frustration.

Hurriedly, she wiped a stray tear from her cheek.

Tess studied her for a moment, her brown eyes searching into her soul. "Maybe Gray didn't tell you about it because he was afraid to admit to his wife that he was failing."

"Maybe." Lizzie shifted on the bench seat. "He didn't like it when any part of our life was falling apart. His standards were very high."

Tess shook her head. "If you want my opinion, your husband set impossible expectations for himself as well as for you. Lizzie, it seems to me that you've lived your life trying to please your husband to make him happy. Maybe now it's finally your time to relax and stop pleasing people. Embrace who you truly are. It's your chance to let go of the past and find your own happiness."

She sighed heavily. "Maybe."

Lizzie thought about Grayson and his high expectations. "My husband did have high — and sometimes impossible expectations. But when he made mistakes, I didn't think he was a failure. I would have supported and helped him."

"I know you would have. You were a good wife to Grayson, Lizzie." Her friend's words encouraged her, but that didn't change the dire straits she was in now.

"What are you going to do?"

With a shaky hand, she pushed a stray tendril of wavy auburn hair behind one ear.

"I'm not sure." Lizzie released a sharp, brittle laugh as the shock of her current circumstances pierced her soul. "I need a job. But I don't know what I'd be good at. It's been too many years since I've worked outside the home."

Tess chuckled, slowly shaking her head. "Out of anyone I know, you have so many talents that are simply natural to you. As usual, you're not giving yourself enough credit for who you are. For years, you've excelled at making meals and hosting dinners for Grayson and doing the same for our Book Club."

"That's all I know." Lizzie grimaced. "I don't think that counts as anything special. All Gray ever wanted was for me to wear the elegant clothes he liked to see on me and to be the gracious hostess for him."

Tess snorted. "It's because you made him look good. He had a beautiful wife that everyone adored and he wanted to show you off. You've always been so graceful, likable, and welcoming to people, Lizzie. Your innate charm has made you the perfect hostess."

A warm glow filled Lizzie's heart at her friend's words. She was puzzled. Sighing heavily, she whispered, "I do appreciate the compliment, Tess. But I don't see how any of those things will help me in the real world."

Tess looked over at her. "Of course, those skills are useful. What you should consider is starting your own bed-and-breakfast. That's something you'd be great at."

"I couldn't do so with the state of my current finances." Lizzie liked her friend's idea, but immediately rejected it.

"I must sell my house, Tess. I can't keep it. And I have to use most of that money to pay my husband's debts."

Tess turned toward her eagerly. "Maybe you'll be surprised. Maybe there will be a little money left over to set up a bed-and-breakfast in a different location." Her friend rubbed her chin with two fingers as she thought. "A place like that island where you grew up."

"Martha's Vineyard?" A picture of the island flew back into her mind's eye. "I don't know about that. I never wanted to go back there to live."

"All I'm saying is you would do well at managing a place where folks come to eat and stay the night. You have a natural gift for hospitality."

"Thanks, Tess."

"Just out of curiosity, why do you hesitate at the idea of living back on the island?"

Lizzie still hadn't told her friend everything about her life before she married Grayson and moved to Boston.

"I dated a guy in high school who I really thought was the one." Lizzie shook her head as she remembered. "But it turns out I loved him more than he loved me. I was a very unsophisticated eighteen-year-old girl."

"What happened?"

"I found him in the arms of our school's cheerleader. He was passionately kissing Cecily after a football game. I saw them behind the bleachers." A tic formed in Lizzie's jaw as memories from that day came back to her. "I wrote him a note saying I was leaving."

A soft gasp escaped Tess's lips. "Sounds like you dodged a bullet."

Lizzie shrugged. "It was a long time ago."

She paused as memories came back to her. "It's strange that even after all these years, I still hesitate to return to that place."

"Not so strange," Tess whispered, her voice hoarse. "Love and heartache effects each of us in unusual ways."

"Yes, well, that part of my life is over. Now that my husband has passed away, I don't think I will ever marry again."

Tess glanced at her sideways. "Never say never, Lizzie. I have a feeling there are more amazing friendships and the love of a good man waiting for you down the road. Sometimes, we just have to be patient. Love will find you, my friend."

Lizzie shook her head in disbelief. "Well, I won't hold my breath."

Tess chuckled and sipped the rest of her drink. "We'll see."

As her friend stood to her feet, Lizzie followed. "I need to get going. But let me know how you're doing from time to time, alright?"

"I will. Thanks, Tess, you're a good friend." Lizzie gave her a quick hug, grateful to have her best friend by her side.

After Tess left, Lizzie poured herself a tall glass of lemon water. She began to think through her situation as she walked past the flowers in her large backyard.

The ringing of her phone startled Lizzie out of deep thoughts.

"Hello?" She answered.

"It's Annie, Mom." Her daughter's sweet voice was the

soothing balm she needed. "I wanted to check on you. Are you okay?"

Tears pricked the back of her eyelid. Her daughter's voice was soft with concern. "It's been difficult since your dad's funeral."

"Mom, I'm here for you. Anytime." Annie had always been such a sweet girl.

"I know, Annie, and I am grateful." Lizzie whispered. "I miss you and the boys. Could you come for lunch on Saturday?"

"We'd love to. I'll tell the others." Annie was always so good at getting her two brothers to family events.

Lizzie smiled. "Thanks. See you then, dear."

BY THE TIME her three children arrived on Saturday, she had already done a lot of work.

She had organized paintings, jewelry, and other valuables ready to sell and had gotten her resume ready for the following week of job searching.

Her children walked in the door earlier than expected.

"Hmmm, delicious. It smells like lasagne."

Will hugged her and kissed her cheek. His tall body with his long arms reached down to envelop her in a hug. "It's good to see you."

As he stepped back, she put both hands on the sides of his face. He grimaced. Her oldest son had never been one to enjoy hugs.

She swallowed as she stared up at him. His dark brown

eyes and brown wavy hair were so much like his father's. "It's good to have you home."

Jake hugged her, squeezing tight. Her youngest son, however, loved affection. He was always up to some sort of fun, unlike his older, serious brother.

"Mom, it's good to be home. I've missed you," he whispered and kissed her cheek.

"And I've missed you too, Jake." She smiled at the light in the green eyes that matched her own.

"Mom, let me carry the food to the table. You sit down and rest." Annie as usual was ready to take charge. She had always been so helpful.

Lizzie pulled her daughter into a gentle embrace. "Thank you, Annie. That would be nice."

As they sat around the table and enjoyed lunch together, she listened eagerly to their news.

"It's so good to have you all home for a little while."

With all three of her grown children's eyes fastened on her, she swallowed and toyed with her napkin.

"As you know, it's been a difficult week for all of us. Not much else has filled my thoughts, other than the sadness over your dad's unexpected passing and trying to figure out a way to pay these debts." Lizzie's gaze swept over each of them before continuing.

"Dad never said anything to you about it?" Jake quietly asked.

Lizzie shook her head. "No. It was your father that managed our finances. To my regret, I didn't even ask. I just assumed everything was okay."

"What will you do now?" Annie's blue eyes held a sheen of moisture.

"I will need to sell this house to pay off the debt." Lizzie sent them a wobbly smile. "Since the mortgage was paid in full last year, I believe that will take care of the debt. Hopefully, with a little income left over."

Annie breathed a sigh of relief. "Good. But where will you live and what will you do?"

"I don't know yet. I will need to find a job and a place to live, I suppose. I need to put the house up for sale. We'll need to plan a weekend where we can go through your things." Lizzie looked at them.

"We'll talk about it and figure out a time that works for all of us." Annie looked at her brothers.

"That sounds good." Seeing the worry on their faces, she said, "Don't worry, I will be fine."

Jake sighed heavily. "I hope so."

Will sighed in exasperation. "Mom, you should have taken more of an interest in what was going on with your and dad's finances. Maybe then you wouldn't have been left with such a massive amount of debt after dad died."

The words ripped out of his mouth impatiently. "This loss doesn't just affect you, but also all three of us — your children."

Lizzie swallowed, her thoughts jagged and painful.

"I know and I'm sorry, Will." Her voice broke miserably. "You're not saying anything that I haven't told myself at least a hundred times. All I can say is that I'm sorry. I hope you can forgive me."

Will's jaw was set in anger, so similar to his dad. "I'll do my best."

"I appreciate that." Lizzie ached with an inner pain,

knowing it would take time for her oldest son to truly forgive her.

"I love each of you very much." Lizzie toyed with the napkin by her plate as her gaze lovingly swept over them.

"We love you too." Jake replied. Her youngest son had always easily expressed his emotions.

She was grateful. It was the encouragement she needed, especially in the wake of her oldest son's anger.

Without warning, her phone rang interrupting her dark thoughts. Hurrying over to the small desk near the door, she reached for her phone.

Answering, she spoke quickly. "Hello, Lizzie here."

"Oh, Elizabeth. I'm glad I was able to get a hold of you." It was her father's only sister calling. Aunt Eleanor's voice sounded raw. Normally, she sounded so cheerful on the phone.

"What's wrong, Aunt Eleanor?" Prickles inched up her spine as she heard the worry in her aunt's voice.

"It's your grandmother, dear."

She gasped, her thoughts now scrambling as she thought about Grams. "What has happened?"

"Your grandmother collapsed at home. When the ambulance arrived, it was too late." Aunt Eleanor sighed. "I'm sorry, but your grandmother has passed away."

Lizzie stood, frozen, and very shaken.

Her beloved Grams, who had raised her and her six sisters after their parents died, was now gone.

"The funeral will be next Saturday at the Community Church on Martha's Vineyard. Call your sisters and let them know, alright?" Her aunt's words barely registered in Lizzie's ears.

"I will," Lizzie whispered. After saying a quick goodbye to her aunt, she hung up the phone.

Annie hurried over. "Mom, what is it?"

"Our beloved Grams is gone." Lizzie choked out the words.

Without warning, tears began to pour down her cheeks as the shock set in.

As her daughter's arms wrapped around her in a gentle embrace, Lizzie sobbed at the loss of her grandmother. She had been the one person who had loved her wholly and completely.

First her husband died and now Grams was gone too.

Her whole world was shaken to the core.

CHAPTER TWO

"Ashes to ashes, dust to dust." The deep voice of Pastor Tim spoke the solemn words.

A sobering hush fell on the large group of friends and family gathered around the gravesite of Elizabeth Stafford.

Lizzie stood motionless as she watched the casket that held her beloved Grandmother's body, slowly lowered into the cold, hard ground.

A lone tear slipped unexpectedly out of the corner of one eye, trailing a path down her cheek.

Annie squeezed her hand tightly and stepped closer to her side. Lizzie looked over at her daughter, the corners of her mouth turning up in a wobbly smile.

As the pastor spoke the final prayer, warm memories of growing up in Grams' cottage on Sweet Beach Cove filled her thoughts.

It was Grams and Gramps who had welcomed all

seven granddaughters into their home after the tragic deaths of their son and his wife in a boating accident.

Lizzie had desperately clung to Grams' strength when it felt like her whole world was falling apart.

Her grandparents comforted and loved them, their actions affirming the importance of family.

Her grandmother had taught them about so many things. They learned practical details of gardening, canning, and cooking.

However, Grams had also trained Lizzie and her sisters to look deeper inside themselves to see the unique personality and talents in themselves that made them special.

During the years of her often turbulent marriage, Lizzie called her grandmother to talk. After every call she had been strengthened by Grams' encouraging words.

She swallowed back emotion at the loss of the one woman who had been like a tower of strength in her life.

As the pastor spoke the final amen, Lizzie lifted her head to peer out at the many people who had come to pay their last respects.

Grams' long-time neighbor, Jeb Whetstone stood with his head slightly bowed, his black bowler hat in hand.

Beside him stood Miss Sadie. She was a beautiful, black grandmother who owned a small diner on the island — Miss Sadie's Place — for as long as she could remember.

Lizzie noticed Ida Cantrell, wearing a stylish black hat with netting that swooped down over the front of her face, covering her eyes. Her black dress was in the latest fashion as Ida never did anything half-way.

Grams had named Mrs. Ida Cantrell the matriarch of the Vineyard.

Her son Ted Cantrell was the same age as Lizzie's dad. They had been friends, growing up on Martha's Vineyard together. After Dad passed away, Mr. Cantrell had faithfully stopped by Grams and Gramps' cottage often.

Not far from Ted, were her father's other two friends from his teenage years, Bobby Sutton and Jerry Hart.

Her father's friends from years ago, with their wives by their side, had come to Grams' funeral. The thoughtful gesture surprised her.

A warmth flooded her as she glimpsed all the familiar folks from the island community.

So many people had taken the time to pay their last respects to her grandmother. Lizzie was overwhelmed by the way they honored Grams.

Their presence here today, only confirmed what she knew in her heart — Grams was well loved by many.

As folks began to slowly walk away from the gravesite, her eyes landed on the tall, handsome frame of the one man she was hoping to avoid.

Her high school sweetheart, Jonathan Brookes.

A soft gasp escaped her lips at the sight of him. She hadn't seen him in person since high school.

He was busy talking to someone, so she took a minute to let her gaze rest on him. His blond hair was a little darker now, with hints of grey throughout the thick waves. He'd always been tall with broad shoulders, even in high school.

Seeing the way his shoulders and arms filled out the

dark blue suit, he looked like a man who worked out and stayed fit.

The truth was, the boy she dated in high school had become a man who was more attractive now than he'd ever been.

A wave of apprehension swept over her as she watched him.

Anxiety spurted through her veins.

Lizzie looked at him half in anticipation, half in dread.

Right now, her heart was hurting from the loss of loved ones.

She was vulnerable. But she'd always been weak when it came to Jonathan Brookes.

That was the real reason she needed to avoid him.

Just at that moment, he turned his head. Their eyes met and a shock ran through her.

His blue eyes focused on her as if she was the only woman in the world.

The tenderness in his expression surprised her.

She wanted to run away, but somehow her feet were glued to the ground.

Jonathan began walking towards her, his long legs bringing him to her side quickly.

"Lizzie, it's been a very long time." His low whisper caused shivers to run up her arm. "You're looking as beautiful as ever. It's really good to see you."

Her composure was a fragile shell at his nearness.

She chewed on her lower lip and stole a look at him.

The intensity in his blue eyes jolted her heart.

Her pulse pounded.

"It's good to see you again, Jonathan." The whispered words drifted out as if on auto-pilot.

Jonathan whispered, "I am sorry for the loss of your grandmother. She was an amazing woman who was well loved by so many islanders."

Lizzie swallowed hard, but tears slipped down her cheeks, anyway. "Thanks."

He reached inside his suit jacket and pulled out a white handkerchief. With gentle fingers, he dabbed her cheeks.

A shaky smile hovered on her lips as she reached for the soft white cloth.

Their fingers touched, and warm tingles spread up her arm.

Quickly, she pulled away and dabbed the soft cloth lightly on her wet eyes and cheeks. She hoped she didn't have puffy eyes like she usually did when she cried.

Being near Jonathan again brought memories back of their senior year of high school. He had been there to comfort her during that time — the year Gramps had died.

There had been many times she cried on his shoulder.

Warmth flooded her as she remembered.

"I'm sorry." Lizzie's voice was raw with emotion and she wiped more tears away that rolled down her cheeks.

Jonathan whispered calmly his voice thick with emotion. "You don't need to be sorry, Lizzie. Not with me. I'm sorry too for the loss of your husband. I'm sure it's very difficult to suffer so much loss in a short time."

The heartrending tenderness in his gaze was almost her undoing.

It would feel so good to have his arms wrapped around her again.

Suddenly, she became aware of the dangerous path her thoughts were taking her down.

She had to fight her overwhelming need to be close to him.

A warning voice whispered in her head.

She couldn't let herself be drawn in by Jonathan's tenderness. She needed to remember, her husband recently passed away and now Grams was gone.

No, Lizzie was determined that she wasn't going to succumb to this man's charm.

His ability to attract women had been what had forced her to run away from the island in the first place.

The vivid scene of him kissing Cecily Whitticombe behind the bleachers had been forever etched into her memory.

Throughout the years, she'd seen photos of him with many beautiful women on his arm.

As a well-known and successful architect, Jonathan Brookes had plenty of gorgeous women to choose from.

However, she wasn't about to become just another woman in a long line of women in his life.

She stiffened. Looking over her shoulder, she spotted her children talking with their aunts.

Her sister Jane waved at her.

"Thanks for your concern. I'll be fine." She swallowed.

"My sisters and children are waiting for me. It looks like I need to get going." Lizzie spoke the words hurriedly.

Looking into his blue eyes, she could see the conflicting emotions there.

"It was good to see you again. Goodbye, Jonathan." The words rushed out of her mouth and she hurried away from him.

A rollercoaster of emotions rioted within her as she hurried to where her children and sisters waited.

Lizzie struggled to refocus her thoughts away from Jonathan, so she could hear what her sister was saying.

"Miss Sadie has invited Grams' family and friends to her diner for a meal." As usual, her sister Jane had a way of organizing events for the family.

"I don't feel very hungry," Annie whispered as they walked towards their vehicles.

"I don't either. But Grams would have wanted us to show respect to all her friends today. We should go for a little while. It's kind of Miss Sadie to offer to have all of us at her diner," Lizzie commented.

She had rented a vehicle for their short stay on the island for her children and her to drive around.

To fit with her tight budget, they had chosen a small, practical car.

Her son Jake opened the car door for her. Lizzie got inside and caught a glimpse of Jonathan watching her as they drove away.

"Mom, I think you have an admirer." Annie spoke softly as she turned her head in the direction of her mom's gaze.

"No, he's simply a guy I used to know from high school," Lizzie replied, doing her best to downplay the past relationship with Jonathan. She refused to believe after all these years there could still be a chance for a real relationship between them.

"I still miss your father," Lizzie whispered.

Annie turned. "Mom, I know you do. All of us know that. But after you've had time to heal, it would be okay if you dated again. You're still young enough to enjoy many wonderful years with someone you love. Wouldn't you agree, Jake and Will?"

Will shrugged his shoulders, a sure sign that her oldest son was feeling upset at her and overwhelmed with changes in his life.

"Maybe. But only if the guy treats Mom really well." Jake responded.

Lizzie smiled at her youngest son's protectiveness. "Well, you don't have to worry that I'll be dating a man anytime soon. Right now, I'm much too busy trying to figure out how to manage my life now that your dad is gone."

She swallowed back emotion as she parked the car on the street outside the diner.

Looking up she spotted the deep red-colored sign with the words, *Miss Sadie's Place.*

Her sisters had already arrived at the diner by the time Lizzie and her children arrived.

Walking into the place, her eyes widened at the number of people who came. This was a much smaller group of people than had come to the funeral or gravesite.

Miss Sadie was busy behind the counter with her workers finishing the food preparations.

The faces were familiar to her. These people were Grams' close friends and family.

Lizzie spotted Aunt Eleanor and swallowed back emotion. It was both good and difficult to see her aunt face to face because her looks and mannerisms were so similar to Grams.

Aunt Eleanor saw her and came to give them hugs. Uncle Herb and their children followed behind, greeting each of them.

"I'm glad you and your children could come today, Lizzie. I've been worried about you. I'm sorry you've lost two loved ones so quickly," Aunt Eleanor's warm voice whispered in her hair and her arms wrapped around her tightly.

Lizzie relished her aunt's warm embrace, welcoming the comfort only her dad's sister could give.

Tears pricked the back of her eyes, but she hurriedly blinked them back. She refused to dissolve into a teary puddle.

"Hello, everyone." At the warm sounds of Miss Sadie's voice, Lizzie stepped out of her aunt's embrace. She was relieved that Miss Sadie was taking charge.

Miss Sadie came to stand near the table, rubbing her palms on the front of the white apron tied around her generous waistline.

Her workers were busy adding the hot food to containers that were held in a long buffet-style table. The aroma of delicious casseroles, fried chicken and tasty vegetable dishes filled the air.

"I just have a few words to say before we start our meal." Miss Sadie began, getting right to the point. "Today, we're all here to honor the life of Elizabeth Stafford."

Lizzie had always adored having the same name as her grandmother. She hoped folks didn't get confused over their matching names.

Names had always been fun growing up in her grand-mother's house.

When they first came to live with their grandparents, Grams insisted on calling each of her granddaughters by their full names, not realizing that the girls were already using their short nicknames.

It seemed to take a lot less time to use the shortened names of Lizzie, Alex, Jane, Charlie, Jules, Katie, and Torrie.

At that moment, Lizzie realized she hadn't heard a word from Miss Sadie.

Mentally, she jolted her thoughts back to listen to words honoring her late grandmother.

The owner of the diner turned around the room until her gaze landed on Lizzie and her sisters.

"As you know, your grandmother was one of my best friends. Oh, the wonderful chats by the fireplace and the laughter we had." Miss Sadie chuckled, her skin wrinkling by her eyes forming smile lines. "But we had our serious talks too. Often, she would give me wise advice and it came at just the right time, too."

Miss Sadie looked around her diner. "As some of her closest friends and family, you know what a treasure she was to us all."

Everyone in the diner nodded in agreement.

"As we eat together today, let us celebrate and remember the amazing life of Elizabeth Stafford and the blessing she was to each of us." Miss Sadie smiled warmly at everyone in her diner.

Rubbing her hands on her apron, she pointed to either side of the long buffet table.

"Well then, it's time to eat. If you'll all form a line on either side of the buffet table, that will help things go easier."

As folks began to get to their feet, Lizzie moved to the back of the lineup to catch up with her sisters.

"We hardly had a chance to talk since we arrived here." Lizzie stood near Alex and Jane as they filled their plates.

Jane replied as they returned to their table. "There hasn't been much time for us to catch up, dear Lizzie."

Lizzie nodded. "I know there hasn't been much time. We'll need to catch up. Will you be staying for a few days?"

Alex turned her head to look at the older man approaching them. "Right now, it looks like our talk will need to wait. I see Grams' old lawyer is walking this way."

Turning her head, Lizzie noticed Mr. Tobias Adams shuffling towards their table.

Stopping at their table, he leaned heavily on his cane.

Bushy, gray eyebrows were lifted high as his gaze swept over the women seated at the table.

"All you ladies look familiar." The older man's grip on his wooden cane tightened as he looked at each of the sisters. "I am sorry for the loss of your grandmother. She was a pillar of generosity and kindness on the island. We'll miss her."

"It's kind of you to say so, Mr. Adams," Lizzie responded, smiling up at him.

Tobias Adams grunted a response before he went on. "As you know, for years I have been your grandmother's lawyer. A week ago, she asked me to pay her a visit. At that time, she updated her will. Elizabeth asked that as soon as possible, that I would share the details of her will with her family."

Lizzie looked around the table at her sisters, noticing a similar surprise on their faces that she felt inside.

Grams' old lawyer continued, "I thought it might work best for everyone if we met at your grandmother's cottage at nine o'clock Monday morning."

Lizzie looked at her children who nodded. "We'll be there." Looking around at her sisters, she saw them nod in agreement.

"Good then. I'll see you all then." Mr. Adams nodded to them once more and slowly walked away.

Alex tucked one of her auburn curls behind one ear. "Well, this will be interesting. I wonder if dear Grams has any more surprises up her sleeve."

"Yes, I was thinking the same thing." Lizzie nodded in agreement. "I guess we'll find out soon enough."

"SINCE EVERYONE IS HERE, let's begin." Mr. Adams stood in front of the large group of people, holding a large file folder in his hand.

The old lawyer sat in a large chair behind the large antique desk that was next to the wall of books in Grams' spacious library.

Lizzie's sisters sat next to her on one side, while her three children were seated on the other. Aunt Eleanor, Uncle Herb, and their five adult children were also seated in the room.

Grams' lawyer began reading the first few paragraphs

of the will. He spoke first of the details of Aunt Eleanor's inheritance as well as what each of her five adult children would receive.

Lizzie thought there must have been a mistake when she didn't hear that the cottage was bequeathed to Aunt Eleanor.

Finally, Mr. Adams began to speak about the specifics of her last will and testament. "Since my son John and his wife passed away before me, I have decided to give his seven daughters — my granddaughters — half of what was mine, and they will also receive the remaining portion of their late father's estate."

The lawyer cleared his throat and continued. "Starting with the youngest twin granddaughters, Katherine and Victoria. This is what I give to them. To Katherine, I leave your grandfather's collection of historical artifacts and some famous art pieces. To Victoria, I leave ten acres of good farm land by Sweet Beach Cove, where she can raise her beloved animals."

Lizzie wasn't surprised at this portion of the will. Grams knew that as a historian, Katie loved the historical artifacts and art. Her twin sister Torrie loved the animals, which was the reason she became a veterinarian.

"To Charlotte, I give you the boats that belonged to your grandfather and father. Along with those two boats, you will receive ten acres of land along the waterfront located next to my land and cottage on Martha's Vineyard."

Grams' lawyer continued. "To Juliana, I bequeath the small cabin and ten acres of land that is located on cottage land. I hope this will give Jules the inspiration she needs to finish writing her novels."

"To my granddaughter Jane, I leave you all my jewels and heirlooms. As a successful event planner, it's my fondest wish that these jewels will bring an added boost to all your events."

Lizzie knew Jane had secretly admired their grandmother's jewels and heirlooms for years. Grams, as usual, knew her granddaughters well.

"To Alexandra, I bequeath my house located near Sweet Beach Cove community. Its prime location would be excellent for a medical clinic. Alex has been a successful children's doctor in Boston for years, but it is my fondest wish that someday she would move here to help heal the children on Martha's Vineyard."

She overheard Alex's quick intake of breath. Her sister turned and stared wordlessly, first at the lawyer and then at her.

Lizzie was still thinking of Alex's gift from their grandmother when she heard her name.

"Lastly for Elizabeth, I bequeath my cottage and the land that surrounds it. Since her sister Jules received the ten acres of land and the cabin that was originally on cottage land, Lizzie's share of land will be ten acres. My fondest wish is that Lizzie will use her gift of cooking and hospitality to make the cottage into a home that many will enjoy.

Mr. Adams cleared his throat. "My stipulation for my granddaughters is that they must keep their inheritance for one year. If, after that time, they decide to sell their inheritance, then they may."

"This is my last will and testament, signed by Elizabeth Stafford."

Lizzie's breath caught in her lungs.

She stared at the lawyer, speechless. Grams had given her the large, rambling beach cottage on Sweet Beach Cove.

Wave after wave of surprise swept over her.

As a young girl, she had dreamed of living in her grandmother's large beach house.

The truth was that with her finances and life in shambles, the inheritance from Grams couldn't have come at a better time.

But fear clenched like a fist in her stomach.

As much as she was grateful for the inheritance, it meant moving back to Martha's Vineyard.

The island was the one place that she told herself she'd never return to live. It was the one place that represented all the wounds and loss in her life.

What was she going to do?

CHAPTER THREE

Jonathan

JONATHAN BROOKES CRUSHED the layout paper in his hands
and threw it in the nearby trash can.

Grabbing another large piece of sketch paper, he
clipped it firmly on his drafting table. This was the fifth
time he had made big mistakes as he sketched the architectural floor plans for a new client.

His thoughts weren't focused today.

Setting down the pencil, he ran a hand through his
hair.

He walked over to the large window of his business
that overlooked the community business area of Sweet
Beach Cove.

As he watched people walking along the sidewalk and

the cars passing by, his thoughts were on the funeral from a few days ago.

Memories of seeing Lizzie at her grandmother's funeral continued to swirl around in his mind.

Her wide, green eyes had been filled with pain.

Even though she was still as beautiful as ever, he couldn't help but notice the way her black dress hung loose on her slender frame.

He remembered the day her beloved Grandfather had died. It had been their senior year of high school and she got the news just as school finished for the day.

He could still remember her tear-filled words.

"Jonathan, my grandmother just told me Gramps died." *Tears streamed down her cheeks, and her voice shook. "It feels like everyone I love suddenly leaves or abandons me — like my parents did years ago. Gramps was my steady rock. He was the one who always encouraged me. Why did Gramps have to die?*

Jonathan had gathered her into his arms, holding her close against his heart.

He hadn't known what to say, so he held her close, whispering comforting words into her ears.

Lizzie had buried her face against his chest, her sobs shaking her shoulders.

Listening to her loud sobs had stabbed at his emotions like the thrust of a sword. He loved her. It hurt him like a physical pain, to see her in such misery.

Back then, he was determined to do whatever he could to bring a smile back to Lizzie's sweet face again.

Remembering Lizzie's pain at the recent funeral, Jonathan resolved again to do what he could to bring happiness to her.

But there was only one problem. It had been over twenty-six years since they had last seen each other. That last time they saw each other Lizzie ran away because the cheerleader had flung herself into his arms.

That was the exact moment Lizzie saw him. Later she wrote him a note and told him they were through.

Jonathan had quickly followed Lizzie to Boston, after her sister Alex gave him the address. But Lizzie's aunt wouldn't let him see her. After trying for a few days, he was forced to go back home.

He continued to write letters, but she never wrote him back.

A year later, Jonathan had been heartbroken when he heard the news that Lizzie had married someone else.

He ran a shaky hand through his hair, his emotions so full whenever he thought of the only woman he truly loved.

Would she forgive him for past mistakes? Would she give him a second chance to restart their friendship?

The loud ringing of his cell phone jerked him out of his deep thoughts.

"Hello, Jonathan here."

Immediately he recognized his friend Sam's voice. "Hey, man. How's it going?"

"Not so great. I just tossed a bunch of sketches into the garbage. I'm sort of distracted today," Jonathan replied.

Sam's curiosity seemed to get the better of him. "Is it work or a woman that's causing the problem?"

Jonathan chuckled. "A woman. I'm concerned, because her grandmother just passed away."

"Are you talking about Lizzie Stafford?" Samuel

Chadsworth had been his faithful friend since elementary school. He knew all about his ups and downs with Lizzie.

"Yeah. But her name is Lizzie Stafford Wentworth now."

Sam's voice turned somber. "I thought her husband recently passed away too."

"He did." Jonathan sighed. "So she's probably going through a lot right now. I probably just need to forget about her."

His friend sighed. "That's not the Jonathan I know. You need to reach out to her. Ask her if she needs anything — if there's some way you can help."

Jonathan thought about that. "I suppose that would be a good idea. But it's too late. I'm sure she's already returned to her home in Boston. It's not likely I'll see her again for a long time." Jonathan sighed heavily.

"Well, then, you must not have heard the news." Sam lowered his voice mysteriously. "My mother spoke to Jane Stafford when she saw her recently. Jane mentioned that their grandmother was very generous to them all and bequeathed Lizzie the beach house on Martha's Vineyard. It's possible that she will be coming back to the island to stay."

Jonathan sucked in a breath. "That *is* a surprise."

He never thought the girl he loved and lost, would return to the island.

"So, now that I've given you some good news, maybe you can get back to work." His friend chuckled softly.

"Yeah, maybe. Talk to you later, Sam." Jonathan hung up the phone, his thoughts scattered.

Lizzie had been given the large, old Stafford beach house by her grandmother.

He smiled softly.

Jonathan hoped that she would decide to move back to the island. If she did move back home, there would be many more opportunities to spend time with Lizzie.

Jonathan knew he was ready to mend the rift between them.

He longed for Lizzie to accept his apology and give him a second chance.

"Here's the last batch of sandwiches." Lizzie set down the plate that was brimming with an assortment of finger food.

Katie followed behind, carrying a large glass pitcher of iced tea.

The sisters sat outside on the large deck at Grams' cottage that overlooked the sandy beach and waters of Vineyard Sound.

The sweet aroma of purple lilac bushes floated along the breeze, mixing with the familiar scent of sea water.

Lizzie sighed. In some ways, it felt like she was once again a little girl living at her grandmother's cottage.

Running her fingers gently along the lilac bushes that reached the height of the deck's railing, she leaned closer to breathe in the pleasing fragrance.

Reminders of Grams filled the air.

Being back here brought back memories of Jonathan.

The summers on the beach, licking melted ice cream together as they sat in the sun.

How they cooled off in the water and kissed each other until she was breathless.

Stop it, Lizzie. Your late husband just passed away. What are you doing thinking about another man? You need to focus on what's important right now.

Shakily, she sat on a tattered cushioned chair between Alex and Jane.

It was mid-afternoon and all seven sisters finally had a chance to sit down together. Aunt Eleanor and her family and Grams' lawyer had said their goodbyes a few hours ago.

"Thanks, Lizzie, for preparing lunch. As always, it's a perfect meal for today." Jane smiled warmly before taking another sip from her glass of iced tea.

"You're welcome." Lizzie looked over at the sandy beach, spotting her youngest son.

Jake was spending time on the beach with Jane's son, Noah, and Charlie's twin boys, Dutton and Waylon. The boy cousins were in their teenage years and looked up to their older cousin.

Her oldest son had told Lizzie he was expected back at the law office where he worked. He'd left the island soon after the reading of Grams' will.

Annie had taken Jules' daughter Emma to see the museum and bookstores.

"It's good to be together again as sisters despite this sad occasion." Lizzie began. Her gaze swept over the familiar faces of her six sisters seated around the outdoor patio table.

Jules, who sat on her other side, dabbed a handkerchief on her eyes and cheeks. "I miss Grams more than I can say. I have so many fond memories of making pancakes in this house on Saturday mornings. I can still taste the syrup."

Katie nodded. "There were many happy times, but sad days too."

"I know what you mean. We were quite the lost souls when we first came to live here, weren't we?" Charlie whispered, a deep crease forming between her brows as she remembered. "I know it's been years since the boating accident, but being here in our grandmother's house makes it all seem like yesterday."

As the oldest sister, Lizzie remembered how Charlie had cried every night for a year when they first lost their parents. Her younger sister had looked up to her father a great deal. The loss of him had stirred in Charlie a desire to take up his profession as a marine biologist.

"It does seem like yesterday." Katie agreed. "I still remember our first week at Grams' house. She insisted on calling each of us by our full names, not realizing that we were already using our nicknames."

Katie laughed.

"We can thank our mother for our long names. She loved learning about history, which I suppose is the reason she wrote so many historical romance novels. It seems she couldn't help but give each of us names of real queens from her history books."

"Now that I'm older, I understand the fascination. I have the same love of history as Mom did, which I suspect is the reason I chose a career as a historic preservationist."

Katie sighed and ran a finger along the rim of her water glass.

"Each of us girls inherited gifts from our mom, dad, and grandparents." Jane ran two slender fingers down her long, light brown hair.

"Do you remember all those elaborate dinners Grams used to have that included guests like a famous actress, an artist, a novelist, and the governor and his wife? I believe my love of big dinners and event planning was inspired by Grams. I love to make special occasions look beautiful and welcoming to others."

"You're very good at it, Jane." Lizzie smiled warmly at her sister. "Gray told me the elaborate dinner you planned for the partners at his law firm a couple years ago was the best event he'd ever attended."

Lizzie admired Jane. She was always so well put together, organized, and had a flair for planning amazing events that attracted a crowd.

"I didn't know he said that. That's encouraging to hear." Jane's smile quickly turned to concern. "I'm sorry for reminding you of Gray, Lizzie. Is it hard for you to talk about him?"

Biting her lip, Lizzie looked down at her water glass for a moment, not sure what to say. Her face clouded with uneasiness. She wasn't sure what to tell her sisters.

"I do miss him. Our relationship had been going through a rough patch for a few years before Gray passed away. I have a lot of regrets and I can't help but feel a little lost without him."

She looked over at Jane, whose face shone with sympathy.

Lizzie was eager to change the subject away from her dead husband and onto something else.

"How's life going for you girls?" Lizzie glanced around the table until her gaze landed on Jane.

"Noah still misses his father, but we are doing fine. So far we enjoy living in San Diego." Jane sighed.

The family had been shocked when the man who Jane married turned out to have another family in Nevada. Her sister had quickly left him and moved hundreds of miles away.

"It's been over a year now. We've settled in and made a few friends. I miss all of you, though." Jane blinked quickly to stop the tears that threatened to flow.

"I'm glad you are settling into your new home and that you've made friends," Lizzie began. Her heart went out to her sister who had gone through so much heartache.

Torrie started to talk, "I have enjoyed living in Maine. Being employed by a small animal Veterinary Clinic suits me. But I have to admit that Grams' gift of a small plot of land on Martha's Vineyard has a certain appeal to it."

"Dare I ask if there's a man you're dating seriously, that inspires this new plan of yours to settle down?" Katie blurted out.

Only her twin could get away with such a blatant reference to Torrie's three broken engagements and the ensuing move to many different states across the country.

Torrie's cool tone revealed her irritation with Katie. "No, that's not what it means." She turned to look at her other sisters, her lips upturned in a small smile.

"But it does mean I will be seriously thinking about Grams' inheritance and about the possibility of moving back to the Vineyard. Besides, I believe islanders could use another veterinarian with all the small pets folks have around here."

Jules nodded. "I'm sure you're right. And I'm glad you're thinking about it, Torrie. I'm open to the possibility of moving back as well. To be able to live in that old cabin where our parents used to spend their days, is a charming idea. We'll see. I'll need to talk to my daughter about it. There are other factors I need to consider as well."

Charlie toyed with her napkin her eyes aglow with an almost hopeful glint. "I wonder. It's almost as if Grams wanted us all back on the island together. What could she have had in mind, I wonder?"

"Perhaps she was remembering the many times her granddaughters argued while she was busy raising us. Maybe she thought it was time for us to learn how to get along with each other better," Katie whispered, before looking over at her sisters.

Awkwardly, she cleared her throat before taking a sip of her iced tea.

The words aroused old fears and uncertainties inside Lizzie's mind and heart. Not only had she remembered their arguments as sisters but also other details that didn't make sense.

"I think bringing our family back together is a big reason why Grams put her efforts towards bringing us all back to the Island." Lizzie nodded in agreement.

Lizzie cleared her throat, her voice shaky. "It's possible that there might also be another reason Grams wanted us all back here. Perhaps, some sort of puzzle she wanted us to solve."

"I don't know, Lizzie. That sounds a little far-fetched." Unbelief circled Jane's words.

Lizzie nodded. "I agree, it sounds ridiculous. But in the last few weeks Grams was alive, when I would call her, she sounded agitated and worried about something. She never did say what bothered her."

"However, Grams did ask me to promise that I would read through her journals after she was gone. Our Grandmother mentioned she had written notes there for me to read."

"Hmm, that is strange," Jane whispered, a crease forming between her brows.

Lizzie's gaze swept across the table to all her sisters, recognizing expressions of unbelief, worry and fear — so similar to her own feelings.

She wanted to put their minds at ease in some way.

"For now, it's important that each of us take it a day at a time. We'll figure this out together. And try not to worry." Lizzie looked over at Jane, seeing the anxious look in her eyes.

Jane huffed. "Easier said than done, dear sister."

Despite her own worries, Lizzie was resolved to help her sisters.

Maybe Grandmother was onto something when she gave each of them something that would bring them back to the island and to each other.

Lizzie turned to look at her sisters again, stopping at Alex. As usual, her sister's emotions were hidden under a stoic expression. Alex had always been the strong one among the seven sisters.

Alex sighed and tucked a tendril of blond wavy hair behind one ear. "I suppose that look means it's my turn."

Lizzie squirmed where she sat. Alex's tone was laced with censure. They had argued about different issues throughout the years. Today, it seemed her sister was on edge again.

"My life continues to be very busy. I work at the hospital from sunup to sun-down, with only one day off a week." Alex sighed. "Lately, my demanding schedule has been more tiring than usual. But it's going okay."

"What do you think of Grams' will, Alex?" Katie asked.

Alex shrugged, her expression stoic. "I found it surprising. I'll have to think about the house she's given to me. As usual, I will need to write down the pros and cons of bringing my medical practice to the island."

"You might enjoy the slower pace here, Alex," Lizzie said, trying her best to support Alex's idea.

Alex huffed, her hazel eyes piercing as she looked at Lizzie. "I might like it. But I wouldn't get as many perks as I do at the big hospital in Boston. On the other hand, I might like the independence of running my own medical practice."

"With Lizzie inheriting the cottage and Torrie and Jules inheriting land, Alex, if you also lived on Martha's Vineyard, most of us sisters would live near each other once again." Charlie grinned. "It might be fun."

Lizzie smiled at the thought. From a young age, her sister Charlie had always loved it when all the sisters were together.

Alex sighed. "Maybe."

Lizzie knew Alex had never done well with change.

That would explain her lack of enthusiasm about moving to Martha's Vineyard.

She could relate.

Ever since the reading of Grams' will, misgivings had plagued her about receiving her inheritance.

"What about you, Lizzie? Now that you know you've been given Grams' historical cottage, do you think you'll be moving to Martha's Vineyard soon?" Katie asked. As ever, her youngest sister adored this historical house.

"I do love Grams' house, Katie. Right now, I'm not sure about moving back to the island. I need more time to think things through." Lizzie swallowed back emotion.

"Why would you not want to move here? It's the perfect place to live." Katie insisted.

Lizzie blinked back tears a heaviness centered in her chest. "It's difficult. I have so many bittersweet memories."

She hesitated, thinking about their shared tragic past.

"There was so much heartache that I remember about living here. First our parents died along the waterway not far from Grams' cottage and then later Gramps passed away. The final straw was when I fell in love in high school with the man I hoped to marry, but ended up with a broken heart instead."

"When you suddenly left us after your high school graduation, I was shocked and hurt that you'd left us all alone." Alex's sharp tone made Lizzie aware her sister was still angry about situations that happened years ago.

Lizzie swallowed hard. When she spoke her voice wavered, "Alex, I am so sorry. I shouldn't have left you all alone after high school. Looking back, I can understand how difficult that must have been for you."

"You didn't just leave me alone, Lizzie. You left both me and Jane to look after our younger sisters. You left all of us." Alex's jaw was set in determination, her voice cool.

Lizzie flinched at the accusation. It was clear, years of resentment and bitterness had been building over time.

Memories came flooding back.

The misery of that night long ago still haunted her. "I remember feeling so heartbroken that I couldn't think straight. So, I ran away."

Swallowing, her voice broke with an inner pain that still ached in her heart. "But that isn't any excuse for leaving you, Alex, and all of you alone. I *am* truly sorry. And I hope someday you can forgive me." Lizzie paused, her gaze clouded with tears, as she looked at Alex.

"Well, I suppose it's all water under the bridge now," Alex spoke in a softer tone of voice.

"No, it's not okay. I can tell that I really hurt you, Alex. All of you." Lizzie looked at Alex and then to all her sisters. "I am truly sorry. I hope you'll give me another chance to make things right."

"Thanks for that. I forgive you, sis." The beginning of a smile tipped the corners of Alex's mouth.

She nodded, sighing with relief.

"I'm sorry for the misery you went through when you lost Jonathan years ago, Lizzie." Jane's voice wavered. "And, of course, I forgive you. I think perhaps we judged you too harshly and I'm sorry for that."

Lizzie's heart warmed at the apology and soon heard the sentiment echoed by all the other sisters that sat around the table.

"I'm grateful. I feel better knowing that we have

cleared the air between us." Lizzie looked around at the beautiful backyard, thinking of her grandmother. "I believe this is the start of the togetherness that our grandmother was talking about. I hope we see each other and talk more often now that Grams is gone."

"We will, I promise." Jane reached over and squeezed her hand. "And I hope you think seriously about accepting the cottage from Grams and living on the island. I think it would be a wonderful change for you, Lizzie."

"I promise to think seriously about moving here, Jane." Lizzie hoped to set her sister's mind at ease. "But I need time to think about it."

❧

THE LOUD RINGING tones of her phone jerked Lizzie out of a daze.

She got up and grabbed her phone that was on Grams' kitchen counter, scooting around Annie who was washing the dinner dishes.

"Hello." Lizzie slid open the patio door, as she talked.

Tess chuckled on the other end of the line. "Hey, friend. You sound distracted. Is now a good time to chat?"

"Tess, how nice of you to call. Yes, we can chat." Lizzie slid the patio door closed, hoping for a bit of privacy.

Since most of her talks with Tess lately were very personal, she didn't want to chance her daughter or son overhearing them.

"Good. I was worried about you, so I thought I'd call." Her friend's warm concern wafted over the phone line, soothing her mind.

"Thanks, Tess. I'm grateful that you thought of me." Lizzie walked along the wooden deck that encircled Grams' cottage as she talked.

Tess snorted. "Of course, I worry about you, my friend." Then she quickly added. "So, tell me how it's been going with seeing people back on the island?"

Lizzie sighed heavily. "To be honest, it hasn't been easy. So many memories have been cropping up from seeing my dad's old friends, some of my old friends and others at Grams' funeral."

"Good memories?" Tess prompted.

Lizzie shrugged. "Some memories were good. But I saw other old friends at the funeral, where the memories were quite painful."

"Like who?"

She swallowed as Jonathan's face flashed across her mind.

"An old boyfriend from high school was there."

"I remember you mentioned a guy named Jonathan before. Is that the man you're talking about?"

"Yes." Lizzie's cheeks heated as she remembered how being near him had unsettled her. "I saw him at Grams' funeral, and he came over to talk to me. He was so tender with me. I'm embarrassed to admit that I had to fight feelings of attraction for him."

"What's wrong with having feelings for Jonathan?"

Lizzie gasped, shocked that her friend needed to ask. "Tess, are you forgetting that my husband passed away only a few weeks ago? What kind of a terrible woman am I to even look at another man?"

"I'd say you're quite normal," Tess spoke gently. "Lizzie,

I'm sorry Gray passed away so suddenly. Yes, it will take time for your heart to heal, but the fact is that you are a widow now. Your husband died, but you didn't. You are very much alive. And I hope someday, you will open your heart to love again."

A heaviness centered in her chest. "I don't know, Tess. I'm not ready for any sort of relationship with a man right now."

"I understand. What you need is time to heal." Tess's voice was filled with understanding. Quickly, she changed the topic. "Tell me, have you had a chance to talk with your sisters?"

Lizzie appreciated when her best friend could sense when to change the subject.

"Yes. After the reading of Grandmother's will, we had lunch at Grams' cottage." Lizzie walked along the deck toward the table. "It was good to chat with my sisters again. I realized, to my regret, that I've neglected to keep in touch with them."

Lightly, she ran her fingers over the wood of the outdoor table remembering their conversation.

Tess replied, "That happens sometimes. I've struggled to stay in touch with my brother too. Life gets busy for all of us. I'm glad you had a chance to talk with your sisters."

There was a pause before her friend spoke again.

"You mentioned learning the details of your grandmother's will. Were there any surprises?"

Lizzie sucked in a breath. Turning, she looked up at the long roof line of her grandmother's large cottage.

"Yes."

"Well, don't leave me in suspense. What did your

grandmother leave you?" As usual her friend was impatient to hear the news.

Lizzie smiled.

"Well, Grams was very generous with the inheritance she gave to me and my sisters. She bequeathed me her beach cottage on the island. She wrote a clause in the will that I need to keep the house for one year. Then, after that, I would have the option to sell it."

"Oh Lizzie. That's wonderful!" A soft gasp escaped Tess's lips. "Now, you will have your own place to go to when your house sells."

Lizzie stomach clenched in a tight ball at the possibility of moving back to Martha's Vineyard.

The island held her best and worst memories.

She turned her head and her eyes were drawn to the sandy beach and clear blue water in front of the cottage.

As her gaze drifted along the beach, she spotted a tall man wearing beige shorts and a blue t-shirt. The set of his broad shoulders and blond, wavy hair looked vaguely familiar.

When he turned to watch his dog run along the beach, Lizzie gasped.

The man on the beach was Jonathan.

Without warning, memories came back.

He had been so thoughtful and kind to her. Helping her through the death of her grandfather.

They had been in love.

At least, that's what she believed.

They had even been talking about a future together.

But all her dreams crumbled to dust the day Lizzie

found Jonathan's arms wrapped around the blond cheerleader.

She swallowed the despair in her throat.

"I don't think I can accept my Grandmother's gift," Lizzie replied in a low, tormented voice.

Her friend's voice erupted in a shocked whisper, "What? Why can't you accept your grandmother's beach cottage?"

Lizzie bit her lip until it throbbed like her pulse. She felt the nauseating sinking of despair.

Staring at Jonathan's handsome face, she whispered in a raw voice, "There's too much pain here."

Lizzie swallowed before continuing. "First, my Mom and Dad died in a boating accident. Without warning, we were orphans. A few short years later, we buried Gramps. Only weeks after that, I learned that the man I loved in high school… didn't love me back."

Deep pain ran through her body from the memories that haunted her. "That's when I ran away from Martha's Vineyard. In fact, I promised myself I would only return to the island to visit Grams, but never to live."

Lizzie turned and walked away so she wouldn't see Jonathan.

She bit back tears. The phone in her hand shook.

She closed her eyes as grief and despair tore at her heart.

"Oh, Lizzie. I'm sorry for all the heartache you've been through," Tess's voice cracked with emotion.

Lizzie nodded and swallowed.

Tess continued in a whisper, "I understand that

moving back to Martha's Vineyard is the last thing you want to do."

Her friend paused.

"Why do I feel like there's a 'but' coming?"

Tess persisted in a soft tone, *"But...* I think it's important for you to consider one thing."

"What's that?"

"The island also holds the best memories of your childhood, your parents, grandparents, and friends. Maybe there's a reason your grandmother bequeathed you the beach cottage. Just maybe, moving to Martha's Vineyard will be just what you need to begin healing from past wounds." Her friend's whispered words were filled with compassion.

Lizzie was silent for a long time thinking that.

Similar words had been echoed not long ago by her grandmother.

The last time she had visited Grams — before she passed away — Grams had said she believed Lizzie needed time and a place to heal.

Her loving Grandmother always told her the truth as she saw it. She advised her granddaughter it was necessary to heal from her husband's death and from the pain of her past so she could move on to the future with open arms.

She clung to the wisdom of her beloved Grams. The wise older woman had always been like a life preserver in the stormy sea of her life.

Could Tess be right? Did she need to come back to the island to heal from the pain of past wounds?

Her mind argued against the very idea. How could she

consider moving back to the same place where she had experienced so much heartache?

Yet, both Grams and Tess had said similar things.

Lizzie sighed heavily. She wasn't ready to commit to moving just yet.

"I will think about what you've said, Tess. But I'm not making any promises about moving back to the island."

Tess sighed. "Good. I'm glad. Remember, you can move into your grandmother's cottage for one year before you need to make a real commitment."

"Yes, I suppose that's true." Lizzie sighed. "It looks like I have a lot to think about. But for now, I've got to get going. I'll call you as soon as I get back to Boston." Lizzie said goodbye to her friend and slipped the phone in her back pocket.

She paused to catch her breath her fears stronger than ever.

Changes in her life were happening so fast.

She felt like everything in her world was spinning out of control. Now, on top of everything else, she would need to think about if she should move back to Grams' cottage.

Her mind said that was the last place she wanted to be.

What if Tess and her beloved Grams were both right?

Lizzie's mind swirled with thoughts of her grandmother's will, even as the hour grew late.

When she noticed Jonathan was no longer walking along the beach, Lizzie decided to take a walk.

She needed more time to think through the decision that was foremost in her mind: *Should she move back to Grams' beach cottage at Sweet Beach Cove?*

To have her home near the place of the boat accident killed her parents would be difficult. However, that wasn't her only resistance to moving to Martha's Vineyard.

The other reason that held her back from moving back to Grams' Cottage was Jonathan. Lizzie didn't know if she would be able to deal with living so close to the man who broke her heart years ago.

The sand squished through her toes as she walked along the beach—a delicious feeling. Smelling the sea air and feeling the sand on her skin, made her feel alive in a way she hadn't felt for a long time.

In some ways, it was comforting to be back.

She had fond memories from when she was a young girl, holding her father's hand as they walked along the water's edge.

Many Sunday afternoons they enjoyed a picnic, laughing and having fun as a family.

Later on, when she was twelve years old, she met Jonathan.

She couldn't forget that memorable day.

This was the exact spot where she had first met him. He'd been a young boy, shy and timid.

She smiled at the memory.

He had fixed her sandcastle that day long ago. After that day, they became fast friends.

Would she be able to truly forgive him?

She wanted to with all her heart.

Pain and anger had weighed her down long enough. She wanted to be free of those crushing weights.

Maybe Grams added that clause in her will to give her the time she needed to make up her mind.

Grams' words swirled in her mind once more. *Lizzie, what you really need is a time to heal from wounds from the past. That's the only way you'll be able to embrace a fresh start with open arms.*

Sighing, she stood on the water's edge.

Lizzie looked across the water. Much like facing her future, the vast breadth of the blue water seemed impossible to cross.

But Grandmother had known that — which was the reason she added the clause in her will.

Her decision was made.

She would move to Martha's Vineyard for one year.

It would give her the time she needed to truly think about the future she wanted.

She would do it.

She would give it one year.

Despite fears of the future, she would work hard try make this work.

With only a small amount in her bank account, she had a deadline she needed to meet. Could she do it?

CHAPTER FOUR

*Folks have settled on Martha's Vineyard for hundreds of years.
One of our prominent families, Henry and Mary Stafford,
settled in the small community of Sweet Beach Cove.
A letter written by Mary to her sister, tells some of the tale.
"It's still difficult to believe that my husband won sixty acres of
land.
His game of chance with Ike Cantrell won him the waterfront
property with a small house along the shore here in Martha's
Vineyard.
Henry tells me when he returns with his ship next time, we'll fix
up the house. I look forward to when you visit us here, Rachel.
With love, Mary."
The Vineyard Historical Letters*

"We're here." Lizzie's voice trembled slightly as she stared at her grandmother's cottage and the sandy beach beyond that.

"Wow. Seeing the blue sky, blue ocean, and sandy beach feels like we've arrived in heaven," Annie breathed out as she came to stand beside her.

Lizzie nodded. "That's why this area is known as Sweet Beach Cove. It's especially beautiful in the summer months."

"I always thought Grams had one of the nicest waterfront homes on Martha's Vineyard." Annie turned to look at her. "It's hard to believe that this place is yours now."

She sighed. "I am grateful for Grams' gift of the beach house, truly I am. But I can't help feeling nervous about what's in store for me as I begin again in this place." Lizzie shook her head.

Will and Jake walked past them toward the house. Each of her sons carried large boxes in their hands.

Lizzie turned to grab some suitcases.

Annie followed behind as they hurried toward the front of the house.

As Lizzie began to climb the front steps, she suddenly stopped.

Standing in front of her were two acquaintances that she knew years ago. Women from her past that she never thought she'd see again.

"Ava Cantrell-Worth and Cecily Whitticombe. I confess, I'm surprised to see the two of you on my doorstep." Lizzie continued to the front porch and set the suitcase down by her side.

Her children unlocked the door, carrying the boxes inside the house.

"Well, we thought it might be nice to surprise you. We personally wanted to welcome you back to Martha's Vineyard." Ava held out her hand with a smile that never reached her eyes.

"Yes, welcome back." Cecily's hundred-watt smile matched her white-blond hair. "I should tell you that my last name changed years ago when I married Ryan Hart. But, since our divorce last year, I've been thinking I might take back the name I had before I married."

"Sorry, I hadn't realized."

"That's okay. You've been gone from the island, so there are many changes in the lives of your friends that you've missed. That's why we wanted to stop by and welcome you back in person," Cecily purred.

Memories still haunted her of how these two women had banded together to bully her and make sure she was left out of fun events throughout middle school and high school.

Lizzie's composure was a fragile shell around her.

Based on past experience, she didn't want to give neither of them the time of day. In the past, these two women had hurt her by their malicious words and actions.

But maybe the two women had changed. Perhaps, as part of this fresh start, she needed to extend an olive branch and give each of them the benefit of the doubt.

Lizzie swallowed. She would do her best to be kind. If they showed they weren't to be trusted, she'd deal with that problem later.

She wanted to start on the right foot with people she knew on Martha's Vineyard from years ago.

"Thank you. That's thoughtful of you." Lizzie shook their hands quickly.

However, she couldn't stop the disquieting thoughts that lingered in the back of her mind.

She shifted on her feet, stirring uneasily.

At that moment, Annie opened the door and came to stand by her side.

"Hey, this would make a great picture of you two in front of the beach house. May I take your photo for the island's welcome wagon?" Cecily asked sweetly.

Lizzie nodded. "I guess that would be okay."

After a quick snapshot with her smartphone, Cecily turned to Ava.

Ava tucked a black strand of hair behind her ear. "We heard you inherited this beach house from your dear old grandmother."

"Yes, I did. It was quite a surprise." Lizzie looked up at the chipped, white paint on the side of the rambling cottage. "But this house is an enormous project. There's quite a lot of work to be done, to fix the place up."

Ava nodded. Suddenly, she asked, "I'm curious. What are your plans for the house? Have you decided to sell it?"

Lizzie sighed heavily, somewhat overwhelmed at all the work that lay ahead. "I'm not sure. Right now, I have an idea I'd like to try before I consider selling this house."

Annie blurted out, a large grin on her face, "My Mom is going to remake Grams' house into an inn. It's going to be amazing."

Lizzie placed her arm around her daughter's waist. "My daughter is very confident in my abilities."

She grinned at her daughter and turned to Ava. "We're going to try to make Grams' beach house into an inn. But we will see if we can manage to get the work done properly."

Ava started, complete surprise on her face. "You're really going to do all the work to re-make this old house?"

Cecily looked at Lizzie with the same disbelief.

"Well, I'm going to try. Who knows how it will turn out. But at least I'll feel good knowing I've taken the first step." Lizzie smiled uneasily, feeling a little unsettled from all the questions.

"Hmm, I don't know, Lizzie. I think this beach house is too old. I really don't want to discourage you, but I think it's a bad idea." Cecilia swung her shoulder-length blond hair. With her long nails, she plucked invisible dirt from her pink shirt sleeve.

Ava stared at the old house, her eyes sharp and assessing. When she turned back to Lizzie, the crease between her brows had deepened.

"Bringing this old house back to life is likely to be an impossible task." Ava's pale eyes were like bits of stone as she stared at Lizzie. "Good luck. I'm sure you'll need it, Lizzie. Cecily, we need to be going."

"Okay, sure. See you later." Cecily waved goodbye as she followed her friend to the car.

Lizzie's face clouded with uneasiness.

Annie walked up beside her. "I think those women were rather rude to discourage you from fixing Grams' old house."

Biting her lip, she turned to her daughter.

She muttered uneasily, "Yeah, they didn't sound very positive about our project, did they?"

Looking up at Grams' sorely neglected beach house, Lizzie sighed heavily. "Do you think perhaps they are right? Is it impossible to fix up this old house?"

Annie huffed. "This is not an impossible project, Mom. Don't listen to those women."

Lizzie leaned over and slipped an arm around her daughter's waist. "Thank you, Annie. I'm grateful to know I have you on my side."

Annie kissed her cheek. "And you always will."

Her heart swelled with warmth.

Jake walked out of the house, followed by Will and Christopher.

Lizzie forced herself to push back the shadowy thoughts of her old friends Ava and Cecily, to focus on her children.

"Mom, we're done."

Lizzie smiled nervously. "I'm glad. That's a relief." She turned to look at them, pleased with how they all helped her move today. "Thanks, Will, Annie, Christopher, and Jake. I don't know how I could have made the big move to the Island without your help."

Will nodded, his expression stoic.

Annie smiled. "We were happy to help, weren't we, Chris?"

"Absolutely." Christopher, Annie's boyfriend, grinned. Looking around the beach house, he shook his head. "This is an amazing house. When you said you were moving to your grandmother's beach cottage, I had in mind a small, two-bedroom home. I never expected a sprawling, seventeen-bedroom, historical home on the waterfront."

"That's my Mom. Always full of surprises." Jake chuckled as he turned to Lizzie. "Mom, in case there was any doubt, we are happy to help you move. What else would we do? We are your children and available to help you anytime."

Jake placed one arm around her shoulders, pulling her close. Lizzie grinned and slipped her arm around her son's waist, her heart swelling with love.

She whispered, "Thanks, Jake. It means a lot to me to hear you say that."

They walked inside.

Lizzie looked around the old house, a warmth flooding her at the familiar surroundings.

Grams had left everything how it was when Lizzie and her sisters were children.

The familiar maple wood grandfather clock stood tall and resolute against the wall, not far away from Gramps' old recliner in the corner.

It was a good thing Grams left the furniture in her house.

Lizzie got rid of her beautiful dining room set and anything else that could be sold.

It had only taken six weeks for her house in Boston to sell.

The first thing she did with the money from the sale was pay off her husband's massive debts.

She released a long sigh of relief. That chapter in her life was finally over.

It felt like someone had lifted a heavy weight off her shoulders.

Her biggest concern now? She needed to earn a regular income.

As things looked now, there was only a little money left over from paying off the debt.

Lizzie needed to figure out a way to make a living.

"Let's go look at the rest of the house," Annie suggested, looking around at everyone.

With the loud ring of her phone, Lizzie stopped. "You all go ahead. I need to answer the phone."

"Hello." Lizzie held the phone to her ear as all four of her helpers hurried off down the hallway.

"Hey, sis, it's Jane." Her sister's cheerful voice on the other end of the phone line brightened her day.

"It's nice to hear from you." Her sister's energetic voice was a happy change to the discouraging thoughts that had been swirling around in Lizzie's head.

"How is everything going with your big move?" Jane's question brought home the reality of her situation.

"Well, we made it here." Lizzie looked around at the old cottage with the faded old-style walls and chipped, wooden floors. "There's a lot in this old house that needs fixing. But I'll muddle through somehow. First, I need to sort through Grams' things."

Jane sighed. "It is true, Grams' house is old. There is a lot to fix up. Do you want some help?"

Lizzie lifted her eyebrows in surprise. "Well, sure, if you've got the time."

"I've got some vacation time coming to me. I also talked with Alex earlier today and it turns out she's due some time off at her job at the Boston Hospital, too. We'll come and help you sort through Grams' things. What do you think of that?"

Lizzie chuckled. "That sounds great. Thanks, Jane."

"All right then, see you soon."

Lizzie hung up the phone, feeling more light-hearted than she had in days. Two of her sisters were coming to help her out. Maybe, in time, as they talked through things, they would start to get closer and be more like the sisters they once were.

Creating a bond with her sisters was something for which her heart longed. Would it happen for them?

Looking around the room filled with boxes, a wave of overwhelm hit her again. Maybe what she needed was a short break.

Needing some fresh air, she walked to the front door, startled when she heard a loud knock.

Lizzie felt startled to see two women standing there.

"Hello, Lizzie. Do you remember us?"

Lizzie nodded. "Of course. Violet and Madison Hayes. It's good to see you. I'll come outside and we can talk there."

As she closed the screen door, there was a loud thump.

The old wooden screen door hung limp with only one tired screw holding it up.

"Looks like I have some fixing to do on this house," Lizzie said as she turned to her visitors.

Violet Hayes tucked a strand of gray hair behind one ear. "Well, that happens with older homes. I understand you recently inherited this house from your grandmother?"

"Yes, I did." Lizzie wondered why had these two women stopped by?

"You might not be aware of this, but for the past ten years, my daughter and I have been successful realtors in the Sweet Beach Cove area." Violet explained.

Lizzie's eyes widened. "I didn't know that. Violet, you used to work as the town administrator, I remember. Madison, I remember you from high school."

Madison chuckled, "Yes, I guess I was bothersome to you back then, following you around. But, as the saying goes, I've grown up."

She recalled that Madison, and her friend seemed to appear wherever she was during high school.

What she remembered most was Madison's competitive nature.

She sighed, wondering why the two women had stopped by her house.

"Yes. But, since inheriting this house, it looks like I'm back." A crease formed between her brows. "Is there something I can help you with?"

"Yes, there is." Violet continued. "Sometimes we buy a piece of property for our own personal use. Your grandmother's old house is one such property we are interested in. We would like to make an offer on your house."

Lizzie was stunned. "I appreciate your interest in this place. However, at this time I'm not interested in selling."

Violet nodded. "I understand. It looks like there is quite a lot that needs to be fixed on the house. To restore this old place will take quite a bit of money. We are willing to buy this house as is — at this moment — to save you all that time and money. Our offer is more than fair. Here's my card. Think about it."

Lizzie took the business card from Violet and nodded.

"Thank you for your offer. But, I'm not interested."

"Fair enough. Madison, we need to be going. Nice seeing you, Lizzie." Violet nodded once and started down the front steps. Madison waved quickly before following her mother.

Lizzie stood on her front deck, puzzled at their visit. Violet had always been a sharp-tongued, determined woman. She hoped Madison wouldn't follow in her mother's footsteps.

She shrugged. Hopefully, the mother, daughter team would soon forget about her grandmother's house and move on to other properties.

Turning back to look at the door, she released a heavy sigh and muttered, "I hope this broken door isn't what I can expect from the rest of Gram's house."

Lizzie wondered how she was going to manage to get everything fixed in this old house, and still keep to her limited budget.

JONATHAN WALKED out of the coffee shop next door to his business, carrying a coffee to-go.

He started towards his workplace, when he heard a woman call his name.

"Jonathan Brookes, I'm glad I ran into you."

He turned to see a long-time resident of the island. Her granddaughter was by her side.

"Mrs. O'Connor, it's good to see you." Jonathan looked over at the gray-haired lady. "Looks like you've been shopping. Do you need help to carry your bags?"

"Would you help? That's kind of you, young man." Mrs. O'Connor handed him a few of her heavy bags.

Jonathan carried them in one hand while he finished drinking his coffee with the other.

Tossing his disposable cup into the trash can, he turned to Mrs. O'Connor. "Show me where you want them."

Jonathan smiled warmly. He was used to carrying shopping bags for his mother.

"Could you come with us, Jonathan?" The grandmotherly lady asked, a bright twinkle in her eyes.

Jonathan nodded. "Where are we going?"

"To the Stafford beach house. It's just a few blocks away. We wanted to give Lizzie these freshly baked muffins and some gifts for her house," Mrs. O'Connor said, the corners of her mouth turning up with a smile.

Jonathan's heart beat faster at the sound of Lizzie's name.

"Lizzie has moved into her grandmother's house?" He asked, forcing himself to sound as detached as possible.

Sarah nodded. "Yes. She inherited the house from her grandmother. She just moved into the house today and we wanted to welcome her back to Sweet Beach Cove."

"I'm at your command, ladies." Jonathan grinned and walked beside them. As he gripped the heavy shopping bags, his thoughts were on Lizzie.

What would her response be at seeing him again? It looked like he was about to find out.

AT THE SOUND of creaking steps, Lizzie turned from the screen door she'd been trying to fix.

She smiled when she recognized one of her grandmother's oldest friends.

Dorothy O'Connor walked up the steps slowly. Her granddaughter Sarah held her arm on one side.

Her eyes widened at the sight of Jonathan Brookes.

He held shopping bags in one hand and with the other hand he held the older woman's arm to help her up the stairs.

"Lizzie, is that you?" The wobbly voice of the older woman reached Lizzie's ears.

Forgetting all about the broken screen door, Lizzie walked over to greet the newcomers.

Mrs. O'Connor had been one of Grandmother's dear friends. The older lady had been so kind to Lizzie and her sisters during their growing-up years.

"It is me, Mrs. O'Connor." Lizzie smiled warmly at the gray-haired lady. "How are you?"

Briefly, Lizzie glanced at Sarah and Jonathan with a small smile.

"I'm well. Right as rain." As the older woman reached the stairs, she stopped to catch her breath.

"Sarah, please give Lizzie our welcome gift." Mrs. O'Connor turned to her granddaughter.

Sarah was a thin girl, with brown hair and wide hazel eyes who was about the same age as Lizzie's son Jake. When her dad died ten years earlier, she'd come to live with her grandmother. Sarah was so quiet, many folks easily overlooked her.

Reaching into the large bag at her side, Sarah pulled out a large container and handed it to Lizzie.

Lizzie lifted the lid and saw June-berry muffins, her favorite. "Mrs. O'Connor, you remembered my favorite treat. Thank you so much."

Lizzie reached over to hug the older lady, warmth flooding her heart. Stepping back, she smiled.

Grams' oldest friend reached over and squeezed her hand. "Ah, Lizzie, it's so good to see you here. You know I've always had a soft spot for you and your sisters ever since you were little girls. Now that your beloved Grandmother has passed, I wanted to be here to give you a proper welcome back to the island."

In that moment, happy childhood memories flooded her senses. "Thank you. Now I know why Grams adored you." Lizzie grinned. "We could all sit and talk at the patio table if you have time? We'll enjoy your delicious muffins."

"Well, only for a few minutes. My daughter will stop by today, so I'll need to get home soon." Mrs. O'Connor sat down at the wooden patio table with Sarah by her side.

She looked over at Jonathan, her cheeks heating as his gaze searched hers. "Do you want to come and join us?"

He was so disturbing to her in every way. Each time she saw him, the pull of attraction was stronger.

Lizzie tried to throttle the dizzying current that ran through her. It disturbed her that she was susceptible to this man's charms.

She would need to guard her heart, but that might prove to be more difficult than she realized.

Jonathan's blue-eyed gaze focused on her, thoughtful for a few seconds, before he replied, "Actually, there's something I'd like to do first. I heard wood cracking near your front door earlier. I thought I'd have a look to see if I can get it fixed for you."

Surprised at his offer, Lizzie was speechless.

After a few seconds, she finally spoke with hesitation.

"Th…that would be wonderful."

Turning, she walked toward the front door.

Jonathan followed closely behind.

"That's where the door cracked." She pointed towards the gaping hole in the old screen door. "The wood is old and is in pretty bad shape. Thanks for offering to fix it. There are tools just through the door and around the corner. Help yourself to whatever you need."

Lizzie watched for a minute as Jonathan got busy. He detached the screen door from the door frame.

"I should get back to my guests." The words rushed out. He simply nodded and continued to work.

She hesitated for a moment, her composure a fragile shell around her. But Jonathan had always had that effect on her.

Lizzie turned away and walked back to where Mrs. O'Connor sat with her granddaughter.

What was the reason for Jonathan's thoughtfulness?

Sitting at the table, Lizzie turned to the older lady in an effort to dispel the fluttering in her chest from Jonathan's attention.

"So, tell me how you've been, Mrs. O'Connor." Lizzie encouraged her grandmother's friend to talk more about herself.

As she listened, she opened the lid to the container.

The scent of the fluffy muffins permeated the surrounding air.

"Help yourselves." Lizzie smiled and took one for herself.

Sarah reached into her tote bag and passed around napkins.

"How lovely." The older lady began to speak, "To answer your question, I am doing well. I continue to stay busy. I host the Sweet Beach Cove community's quilting and knitting club every week in my home. We still create little booties and blankets for baby showers and weddings. It's quite fun." The older lady had a spark in her eyes as she talked.

"I'm glad you've found something that you love." Lizzie smiled warmly. Her words rushed on, "Sometimes, one of the most difficult things in life is to have the courage to try something new."

"You are an inspiration, Mrs. O'Connor. You've done that. And you've helped others do what they enjoy too. I think your crochet and knitting club is a really good thing for folks who live in this area."

"Thank you, dear." The older lady reached over and squeezed her hand.

Turning to the older lady's granddaughter, Lizzie asked. "How about you, Sarah? What keeps you busy?"

A shy smile formed on her lips. "Well, I write a weekly column for a new start-up newspaper here. My articles are all about crocheting, knitting and other creative activities that islanders enjoy."

"That sounds lovely. I'd love to read your column

sometime." Lizzie couldn't help but be interested in the articles this shy girl wrote. By reading them, she hoped to get to know her better.

Sarah replied. "I'll stop by and give you a copy of next week's newspaper."

"That would be great. What's the name of the newspaper?"

"The Vineyard Tales."

Lizzie smiled softly. "That sounds appropriate. I look forward to reading it."

Mrs. O'Connor commented, "I am proud of my granddaughter. And I am proud she's writing about my quilting, knitting and crocheting club. In fact, I think the real reason we've had more people join us in the past six months is because of her newspaper column."

A becoming blush formed on Sarah's pale cheeks at her grandmother's praise. "That's high praise indeed."

"It is. I know my son Sean — may he rest in peace — would have been proud of his only child." The older woman blinked away tears that formed in her eyes as memories of her son rose to the surface.

Lizzie remembered Sean O'Connor. He, too, had written for one of the newspapers on Martha's Vineyard. His death in a boating accident ten years ago had come as a shock to many islanders.

She reached over and squeezed the older lady's hand. "I have no doubt Sean would have been proud. Seems like Sarah has inherited her father's gift of writing."

"She has, and I'm happy about that." Mrs. O'Connor swallowed and asked. "Speaking of children, what are your children doing now?"

Talking about her children always brought joy to Lizzie. "My oldest son, Will, just graduated with a degree in law. He works at a Law Firm in Boston. It keeps him busy."

"Our daughter, Annie, just completed her design degree and an agency in Boston has hired her. And our youngest son, Jake, has been helping me. Jake's been working as an apprentice in house construction. I am grateful for his help as I need a lot of help lately, it seems," Lizzie whispered, feeling vulnerable at her admission.

"Nothing wrong with asking for help, Lizzie. We all need that from time to time." Mrs. O'Connor assured her.

Memories of her husband rose to the surface, and a crease formed between her brows. "My late husband, Gray, didn't like it when I asked for help. Yet, he insisted that everything be in excellent order at his work and at home."

Lizzie shook her head. "I worked hard to keep everything as perfect as possible, but there were many times I failed."

"Oh, my dear. Nobody should have such impossible expectations placed on them." Mrs. O'Connor shook her head.

Lizzie's heart ached with an inner pain at the truth of her words.

The older woman's expression turned serious. "Your Grams worried about you, Lizzie. She mentioned to me once that after your marriage, you clammed up, and she thought you wanted to hide yourself away from people who loved you."

Lizzie's cheeks heated uncomfortably. "I suppose that

was true. Gray was very particular in the way he wanted things done. Even though I tried my best, I ended up failing."

"If I'm not mistaken, this also included his expectations of you."

Lizzie shifted uncomfortably in her chair and silently nodded.

"Well, before your beloved Grandmother died, she made me promise I would be there for you. She said: *It's important that Lizzie breaks the chains that are holding her down. She needs to embrace the beautiful woman she is, so she can find healing to live life fully and love again."*

Lizzie caught her breath. "That sounds like Grams. My friend Tess said something similar not long ago."

"Then your friend is a wise woman." Mrs. O'Connor nodded. "You know your grandmother loved you and wanted the best for you."

Lizzie swallowed and nodded. "I know. My grandmother had a strong desire to see all of her grandchildren happy. Sometimes though, life can deal a person so many painful blows that you end up shriveling up on the inside."

The older lady nodded. "Sadly, that's very true. I want you to know I'm sorry for the pain you've gone through, Lizzie."

She nodded, swallowing back emotions.

"I think your decision to move back to your grandmother's beach cottage has come just at the right time." She whispered.

"I have a feeling that healing and love are waiting here for you." A secretive smile turned up the corners of Mrs. O'Connor's mouth as she glanced over at Jonathan.

Lizzie smiled nervously. Change had never come easy for her. "I'm not so sure about that. But I will say that I'm very glad to have you on my side, Mrs. O'Connor."

"That's one thing you can be sure of — I am on your side, my dear." The older lady stood to her feet. Sarah hurried to her grandmother's side, a support for your grandmother. "We must be getting back home, but let's talk again soon, Lizzie dear."

"I look forward to it." Lizzie waved as the two of them walked away.

At the sound of a hammer pounding wood, she turned.

Jonathan was hard at work fixing her broken door. Her son Jake worked with him.

"Hey, Mom. Look who stopped by to help us fix up Grams' house." Jake grinned over at her. "Now, the screen door is all fixed."

"Thank you. I'm very grateful." Lizzie looked at Jonathan. He nodded and smiled.

Her son continued, "Jonathan said you two are old friends."

Jake's comment caused an extra worry to rise inside her.

She didn't want her son thinking there was more to her relationship with Jonathan than there was.

She was grateful that Jonathan had offered to fix the screen door. But it made her uncomfortable that her son was working alongside her old boyfriend.

Lizzie had already decided that she wasn't ready for a relationship with any man.

Maybe she never would be ready.

Her experience with marriage meant a life of someone trying to re-make her into their image of the perfect wife.

She decided she didn't want that kind of life ever again.

"Yes, we grew up on the island together." Lizzie glanced at Jonathan, who tilted his head to one side, stealing a slanted look at her.

Nervously, she moistened her lips.

Jonathan leaned against the wall of the house.

"Did you know my Mom well?" Jake asked.

A small smile formed on Jonathan's lips. "I met your Mom when I first moved to the Vineyard when I was twelve. I got to know her better and better through the years until we graduated high school together."

Jonathan's blue gaze lazily appraised her.

A blush like a shadow crossed Lizzie's face, but she forced herself to remain still.

"I didn't think your Mom would ever return to the island." Jonathan looked at her son, before turning to look at her. "However, I'm happy to see that I was wrong."

Jake turned his head to Jonathan, his face filled with curiosity. "I think I'd like to hear this story."

Lizzie interrupted, "Maybe someday. I'm sure you'll get a chance to hear that story some other time, Jake. But for now, I'm sure Jonathan is very busy and needs to return to his office."

"Ah, Mom." A crestfallen look fell on her son's face.

Lizzie wasn't ready to rehash the pain of her past.

"I guess I'll see you later, Jonathan." Jake sighed.

Jonathan nodded. "It was good to meet you, Jake."

As her son went inside the house, Lizzie turned to

Jonathan. "I appreciate you taking the time to fix the screen door. That's one item off of my long to-do list for fixing up Gram's old house."

Lizzie realized she was babbling it was what she often did when she was nervous. "But I know you must be eager to get back to your office. So, I'll let you go. Thanks again."

She nodded and began to walk towards the door when Jonathan spoke.

"I know there's a lot of work to fix up your grandmother's beach house, Lizzie. A project like this would be something I would love to be a part of. After all, a big part of what I do as a restoration architect is to bring new life to old things," Jonathan murmured.

His gentle words were coaxing.

"I'm sorry, but it's not in my budget to hire you, Jonathan," Lizzie croaked out the words, a feeling of embarrassment flooding her soul.

Jonathan stepped closer, his blue eyes searching hers with an intensity that forced her to stand motionless.

"Let me do this for you, Lizzie. I promise, there is no cost involved and no expectations. I just want to help you. What do you say?" At Jonathan's soft entreaty, a small piece of the icy block around her heart fell away.

His heartfelt offer melted her resolve.

How could she say no to his offer to help her for free — when it was so desperately needed?

Lizzie nodded. "I accept your kind offer on one condition."

"What's that?"

"I'd like for us to agree we are simply old friends,

working together to fix my grandmother's old house." Her cheeks heated at the request.

More words tumbled out of her mouth. "I…I just don't want to confuse my children about the relationship between us."

Jonathan lifted one corner of his lips. His rogue smile was back. She remembered it well from years ago.

It was the same smile that had won her heart years ago. Now, it only made her wary of him.

"I promise that I won't do anything that you don't agree to first." His words meant to set her heart at ease, instead set her pulse pounding.

She didn't really know what to say, so she simply nodded and whispered, "Thanks."

Just as Jonathan walked, he spun, his heart in his eyes. "And, Lizzie?"

Lizzie's heart turned over in response. "Yes?"

"We—we need to have a conversation about what happened between us years ago. I'm sorry for any pain I caused you. And—and I guess I'm asking you for a chance to hear my side of the story." Jonathan stuttered a little as he spoke, emotions of hope and regret flooding his face.

Lizzie's spine stiffened, and she swallowed back emotion. "I don't think we need to rehash the past."

She believed that there wasn't any use dredging up the painful past. She just wanted to move on.

"Please, Lizzie. This is important."

Her heart ached from memories that haunted her. But Jonathan's heartfelt request stirred her emotions.

Reluctantly, Lizzie agreed. "All right. At some point later on, we can talk."

She didn't have any hope that it would do any good to hear his side of the story. But maybe if they talked things out, there wouldn't be any more awkward moments between them.

It was useless to hope that might happen.

"Thank you, Lizzie. I'll see you soon."

She was caught off guard by the look of relief and the tenderness in his gaze.

"See you later." Lizzie watched him walk away. She turned abruptly, hurrying into the house.

She was desperate to escape the emotions that arose inside whenever he was near.

Somehow, she had to conquer her involuntary reactions to that tender look of his.

A knot formed in her belly as she thought of the two of them working side by side to fix the house.

How would she be able to stop this attraction she had towards Jonathan? It seemed her traitorous heart was working against the decision she already made.

Would her resolve hold out?

Lizzie worried it wouldn't.

A wave of fear coursed through her.

Lizzie believed she wouldn't be able to handle falling in love only to have her heart broken again.

If that happened, her heart would shatter into a million tiny pieces and never recover.

CHAPTER FIVE

Another well-known family on Martha's Vineyard was established when Ike and Clara Cantrell bought their sixty acres along the waterfront.
Ike penned these words in a letter to his brother, George.
"Brother, I made a grave error. During a night of imbibing too much strong drink at the local tavern, I lost sixty acres along Martha's Vineyard shoreline, in a game of chance.
Now, Captain Henry Stafford holds the deed to that land.
But I have a plan. A friend of mine has heard of a ship carrying gemstones and jewels that is coming towards the island. Maybe there will be a way to recover what was lost after all, eh? Come and visit me and Clara soon.
Your brother, Ike."

The Vineyard Historical Letters

izzie's hands shook. Dropping the newspaper in her hands, she gave a wide-eyed glance at her two sisters.

"Have you read this article written by Miss Knowing?" Lizzie threw the words out, her temper soaring.

Both Jane and Alex reached for their newspaper that lay on the wooden table on the outside deck.

Her sisters had only arrived a couple of hours ago. She had prepared a snack of muffins and coffee so they could sit on the sunny deck and chat for a while.

Sally had stopped by earlier in the day with extra copies of the promised newspaper. The young girl had been eager for Lizzie to read the piece she'd written.

"What article?" Jane quickly turned to page two and scanned down the page until she found the offensive article. "Ah, I see it now."

Jane read it out loud. *"The oldest sister of the seven Stafford sisters has returned to our beloved island. Lizzie Stafford Wentworth has arrived fresh from Boston to take over the beach house she inherited from her grandmother, Elizabeth Stafford.*

If the rumors that have reached this writer's ears can be relied on, all seven sisters received a very generous inheritance from their grandmother when she passed away only weeks ago.

The Stafford family is a very old and prominent family here on Martha's Vineyard. Islanders recognize William and Elizabeth Stafford as well-known benefactors not only on Martha's Vineyard but elsewhere.

After the death of their son John Stafford and his wife Anne in a boating accident years ago, the grandparents raised the girls.

Many long-time residents in the Sweet Beach Cove community feel like the mystery of what happened on that stormy night long ago was never fully solved.

Lizzie, the oldest girl of the seven Stafford sisters, recently inherited her grandparent's beach cottage.

With the recent passing of her husband, Lizzie has chosen to move back to Martha's Vineyard.

Her three young adult children remain in Boston.

One islander told this writer that she spotted architect Jonathan Brookes fixing the front door of the Stafford beach house.

It makes this writer wonder if Lizzie has plans afoot for that old house? We will watch closely to see what transpires in the coming weeks."

Jane continued. "It says this article was written by, Miss Knowing."

"Why would this unknown writer want to gossip about me?" Lizzie muttered hastily.

Her sister Alex regarded Lizzie stoically. "Maybe you should take it as a compliment. Someone at this newspaper clearly finds you and our entire family a fascinating topic for gossip."

Lizzie huffed, folding her arms across her chest.

"This article really isn't so bad, Lizzie." Jane smiled widely. "It seems to me like the writer is simply curious about your plans for Grams' cottage."

Lizzie snorted. "There is that. But this author is also writing about our parent's deaths as an unsolved mystery. It was an accident. The sheriff said so."

"Last week when I was talking to friends from this area, they told me they think the sheriff should have done more digging into what happened," Jane whispered.

"Well, it happened years ago, so it must be too late for that now." Lizzie sighed heavily. "However, what isn't okay is when an unknown writer at the newspaper gossips about our parent's deaths to get more newspaper sales."

Alex's calm demeanor was the opposite of the outrage that stirred inside Lizzie.

"I don't like it either. On the other hand, this is what newspapers usually do to gain followers, isn't it?" Alex's matter-of-fact response to the matter was irritating.

Jane nodded. "It's sad, but all too true. Well, perhaps our family is simply this week's news. I suspect next week, Miss Knowing will have a new person to target for her society column."

"I truly hope so." Lizzie swallowed, attempting to bring a calmness to her mind that she didn't feel.

"Moving on to a much happier topic. Did you happen to read Sarah's article?" Jane questioned.

Lizzie turned, still frustrated by the newspaper article. The selfish part of her wanted to vent all her frustration.

But Jane, as usual, could sense the emotions of the people in the room. Which was likely why she insisted on changing the subject.

Nodding, Lizzie replied, "I did. From her thoughtful article, I can tell Sarah is very proud of her grandmother's club. Mrs. O'Connor must be happy about that."

"I'm sure she is. Her granddaughter is following in her father's footsteps by writing for the newspaper as well as attracting more interest in her club," Jane commented.

Alex nodded. "I remember Mrs. O'Connor's son, Sean. He was always writing about folks on the island who were meddling in other people's affairs."

"His newspaper column was always interesting. I always thought it was strange that he died suddenly in that boating accident years ago."

"I agree. That was weird."

Lizzie shook her head. "Well, that was a long time ago. I don't think we'll ever know what happened to Sean."

"Maybe not." Alex shrugged her slender shoulders. "But I do like hearing that Sean's daughter has followed in her father's footsteps and is carrying his torch, so to speak."

Lizzie nodded, thinking that was a good way to think of it.

The creaking of the wood steps jarred her out of her reverie.

Lizzie turned her head to see Grams' neighbor.

Old man Jeb Whetstone walked up the back porch stairs carrying something.

Lizzie stood to her feet and hurried over to him.

"Mr. Whetstone, it's nice that you've stopped by." Lizzie reached out to help the eighty something year old man to the top of the stairs.

But it turned out he didn't need her help. He was spry enough to reach the landing on his own.

"Lizzie, that you?" Mr. Whetstone's voice rasped as he peered over at her. The crinkle lines by his grey eyes grew in number with his wide grin.

"It's me."

"Well then, you're just who I wanted to see." His two wrinkled hands handed her a fresh fish wrapped in clear plastic. "This is for you. Just caught some fish this morning. Thought it would be neighborly to stop by. Give you a welcome home gift, you might say."

"Mr. Whetstone, that's kind of you." Lizzie wrapped her hands around the plastic wrapped large fish. "You were fishing this morning?"

The older man nodded. "Yep. I take my boat out every morning. I have for years. Caught this bluefin tuna near the water over by Gordon's Gully. A fine morning for fishing."

"I remember when you used to bring my grandmother your catch of the day. It was always a real treat for our evening meal."

The old man chuckled. "Good, I'm glad. I remember your grandmother would make a big dinner for all you girls from the fish I would bring over. I have fond memories of those days."

The old man sighed heavily before he turned to her. "Your grandmother would have been happy that you came home at last, Lizzie. I don't mind telling you I'm glad about it too. Seems fitting somehow, you being back home." He patted his hat. "Well, I should go. I have more fish waiting for me to set to rights at my place. Talk to you later, Lizzie."

He tipped his hat with two fingers and walked down the stairs.

Lizzie stood silent for a long while, pondering his words.

As he walked away, she called out, "Thanks again for the fish."

He waved back before heading on his way.

Alex and Jane walked up to stand on either side. All three of them watched as the older man limped beyond the trees into his large waterfront property next door.

"I'm surprised, Mr. Whetstone continues to fish at his age," Alex spoke up.

"That's the doctor in you speaking, Alex. From the look of Jed Whetstone, he seems to be quite agile for his age," Jane commented.

Lizzie smiled warmly. "I think it's wonderful that he's enjoying going out on his boat while he still can. It was kind of him to bring us this large fish. I'll cook it up for supper."

She turned to her sisters. "Let's go inside. I'll set the fish in the fridge. Then we can start going through Grams' things."

"Sounds good." Jane and Alex followed closely behind.

As Lizzie stepped into the kitchen, she saw Annie, Chris, and Jake.

"What are you three up to?" Lizzie questioned as she opened the fridge, setting the fish inside.

"We were hoping to talk to you, Mom." Jake finished eating his apple, and, after he threw it in the garbage, turned to her.

"Oh? What's up?"

"We wanted to fix up the upstairs bathroom. The shower is broken. I found that out this morning. And the toilet isn't working properly, either." Jake's announcement caused an inner turmoil.

"Well, we should fix that up then, because we'll need all bathrooms to work properly if we want to get this house in working order." Lizzie swallowed as she thought of more money going out of her bank account for repairs.

"Yes, we do. Chris says he'll search for the materials we need for the bathroom at a lower cost."

"Good. That would be very helpful." Lizzie found her purse on the counter and, finding her debit card, she gave it to Jake. "Get what you need to fix the bathroom."

"Okay thanks, Mom."

After the three of them left, Lizzie turned to see her sisters staring at her, concern written on their faces.

"Lizzie, are you okay?" Jane spoke in calm tones as she looked at Lizzie with a searching gaze.

"To be honest, I am feeling a little overwhelmed." To her chagrin, her voice cracked a little. "There is so much that needs to be fixed in Grams' rambling old house. And I am on a tight budget to try and get it all done."

Reaching over, Jane gently squeezed her hand. "Start by fixing only what is necessary. Then, look and see where your budget is at."

Lizzie nodded. "Yes, that's a good idea."

Another wave of overwhelm hit her. "I think I am stressed about how to transform our grandmother's old house into an inn. The truth is I feel a lot like this old house right about now. Broken down. Weary. And fraying at the ends."

"Why's that?" Alex's eyebrow rose a fraction.

Lizzie bit her lip and swallowed back emotion. "I think it's because my life has been turned upside down in the last few months. Fixing this house is another fresh change in my life that I feel very inadequate and unskilled to handle."

Both sisters were quiet for a long while, deep in thought.

"I'm sorry, Lizzie, that you've been through so many difficult life changes in the past few months," Jane whispered.

Alex cleared her throat. "I've thought of something. Would it help if you had someone to help guide you in this project of turning Grams' house into an inn?"

Lizzie nodded. "That really would make things so much easier. But I can't think of anyone who would help."

"I can. Mrs. O'Connor comes to mind. I remember when she turned her house into a bed-and-breakfast. I think she operated that business for twenty years or so before she sold it."

Lizzie nodded. "Of course. I should talk to the dear old lady. Thank you, Alex."

"Now that we have that sorted, let's go see what we can find among the many boxes that Grams left behind." Lizzie turned, walking down the long hallway to their grandmother's bedroom.

They entered the large room. The familiar wallpaper, decades old, with its dark green background and pink and white flowers, gave her a warm feeling inside.

The tall ceilings in the room made the room seem more spacious than it really was.

Lizzie walked over to her grandmother's large closet.

Opening the door, they saw many large boxes.

"By the look of things, we'll be here awhile." Alex sighed as she reached for one box.

Since there was lots of floor space, they sat on the wood floor.

Alex reached inside her box and found the photo albums.

"Oh good. Here are some terrible pictures of me as a child with my buck tooth problem." Opening the first photo album, she started looking through it.

"This is when Dad and Aunt Eleanor were children. Here's a picture of Dad and Gramps going fishing on Grandfather's old boat."

Jane smiled. "I love looking at these old photos. It's a wonderful way to get a glimpse of how life was for Dad and our grandparents when they were younger."

"Here's a picture of Dad with his friends. They look like they are teenagers. Who are his friends, I wonder?" Alex pulled the picture out from the album so she could study it closer.

"Can I look?" Lizzie asked. When Alex passed the photo, Lizzie recognized the faces. "These are the buddies Dad always hung around with when he was a teenager."

"You might remember Grandmother mentioning their names." Lizzie pointed to each person in the picture. "This is Ted Cantrell, Bobby Sutton, Jerry Hart, and Matty Bellanger."

"I remember Grams talking about Dad's friends. Didn't Matty die about the same time Dad and his friends went diving in that shipwreck?" Alex turned to Lizzie for confirmation.

Lizzie nodded. "Yes, sadly, that's true. Grandmother said something happened when Dad and his four friends went diving that day. They were searching for treasure.

She told me Dad wasn't the same after that day. Grams asked Dad what happened, but he refused to talk about it."

A look of tired sadness passed over Jane's features. "That sounds like our Dad. Remember how he always tried to make things happier for us kids? He didn't like to talk much about what bothered him."

Lizzie swallowed back emotions. It still hit her hard to talk about their parents. She missed them, even after all these years.

As the three sisters continued to pull books out of the boxes, Lizzie spotted a stack of many large notebooks.

Picking up the top one, she opened to the first page.

"Oh, my." Lizzie's quick intake of breath caused her sisters to turn their heads in her direction.

"What is it?" Alex asked.

"I think I've found Grams' journals. There's no doubt this is her handwriting. It's a really old journal. This first book in this collection dates back over sixty years ago." Lizzie sat amazed as she rifled through the pages.

"Well, then. It sounds like you've struck gold." Jane grinned. "Didn't you tell us that in the last few weeks Grams was alive when you called her, she sounded agitated and worried about something? Didn't Grams ask you to promise that you would read through her journals after she was gone?"

"Yes, she did." Lizzie nodded and grabbed a few more of the handwritten journals. "Looks like I will be doing quite a lot of reading in the next few weeks."

Alex smiled. "Well, let us know if you find some interesting tidbits in Grams' notes."

"Will do." Lizzie replied as she continued to add more

of Grams' notebooks to the growing pile in front of her. "My evenings will be busy for some time to come."

Suddenly, they heard footsteps hurrying down the hallway.

❧

ANNIE POPPED INTO THE ROOM. "Mom, can I talk with you for a minute?"

Lizzie stood to her feet.

Her daughter led her into the hallway to talk with her privately.

"I overheard something when I stopped in at the grocery store." Annie tucked her hair behind one ear, looking a little uneasy.

"What are you worried about?" Lizzie whispered, concerned by her daughter's nervousness.

Annie's wide-eyed gaze focused on her mother. "It was a conversation I overheard at the grocery store. I was in one aisle looking for beans and two women were in the next aisle. The two women didn't see me."

A crease formed between Lizzie's brows. "What did they say?"

"I heard their voices," Annie continued. "I heard one person say this. *I am good at what I do. You've taught me well, mom.*"

Annie continued. "Then the other voice said. *Well, you still haven't been able to buy that property on the waterfront yet, so maybe you are losing your touch.*"

"That's when the first person spoke again." Annie explained. "She said: *Don't worry. After I help her understand how unfit she is to run that place, she'll come running to me, begging me to buy the place."*

The crease deepened on Lizzie's forehead as she listened.

"Do you think they were talking about me?" Lizzie asked her daughter.

Annie shrugged. "They didn't say your name. But they talked about the waterfront property, which is what you have. I'm just worried they might target you."

Lizzie sighed. "Well, you didn't get their names, so we won't worry about it for now. Thank you for looking out for me, Annie."

Annie nodded and gave her mom a big hug.

Without warning, there was a loud knock on the door.

"That might be Jonathan," Annie said. "He said he might stop by later."

Lizzie's cheeks heated from simply thinking of him.

She whispered, "I'll be back as soon as I can."

Sighing, she walked toward the front door. She remembered how Jonathan's presence had been affecting her lately.

Lizzie sighed and smiled as she walked toward the front door.

Tossing and turning most of last night, she'd barely slept.

All night long, her thoughts were of Jonathan.

Yesterday, his offer to help her fix her grandmother's house touched her heart.

She didn't want to think about him.

Despite that, memories of him came back to her.

His handsome face. His gentle voice. His intense blue eyes.

When Jonathan riveted his attention on her, her pulse raced.

Yesterday made her all too aware of him.

She didn't miss his obvious examination and approval of her.

But she wasn't about to give in.

Such an attraction would be perilous.

JONATHAN TURNED his head at the sound of footsteps.

Seeing Lizzie's shoulder-length auburn hair and her big green eyes as she opened the door caused him to catch his breath.

Even after all these years, she was still the most beautiful woman he'd ever seen… both inside and out.

He forced a calm demeanor that he didn't feel. His heart was beating double time at the sight of her.

"I thought I'd stop by. I was thinking we could talk about what plans or changes you have for the house? That would help me as I draw up a blueprint for design changes," Jonathan spoke with an assurance that came from years of experience as a successful architect.

Lizzie held a gigantic pile of notebooks in her hands. She looked a little flustered from her busy day, even though it was only early afternoon.

"Oh, of course. That would be helpful. Come in, please." Lizzie backed up, waiting as he stepped inside the house.

"Looks like you have a lot of reading to do." Jonathan grinned, staring pointedly at the bunch of notebooks in her hands.

Lizzie looked down. "Oh, I forgot I was holding onto Gram's journals. I do plan to read each one, but I expect it will take some time."

"That's a wonderful gift from your grandmother. Many times, it's the memories of those people we love most that become our most valuable treasure." Jonathan spoke from the heart as he thought of the people in his life he loved. His grandmother and, of course, Lizzie herself.

Nervously, he watched as she set the notebooks down on the desk nearby.

Every movement of hers was graceful. She made understated elegance a fine art form.

Her cheeks stained a dark pink as he studied her.

Did his comment cause that blush?

Jonathan couldn't help but notice she wore a designer navy blue tank top with dark brown capris pants.

As always, she looked beautiful.

Yet, he couldn't wait to see her in lighter colors like the greens and pinks she used to wear when they were younger.

Colors that were more relaxed.

Colors that were peaceful.

Colors that were filled with light.

The colors brought to mind the light-hearted Lizzie he remembered from long ago.

"Where should we begin?" Lizzie's soft voice interrupted his wandering thoughts.

Jonathan rubbed his chin thoughtfully. "Perhaps we

should start with the most important changes you want to make first."

"Sure. Come with me to the dining room." Lizzie turned and walked down the hallway.

Jonathan pursued Lizzie to the large dining room. He looked around at the brown walls with its decades old wood panelling.

"I think this room needs to be updated." Lizzie looked around the room with a frown between her brows. "It simply feels too dark and dreary here. And I think the wall needs to be removed, to make it larger and make the dining room more open." Lizzie turned to Jonathan. "Could we remove it?"

Jonathan walked over to the wall. Knocking on the wall, he listened for the sound. "We can remove most of the wall. However, we'll need to leave this load bearing beam here. I think the rest of the wall can be removed."

"Good, I'm glad." Lizzie clasped her hands together. "That way, we can make the dining room much larger."

"Yes, it will increase the number of guests you can have in the dining room at the same time." Jonathan looked towards the solid wood door that led to the deck. "Hmm. I have an idea. What do you think of replacing that wooden door with two large French doors that lead onto the deck?"

Lizzie walked towards the wood door. "I would love it if guests could eat on the deck on sunny days. That's a great idea."

"Good. I'll draw up those changes and we can get to work." Jonathan wrote notes down on his smartphone, capturing his ideas quickly.

Lizzie hesitated, stumbling over her words, "I'll need to double check if my budget can handle this renovation."

Jonathan named a price.

Lizzie sighed in relief. "Oh, that's very reasonable. Alright then, let's go ahead with the dining room first."

"Sure. For an inn, that's a great place to start. How do the bedrooms and washrooms look to you?"

"Well, to be honest, the bathrooms need a lot of work. In fact, this morning Jake and Annie went to purchase supplies to fix one of the upstairs bathrooms." Lizzie sighed heavily.

"Sadly, Grams' old house needs a lot of work to get it ready for guests. I don't know if I'll be able to get it all done."

"Don't worry, Lizzie. We'll tackle each problem one at a time and find a solution. We will get this house ready and it will become the inn you envision." Jonathan's steady gaze focused on her, his words filled with promise.

He told himself he would do everything in his power to help Lizzie make her goal of fixing up this house come true.

He would do almost anything for this woman who, even after all these years, held his heart in her hands.

"Thanks for saying that. I am grateful for your help, but I just don't know if I'll have the skills or the resources to make this inn become a reality." Lizzie shrugged her shoulders in resignation.

Jonathan responded, doing his best to reassure her, "Sure you do. Besides, you have a few people around you who dedicate themselves to helping you. Next steps would be about getting approval from the Select Board and then getting a business license."

"I don't know if I will get approval from the board of selectmen of Sweet Beach Cove. I've never run an inn before or even a restaurant." A crease formed between her brows. "It's all a little overwhelming."

"I do understand about being overwhelmed. But remember, you have people to help you." He could see a glimmer of light in her eyes. "And just remember, there are many people on the island whose businesses have been approved and the owners don't have the experience needed. I'm confident they'll approve you as well." Jonathan reassured her.

"Thanks for saying that, Jonathan." Lizzie smiled. "But there are others on the island who don't think I can do this."

"Like who?"

"Well, when we first arrived, I was surprised to see Ava Cantrell-Worth and Cecily Whitticombe waiting on my doorstep. Both of them thought that my efforts to re-make Grams' beach house into an inn was a bad idea." Lizzie sighed heavily.

"I wouldn't listen to those two, Lizzie. Both of them don't have any idea about the work you're doing with this project. And they don't have any idea about what a resourceful and determined woman you are. In fact, I think those two will have to eat their words when all is said and done." Jonathan lounged casually against the door frame, watching her.

Lizzie's cheeks stained a deep pink. She reached over and placed one hand on his forearm.

"You've given me such confidence. Even though I doubt my abilities, you still believe I can do this." Withdrawing her hand quickly, she turned to look out the dining room window.

When she turned back, there was a frown on her face. "What's wrong?"

Lizzie swallowed and blinked rapidly. "It's just been a really long time since someone believed in me like that."

Her words surprised him.

Didn't her late husband believe in her? What would make Lizzie say that?

Jonathan noticed her green eyes were bright with unshed tears. As usual he didn't know how to handle it when a woman was teary-eyed. It had been the same whenever his mom or sisters cried.

Unsure of what he should do, he stepped closer to her.

With gentle fingers he lifted her chin to search her eyes. A single tear trailed down her cheek.

Her large green eyes glistened with unshed tears as she looked up at him with soulful eyes.

"I will always believe in you, Lizzie," Jonathan whispered softly.

At his words, Lizzie smothered a sob.

Pushing her hands against his chest, she pulled away her gaze clouded with tears.

Jonathan could see the confusion in her beautiful green eyes.

He wanted to hold her in his arms again, but she pulled away from him.

Her cheeks colored under the heat of his gaze.

Lizzie swallowed multiple times before the words rushed out, her voice cracking, "I must go."

Jonathan sighed helplessly as he watched her hurry away.

As her footsteps faded away in the distance, he found himself standing motionless, his thoughts swirling in confusion.

What had just happened? Why did Lizzie accept his embrace and then run away?

One thing he knew for sure was he would need to sort this out. He was determined to solve the mystery of Lizzie Stafford Wentworth.

He only hoped to only somehow get past the thick walls she placed around her heart.

CHAPTER SIX

Mr. Ansel Bellanger bought a small cabin on Martha's Vineyard. Ansel worked on one of the shipping boats, while his wife, Abigail, was a seamstress for a few of the ladies on the island.

This is a letter Abigail wrote to her mother in those early years. "I wish you could come visit us on Martha's Vineyard, Mama. Our sons Matthew and Ezra are almost as tall as their father. We work long hours, but we finally have a little cabin of our own. Ansel tells me he wants to leave this cabin and more besides to our sons when we leave this earth. It's my wish as well. Your grandsons would love to see you in the summer if it works for a visit. We will make all your favorite foods when you come. With love, your daughter, Abigail."

The Vineyard Historical Letters

*L*izzie yawned as she followed Annie up the stairs to see the work they finished yesterday.

"Mom, you seem tired. Didn't you sleep?"

"I slept, but only for a few hours," Lizzie whispered.

"Are you feeling well?" Annie stopped at the top of the stairs and turned to Lizzie, a frown creasing her forehead.

"I feel fine. There's just so much on my mind lately that I stay awake thinking." Lizzie sighed heavily.

Annie gave her a quick hug. "Everything will be okay,"

Lizzie simply nodded.

She didn't want to get her daughter worried about her problems.

Yesterday haunted her. She had truly embarrassed herself in front of Jonathan.

Her face grew hot with humiliation at the way she cried in front of him.

Memories of being held in his strong arms caused her cheeks to burn.

Worse, she had wanted to stay in Jonathan's arms for a really long time.

That's what worried her.

How could she face him again?

Lizzie promised herself she would not get involved with any man.

But whenever she was near Jonathan, her resolve weakened.

No. She reminded herself she wasn't about to let that happen.

At Annie's words, Lizzie refocused on her daughter.

"Mom, what do you think of this?"

Annie was pointing to all the work they did in the upstairs bathroom.

"This looks really good, Annie. You, Chris, and Jake did a good job on it." Lizzie's gaze went over the white and dark teal-colored walls.

They had installed and set up the new bathtub and shower head. Everything worked as it should.

"I'm glad you like the changes we made, Mom." Annie smiled, a satisfied gleam in her eyes.

Lizzie reached her arm around her daughter's shoulders and squeezed. "I really appreciate all the work you've done."

"I know you do, Mom. And we're happy to help."

As they walked down the long hallway, Lizzie looked quickly inside each bedroom.

"In the past few days, I've been looking around Grams' house. I noticed there is so much to fix to make this house ready for guests. It feels very overwhelming." Lizzie shuddered inwardly at the reminder of everything she had yet to take care of in order to reach her goal of opening the inn.

"Don't worry, Mom. We'll get it done." Annie poked her head inside the next upstairs bedroom. "There is a total of seventeen rooms, but only fourteen bedrooms that we can use for guests.

"Yes. At some point, hopefully we will have a lot of guests. I look forward to that." Lizzie looked at the large bed in the room. "It might be a good idea to buy new bedding for each room. Some good quality, cotton sheets with spring colors. Some light browns, purples, pinks, greens, and blues. What do you think?"

Annie nodded, smiling. "Yeah, that's a good idea. Maybe we should add bedspreads with similar colors?"

"Yes. That will be perfect for our beach house." Lizzie sighed happily. "I want each guest here to feel like they are very welcome. I think some spring colors will help."

"I do too." They turned to walk back down the stairs and ended up in the cozy den with the fireplace and large desk.

Lizzie had her desktop computer on top of her grandfather's old desk.

They sat down on chairs by the fireplace.

"Mom, have you thought of a name for your inn?" Annie took out her phone and wrote some notes.

Lizzie smiled. "I have thought about it. I was thinking of naming this place, *The Vineyard Inn*."

"That's a good name. Simple and elegant." Annie smiled.

"The only thing is, I'm not sure what is all required for a business here on the Island." Lizzie made a mental note to visit the Sweet Beach Cove town office.

"Let's see what we can find out." Annie walked behind the desk and turned on the computer. After a minute, she turned to Lizzie.

"Mom, it says here on the town's website that you'll need to get approved for your inn by the board of selectmen. Also, to serve food and to have guests, you will also need to have the kitchen approved for health regulations and have your house approved for overnight guests."

"Does it say on the website when the board meets to approve new businesses?" Lizzie took out her phone and made some notes.

"The first Wednesday of the month," Annie continued, "which means the next meeting will be at the start of September. That's in three days."

Lizzie nodded and jotted the information down in her digital notes. "Wow, that seems fast. I'll write that down."

"Mom, I have a bunch of ideas for your website." Annie grinned.

Lizzie smiled at her daughter's enthusiasm. "I'm grateful that you are willing to design my website. But I think I need to be approved first to run a business on the island, before I can have an official business website."

"Alright. But, in the meantime, I'm going to create a marketing strategy to get the word out about your inn." Annie tapped a finger against her chin. "Let's see. We'll need videos, nice photos of each room, and the view of the beach. Also, we should add some photos of food that guests can expect when they come, don't you think?"

Lizzie smiled. "Sure, we could do that. I'll make us some enjoyable meals and you can take photos before we eat. How does that sound?"

"Yum. Research can be fun and delicious." Annie grinned.

Lizzie smiled. Her daughter had always loved home-cooked meals they had over the years.

She made a mental note to make more meals.

Without warning, her phone rang. "It's Tess. I'll talk to her outside."

"Alright, Mom. I'll be busy planning your website." Annie gave her a small wave as Lizzie walked outside onto the deck.

&

"Hi, Tess. It's so good to hear from you." Lizzie was eager to hear her friend's voice. "How are you doing?"

"I'm good. Keeping busy as usual. How is everything going for you now that you've moved into your grandmother's house?" It was so good to hear Tess's happy voice.

"Where do I start?" Lizzie replied. "Jake, Annie, and Chris fixed the upstairs bathroom. My sisters are here helping me sort through Grams' things. And Jonathan Brookes stopped by and fixed my broken screen door. He also offered to draw up blueprints for any changes I want to make to Grandmother's house."

"Wait. I'm aware your children and sisters are helping you. But Jonathan, is doing all that work for you, for free?" Tess's voice rose a notch in unbelief.

Lizzie flushed. "I didn't ask for help. He offered."

"But that's the part that is so incredible." Tess sighed. "Lizzie, no man in his right mind would simply offer to help you for free, unless he's a relative or he's falling for you. Clearly, the man is smitten with you."

"No, I don't think so." Lizzie rejected the idea out of hand. "No, he's simply an old acquaintance who also happens to be a talented architect that's good at restoring old houses."

"Are you saying there have been no moments of closeness between you and Jonathan?"

Heat rushed from Lizzie's neck up to her cheeks as she remembered what happened yesterday. "Well, yesterday when he was helping me plan out the changes to the dining room, I became overwhelmed with this project. Jonathan told me he believed in me, and I got tears in my eyes. It was such a silly thing, really."

"No, I get it, Lizzie." Tess's words were whispered. "Your late husband, God rest him, always had these high expectations. And I think you felt like you failed somehow. That you could never live up to his expectations. Am I right?"

"Yeah." Lizzie swallowed back emotion. Even now, weeks after his death, whenever she remembered Grayson, her mind would shift, and she'd look to see if her clothes were just right or if the house was in perfect order.

"So, when Jonathan said he believed in you, his words must have touched your heart," Tess replied. "So what happened?"

"He saw my tears and put his arms around me. Being in his arms felt too good. And that scared me." Lizzie sighed. "So, I quickly pulled away and hurried from the room."

Tess gasped in her ear on the other end of the phone line. "Oh, my goodness. Lizzie, it sounds to me like there's romance in the air."

"Tess, don't even say that. I am recently widowed. I shouldn't even be thinking of another man. On top of that, I am trying to re-make Grams' house into an inn. Anyway, I work too many hours a day to have time to date." Lizzie assured herself.

Her friend sighed. "Lizzie, I think you are trying to come up with reasons to deny your attraction to Jonathan. Your high school boyfriend is back and has wheedled his way into your heart, despite your protests. And now you're running away scared. Am I right?"

Heat crept up Lizzie's cheeks.

Her friend had always had a way of getting to the core of the matter. Tess knew her well.

"I don't know. Maybe." Lizzie sighed heavily. "I'm just not ready for another relationship, Tess. I'm still trying to heal from the loss of my husband and the wounds of the past."

Tess sighed. "I know you need time to heal, my friend. All I'm saying is, don't close your heart off completely to a second chance at love."

Lizzie was quiet for a long while, deep in thought.

Her head swirled with doubt and fear as she thought about a relationship with Jonathan.

Lizzie couldn't deny her attraction to him. However, memories of what happened years ago haunted her still.

"I'm not completely closing the door. I'm hesitant. I need to know that he's changed. I worry about that, you know." Lizzie had her doubts.

"I know you do, Lizzie. But I really believe he's already showed you he's changed. You just described a man who has been helpful, thoughtful, and kind to you."

"It's true he has been very helpful and kind to me." Lizzie breathed in deeply. "But I still have doubts."

Tess replied, "Well, I believe if you give Jonathan time, he'll continue to show you he's a good man."

"I hope that's true, Tess." Her face clouded with uneasiness as she thought about the weeks ahead working with Jonathan on the house.

"It is true. I'm confident of that."

Without warning, the front door shut loudly.

"I've got to go. There's a loud racket by the front door. I need to see what it is. I'll talk to you later." Lizzie had just hung up the phone when the door to the dining room opened.

Her eyebrows flew up in surprise when her son Jake and Jonathan walked into the room.

Both men carried armloads of wood.

A telltale blush heated Lizzie's cheeks as she stared wide-eyed at Jonathan.

LIZZIE TUCKED her hair behind one ear as Jonathan set the boards down against the one wall.

A nervous jitter sliced through her veins, causing her hands to tremble slightly.

Being near Jonathan made her feel vulnerable.

Quickly, he turned and walked over to her. His blue eyes looked at her with a new intensity.

There was a spark of some indefinable emotion in his gaze.

Lizzie swallowed.

Placing his hand on the wall behind her, he leaned close.

His warm breath tickled her ear as he whispered, "Are you doing better today?"

She nodded, heat rising up her neck to her cheeks. "Sorry about melting into a puddle yesterday. You didn't need the extra burden of dealing with my messy emotions."

Lizzie tried to throttle the dizzying current racing through her. He was so close that she could touch him.

The smoldering flame she saw in his eyes startled her.

"You, my Lizzie, are never a burden. And if you ever need to talk, I want you to know I'm here." Jonathan's compelling eyes riveted her to the spot.

Her heart hammered in her ears.

Tingles swept up her arms as he said her name like an endearment: *My Lizzie.*

She told herself it was just a slip of the tongue.

Her voice trembled slightly, and nervously she cleared her throat. "Thank you for that."

Jonathan's low voice continued, "In fact, I was hoping we might have lunch soon. Perhaps on Saturday? I thought we might talk about ideas for the redesign of your beach house."

"Sure. Lunch would be good. It would be helpful to talk about more ideas to fix up the house." Lizzie hesitated, looking him in the eye. "But, just so we're both clear, this isn't a date."

His eyes danced in merriment. "Whatever you say. I'll pick you up at noon on Saturday for our non-date."

Despite his teasing tone, she was glad he agreed to her conditions. In her mind, this wasn't a date, but a business lunch to talk about their shared project.

Interrupting their conversation, her son called out, "Jonathan, would you come and help me measure this?"

Jake was measuring the width of the new French doors they wanted to add to the dining room.

"Coming," Jonathan replied. Turning back to Lizzie, he

grinned and whispered, "I'm looking forward to our lunch together."

Looking into his deep blue eyes, she shivered and silently nodded in response.

He was so disturbing to her in every way.

Lizzie watched him walk away, her emotions at war inside her.

Deep inside, she knew her feelings for him were intensifying.

A quiver of worry surged through her veins.

Lizzie's mind told her to resist Jonathan's continued interest in her, but her heart refused to listen.

As she watched Jonathan work alongside Jake, her heart warmed by the kind treatment of her son.

How would she be able to resist this man who was attractive and so helpful and kind to both her and her children?

Wrenching herself away from her ridiculous preoccupation with Jonathan, she hurried out of the room.

It wasn't until later that day that Alex and Jane finally arrived back at the beach house.

Lizzie was busy in the kitchen cooking. For today's dinner, she had made Beef Wellington. Whenever her emotions were overwhelmed, she resorted to cooking.

Cooking, in her experience, was something that was safe. If she followed the recipe, the meal usually turned out fine.

Unlike real life.

Sighing, she added the final touches on the meal. After she rolled the beef onto the puff pastry and mushroom mixture, she crimped the sides with a fork.

"Hey, sis. It smells good here. You've been busy." Jane's eyebrows shot up as she eyed Lizzie busy at work on the small kitchen counter. Alex walked into the room behind her.

"Yes, I've been busy cooking as usual. Annie reminded me that I should have photos of meals that guests can expect when they come to the inn. So, I thought I'd make Beef Wellington for dinner." Lizzie wrapped the beef and pastry mixture tightly in plastic wrap and set it inside the fridge.

"Yum. My favorite," Alex commented as she removed her sunglasses.

Lizzie washed her hands before turning to them. "So, did you two have fun re-visiting Martha's Vineyard?"

"We did," Alex commented. "We did a little shopping and then I stopped by Dr. Waverly's medical clinic downtown. The good doctor announced she was going to retire in the coming year. She said so many families have told her they wish there was a good pediatrician on the island to take care of the sick children. Then Dr. Waverly asked if I would consider moving back."

Alex continued, "I told her I've thought about it. With my inheritance of Grams' house near the busy downtown on Martha's Vineyard, it's been on my mind. That old stone cottage really is an ideal location for a medical office."

"So, you'll move back here?" Lizzie asked, as she wiped the countertop clean.

Alex responded, "I haven't committed yet, but the idea is growing on me."

"Oh, I hope you move back," Jane replied. "Perhaps I should seriously think about moving back. My son could benefit from being away from the city. Living here, he would be in a smaller town and closer to nature. And we would be closer to family."

Lizzie's eyes brightened. "Wouldn't that be something if all of us sisters moved back to Martha's Vineyard?"

Jane nodded. "That way, we would have a lot more time to search through Grams' things."

"True." Lizzie took her apron off and stared at her sisters. "Speaking of searching through Grams' things, I was hoping to show you something from her journal. Since both of you leave tomorrow, tonight might be our last chance to talk about it. Should we go to the den?"

"Of course." Jane and Alex turned to walk to the den. Lizzie quickly grabbed three glasses of ice water and followed close behind.

After she handed them a glass, Lizzie sat down on her grandfather's chair close to the fireplace.

"Thanks for the water, Lizzie. I didn't realize I was thirsty." Alex smiled and took another sip of water before shifting in her chair.

"This room brings back so many memories." Jane sighed as she looked around. "There were many days when I would run into Gramps' den crying. He would grab me into his arms and hug me. Telling me that everything was going to be alright."

Alex nodded. "Gramps would show me his maps of the places our great-grandfather and he visited with their ship. It felt like the world opened up to me in a bigger way whenever we talked."

Nostalgic memories wrapped around Lizzie like a warm blanket. "I loved sitting close to him. I remember telling Gramps about all the big mistakes I made in my life."

"He never judged me. I always felt safe and secure whenever I was near him. It seemed like nothing could hurt me when Gramps was nearby."

Tears pricked at the back of her eyelids and she quickly blinked them away.

Alex's expression stilled and grew serious. Lizzie was keenly aware of her sister's scrutiny. She had a feeling her younger sister wanted to ask her more questions about her comment.

Quickly, Lizzie continued talking, hoping to distract her sister.

"Our grandparents were so good to us, taking all seven of us into their home after our parents died. I'll always be grateful to them." Lizzie offered a wobbly smile to her sisters.

Alex paused, and a look of tired sadness swept across her face. "I agree."

"Me too." Jane, usually so upbeat, sighed and clasped her slender hands together as she looked at both her sisters.

Lizzie grabbed the tattered leather journal that rested on her grandfather's old desk.

"I wanted to read something that Grams wrote. She left behind a note at the start of her first journal." Lizzie opened a worn leather book and fingered through the yellowed pages.

Jane smiled warmly. "I'm glad you've already started reading through it. I'm sure you've been finding our family stories interesting."

"I've been really surprised so far," Lizzie said, "at how our family's history is littered with secrets and mystery."

"Oh? Do tell." Alex leaned closer, a sideways grin on her lovely features. Lizzie sighed. "It sounds exciting, but from Grandmother's notes, she seemed very disheartened at what she learned."

"Let's hear what she has to say." Jane pressed for more information.

"Alright. Here is what Grams writes." Lizzie brought the journal closer and started to read.

"To my seven granddaughters. I am writing you all this note and I'll leave it for you to find in one of my earlier journals.

So my lovely granddaughters, if you're reading this, then I have already left this earth. I'm sad to be leaving you because I'll miss your warm hugs and laughter. But I'm happy I will finally be together with my William, your grandfather."

All three sisters sighed heavily before Lizzie continued to read.

"But now I want to tell you about what you'll discover in the pages of my journals. You will find colorful and heartfelt memories of when your father and your Aunt Eleanor were children and as they grew up. I also share different stories of each of you girls as your grandfather and I raised you in our home. As you read through the pages, you'll find that I share the happy and sad parts of our lives in equal measure.

Some of the secrets and mysteries I wrote about, I didn't truly understand until the last couple years of my life here on earth.

In fact, I must say I was very discouraged by what I learned about the Stafford family history and our connections to other families on Martha's Vineyard.

I believe it affects all of our family today.

As you read through the pages, you'll learn about the mysterious death of your dad's friend, Matty Bellanger, when they were teenagers. I have so many questions. Was it simply a drowning as the police told us? And, of course, you know that your dad and mom's boating accident was ruled by the police to be a simple boating accident. But, was it really an accident?

These are troublesome questions that have gone unanswered for years. There are some people — like Matty's mother for instance — who has been waiting on answers for decades.

One last thing, as you keep reading, you'll discover that a certain group of people on Martha's Vineyard have continued to attack the Stafford family over the years. I don't have proof, but I've seen enough connected coincidences to believe it to be true.

Anyway, that's the reason I wanted to ask you all — my granddaughters — keep searching and digging until you find the truth.

This is my last request. I'm confident that there will finally be justice and peace when the truth is revealed at long last.

I love you, my granddaughters with all my heart. I will be looking down from heaven, waiting for the day when each of you return to Martha's Vineyard.

My hope is that all you sisters will grow closer than ever this time and that you'll each be given your second chance at love. I believe both are waiting for you on our beloved island. All my love, Grams."

Lizzie's eyes misted and she wiped a stray tear that fell down one cheek.

She noticed both Alex and Jane's eyes glistened.

Grabbing the box of tissue from the desk, she passed it to Jane.

"Look at the three of us." Lizzie stared through the haze of tears at her sisters. Wiping her eyes, she gulped hard. "Our grandmother still has the ability to cause us girls to get all misty-eyed."

Jane giggled. "I was reminded how much I missed our grandmother. I think she wants all us sisters to come back to Martha's Vineyard. To be a real family again."

Alex nodded. "But not just for us sisters to be a family again. From the letter, it seems Grams wants us to do some digging into what really happened to Dad's friend Matty when they were teenagers. On top of that, we've been asked to research some dark secrets from our Stafford family history."

"Yes, it's true." Lizzie's hands twisted nervously in her lap. "I can't help but feel a little worried. I mean, why would Grams say she believes Matty's death and our parents' death weren't accidents? What did she discover?"

"Hmm. It does seem very dark and mysterious." Jane agreed. "Well, each of us will need to do some digging into the Stafford family history to find answers."

A shiver of fear rippled through her body.

Panic welled up in her throat.

Was there someone — or a group of people — like

Grams hinted at, that were attacking everyone related to the Stafford family?

It seemed like they had no choice.

Together the sisters would find out what was going on — no matter what.

CHAPTER SEVEN

Another well-known family in Martha's Vineyard, is the Hayes family.
Silas and Edith Hayes sold their Boston business to a good friend, and bought a large house on the island.
Just after their move, Silas wrote to his friend Nelson Wilson.
"Dear Nelson, I hope all is well with your family and that the business is going well. Edith and I have been making the acquaintance of many good families here. I believe my skills in buying and selling property will be much needed on this island. I look forward to telling you more when I visit you in the spring. Your friend, Silas."
The Vineyard Historical Letters

"Mom, it looks like there are a lot of people here," Annie whispered in her ear.

Lizzie looked around the room to see more than half

the chairs filled in the community center. She didn't think this many people would attend the Sweet Beach Cove Board of Selectmen Meeting.

She muttered uneasily, "I know. It feels very intimidating to me."

Jake slipped his hand into hers and gently squeezed.

"Mom, you don't need to feel intimidated. Your inn is a great business idea for this area. Hopefully, people will be able to see that tonight." Jake's words encouraged her.

"Thanks, Jake."

Lizzie stared wordlessly when she spotted Jonathan seated in the row in front of them.

She didn't realize he would be attending this meeting.

The moment Jonathan saw her, he stood to his feet and walked back to their row.

"Mind if I sit next to you?"

She took a quick breath at the sound of Jonathan's low voice whispering against her ear.

"Not at all." Lizzie moved over so he could sit on the chair that faced the aisle. His long legs probably needed the extra room to stretch out.

Jake turned to Jonathan, "Have you been to one of these meetings before?"

Jonathan nodded. "Yes, a few times. The first time was when I set up my architectural business years ago. Then I came a couple of other times to support some friends of mine who wanted to get their businesses approved."

"They were successful?"

He nodded. "The one friend had to wait two months for his approval, but eventually he did get approved.

Sometimes it takes longer. We'll just have to wait and see what happens tonight," Jonathan explained.

"I suppose." Annie squeezed her mom's hand.

Doubt and worry filled Lizzie's thoughts.

She turned to look at the people still arriving in the room. She was surprised to see Mrs. O'Connor and her granddaughter Sarah had also showed up to the meeting.

Waving at them, she smiled warmly. Sarah saw her first and immediately whispered into her grandmother's ear. Mrs. O'Connor turned her head and waved back.

It was comforting to know she had friends here.

Ava Cantrell-Worth was seated in the middle row of chairs. Sitting beside her was Cecily Whitticombe.

In the row of chairs behind them, she saw Violet and Madison Hayes also in attendance.

Lizzie was curious as to why those women decided to attend the meeting.

She also noticed friends of her dad from years ago in the crowd. Bobby Sutton, Jerry Hart, and Ted Cantrell were seated together on the far side of the room with their wives.

Looking around the room again, Lizzie sighed. "There are so many people here. I'm surprised."

"Folks want to have their say in what goes on in their community," Jonathan commented.

A man in a dark blue suit walked to the front and grabbed the microphone.

"Hello, everyone. Welcome to this month's board of selectmen meeting for the community of Sweet Beach Cove." The man's voice droned on.

Jonathan leaned over and commented in a low voice, "The name of the man speaking is Mr. Arthur McTavish."

"Thanks for telling me. That's helpful to know." Lizzie smiled and nodded. She was glad to be seated next to Jonathan. He had lived on the island longer and knew more about the people here than she did.

Mr. McTavish continued to speak, "We like to begin promptly. So, if the selectmen will take their places at the front of the room, we'll begin."

The handful of men and women took their places where everyone could see them at the front of the room.

The meeting began.

Lizzie was happy to see Miss Sadie on the board. She noticed Vera Cantrell was also on the board. Vera was the daughter of Ida Cantrell. The Cantrell family had been acquaintances of the Stafford family ever since she could remember.

The people on the board began to talk about what transpired at the last meeting and went on to discuss other issues from previous meetings that they needed to take care of.

Lizzie shifted in her chair, uneasily awaiting her turn.

Finally, the board turned to the topic of requests for approval.

There were three requests that they needed to discuss for this meeting.

To start with, Ramona Forsythe had a request for approval of her start-up accounting firm at a small older house which was located near the center of the business area in Sweet Beach Cove.

Mr. McTavish, the lawyer, began to give details of the request. The lawyer spoke about the fact that this area of Sweet Beach Cove was focused on business and that her accounting practice would be an asset to the area.

He asked for comments from the crowd. No one objected.

After a short discussion among the board, Ramona's request was approved.

Lizzie was encouraged by that.

Next, was Mr. Frank Elward. His request was for approval of a new sports equipment shop.

Mr. McTavish explained that Mr. Elward wanted to bring more surfing and other water sports equipment to the area. After he was done explaining, again, the man at the microphone asked if anyone wanted to comment.

One woman complained, but it sounded like her objection was about the added competition to her own water equipment store.

The board of selectmen approved Mr. Elward's request.

At last, it was Lizzie's turn for approval.

Lizzie's gaze flew expectantly to the lawyer who began to speak about her request for a business license.

"The last request for tonight is from Lizzie Stafford Wentworth. Lizzie would like to run an inn out of her home. Most of you will know of the old Stafford beach house along the waterfront," Mr. McTavish explained.

He continued to explain, "Lizzie would like to call this place, The Vineyard Inn. There are fourteen rooms for guests. These rooms are available to rent on a daily, weekly, or monthly basis throughout the year. Lizzie doesn't have any experience in running an inn or a bed and breakfast."

Mr. McTavish looked at the crowd. "If there are people from the community of Sweet Beach Cove, who have something to say about this request, please speak now."

Lizzie's gut clenched with worry when three hands flew up.

An older lady with short red hair with silver streaks stood to her feet. "I don't like the idea of a hotel-type of business at the old Stafford place. It's too close to my own home along the waterfront. I'm worried about the increase in traffic. Where will all the cars park from all these guests? And the noise from all these guests that show up at this new inn will be too much for our quiet neighborhood."

Mr. McTavish spoke again, "Thank you for sharing your concern, Mrs. Donnelly. Would you like to talk to Mrs. Donnelly about those concerns, Mrs. Wentworth?"

Lizzie nervously cleared her throat and stood to her feet.

Looking over at Mrs. Donnelly, she addressed the older lady's concerns, "I do understand your concern about increased traffic and loud noise from the guests. To help reduce unwanted noise, here are my guidelines."

"Guests must be quiet from eight in the evening until eight in the morning every day. As for the issue of parking, Stafford house is located on ten acres of land. My plan was to make one acre of that area into parking. That way no one parks on the street and none of my neighbors will be negatively affected by the increase in the number of guests." Lizzie explained.

"Thank you, Mrs. Wentworth." The lawyer nodded at Lizzie before turning to look at the next person who raised their hand.

"It's your turn to speak of your concerns, Mr. Bateman." Mr. McTavish nodded to the man who had raised his hand.

Mr. Bateman shifted on his feet. "It's my belief that this new inn would only be another hotel that we don't need. My bed and breakfast isn't that far from Sweet Beach Cove, we're only three miles away. New guests can come to my place. I say there's no need for another hotel or inn for more guests in this area."

Again, Mr. McTavish turned to Lizzie. "Would you like to reply to Mr. Bateman's concerns, Mrs. Wentworth?"

"Yes, of course." Lizzie looked over at Mr. Bateman, hoping she could explain herself well enough. "I understand your concern about having an excess of hotels or inns, Mr. Bateman. I would like to explain why my inn would be unique. My place is private and away from all the noise and traffic areas."

"Guests will have amazing views from their bedrooms as well as when they dine in our newly remodeled dining room. I would also like to mention that your bed and breakfast is located a good distance away from Sweet Beach Cove. Because of that, I believe there is a unique opportunity for what my inn will offer to this community."

"Thank you, Mrs. Wentworth." Mr. McTavish then

pointed to the woman in the front seat. "It's your turn to speak your concerns, Mrs. Cantrell-Worth."

Lizzie eyebrows went up as she saw the woman was Ava. What was her objection?

"Much like Mr. Bateman, I believe turning the Stafford house into an inn would not be a good idea. We have too many B & B's and inns on the Martha's Vineyard already. Not only that, but that house is very old. I would be worried that it would collapse on the guests. But I have another objection to this request for the establishment of this inn."

"I did some digging and have learned that Mrs. Wentworth hasn't worked in over twenty-five years. So, if she has no experience in the hospitality industry, and has basically no working skills, how can we expect this proposed inn to be successful?"

"I believe we should save Mrs. Wentworth and the people in this community the trouble and vote no to her request to approve this new business."

"Would you care to speak to those concerns, Mrs. Wentworth?" The lawyer asked.

Startled at the attack against her character from Ava, she bristled with indignation.

But after a minute, she forced herself to cool down.

Lizzie told herself to respond with a cool head. "Yes, I would like to address Mrs. Cantrell-Worth's concerns."

Turning to Ava, Lizzie replied in a cool voice, forcing herself to speak in a calm and clear voice, "Mrs. Cantrell-Worth you mentioned two objections. As I previously addressed the concern of excess hotels or inns with Mr. Bateman, I will again say that The Vineyard Inn would be unique in that it would be the only one of its kind in Sweet Beach Cove."

"We are also working on renovations to the old house that will make this inn, a strong and stable place for guests. As to your other concern regarding my lack of experience, I would like to speak to that."

Lizzie took a deep breath to calm herself before continuing.

"It's true that I have not worked outside of the home in over twenty-five years. During that time, I was raising my children and I was hosting large dinners for my late husband's law firm in Boston. Many people that came to me later assured me that my dinner parties — that I cooked and hosted — were some of the best meals they'd ever had."

"My job as a waitress before I was married also has been useful in learning how to serve people better. It's my belief that those are just a few of the skills that will help me make The Vineyard Inn successful."

"Thank you, Mrs. Wentworth." Mr. McTavish looked over at the crowd. "Would anyone else like to make a comment?"

Lizzie waited with bated breath and was relieved when nobody raised their hand.

"We'll take a few minutes for the board to talk together about the business proposal from Mrs. Wentworth." Mr. McTavish turned to the board, who began to talk together.

Lizzie grabbed Annie's hand as she waited for their decision.

Finally, after a few minutes, the chairman of the board spoke into the microphone.

"The board for Sweet Beach Cove has made the decision not to approve Mrs. Wentworth's application at this time. As was mentioned in the concerns spoken by some, there are a few obstacles we feel need to be addressed before we can grant approval."

"Namely, the fact that the house is old and the proposed idea of creating new parking space. We would like to see progress made on the new parking space and the renovations to the old house before we feel we can approve this request." The chairman nodded at Mr. McTavish.

The man leading the board meeting closed the event for the evening.

Lizzie's heart sank to her stomach, and she didn't even hear the closing comments.

They had rejected her proposal to open her business.

Discouragement filled her thoughts, so that she didn't even hear the closing comments.

As everyone started to leave, Jonathan spoke to her, "I can't believe they didn't approve your request. I have a feeling there is another reason why your request wasn't approved."

"What would that be?" Lizzie mentally went through all the work they had done on the house, trying to think of what they missed.

Unexpectedly, a woman's voice interrupted her thoughts.

Lizzie turned to see Madison Hayes walking her way.

"Lizzie, it's really too bad the board didn't approve

your request to start your business." Madison's voice didn't sound like she was disappointed.

Jonathan sighed. "Miss Hayes, I'm not convinced you are truly disappointed. Tonight, you were nodding your head in agreement with the objections presented about Lizzie's proposed inn. To me, that sent a clear signal that you agreed with their objections."

"Well, I'm glad people spoke up. We needed to be clear on the facts." Madison responded to Jonathan before turning towards Lizzie. "Lizzie, I need to tell you the truth. I agree with Ava, that you simply don't have the skills needed to start this inn. I think the board of selectmen realized that tonight when they denied your request."

Madison's tone was cooly disapproving. "But all is not lost. You could sell your beach house to me and you wouldn't need to worry about needing to fix up that old house. I'm prepared to give you a more than fair offer. Think about it."

Madison handed Lizzie her business card.

Lizzie sputtered. "I haven't thought about…"

She abruptly interrupted. "Consider the offer, Lizzie. It might be the best thing for you. Call me."

With that last comment, Madison gave a quick wave and walked away.

Lizzie was too shocked to do anything more than simply stand there.

"Well, I guess that answers our question about whether there is another reason why the board didn't approve your request." Jonathan clenched his jaw as he watched both Madison and her mother walk away.

"What are you saying?"

"I believe your request wasn't approved because of these types of politics between residents. It makes sense to me now."

Annie sighed. "Tell us what you mean, Jonathan."

"Well, I think there is something going on where someone is convincing the members of the board to vote against your mom." Jonathan's voice was taut with anger.

Jake's jaw tightened. "Why would anyone do that?"

Lizzie wondered the same thing.

"I'm not sure, except that for years, Violet or Madison Hayes haven't liked the Stafford family for some reason. Not only that, but they are also good friends with the Bateman and Donnelly family. It's obvious they all had objections to your mom starting her inn." He cleared his throat.

"The real issue here is that sometimes these decisions come down to those who have more influence or power who show favoritism to a specific person or group." Jonathan explained.

"That's not right." A furrow formed between Jake's brows.

Lizzie put a hand on her son's arm. "It isn't right, son. I don't understand why they would do that."

Together they started to walk outside towards their vehicles.

"Because they can. There are powerful families on this island. They can usually sway most folks to their way of thinking." Jonathan shook his head.

"I suppose." Lizzie had never understood politics and family dynamics on the island. "I just don't understand why Madison Hayes is being so awful to me. And Ava was discrediting me in front of everyone tonight. I know the beach house is old and that I don't have experience running an inn. But we're working to fix things up."

She sighed heavily, discouragement weighing her down. "Maybe she's right and it's not worth it to fix up Grams' old house. Maybe I should stop trying to make this inn idea work. Perhaps, I should take her advice and sell the house."

Lizzie fell silent, feeling defeated. She was surprised that the thought of selling Grams' house brought sadness to her. Before she moved here, it would have been easy to sell the house.

Now, she was becoming attached to the old house, the memories, and even the people in the Sweet Beach Cove community.

Her throat ached with despair at the thought of selling the beach house.

Arriving at her car, she opened the door.

Turning to Jonathan, she sighed. "I'll see you tomorrow for lunch."

Jonathan leaned over and whispered, "Don't give up yet. We'll talk tomorrow alright?"

"Sure." Lizzie nodded in agreement, even though her heart convinced her that all those dreams of turning the beach house into an inn were crumbling to dust.

She got into her vehicle along with her young adult children and drove home.

As they walked into the house, Annie whispered, "Do you think it was Violet and Madison Hayes that I overheard speaking about the waterfront property?"

Lizzie sighed wearily. "I don't know. I doubt it. I can't think of what reasons they would have to want to buy Grams' old house."

Annie shrugged. "I don't know either."

"We won't worry about it." As they walked into the house, Lizzie's thoughts turned back to Jonathan.

She was convinced talking with him wouldn't change the truth.

The truth was she didn't have the money to renovate the old beach house completely, which was what was needed. The other truth was that she didn't have the experience needed to run an inn.

Her misery was so acute it was a physical pain.

A new anguish seared her heart as she thought of giving up the beach house that had been entrusted to her by Grams.

How would she be able to do it?

THE NEXT DAY, Jonathan drove her to a popular cafe along the coast of Martha's Vineyard.

A waitress led them to a table with an ocean view. Like a gentleman, he pulled back the chair at their table.

"Thank you." Lizzie nodded with a shaky smile.

Nervously, she chewed on her lower lip and stole a look as he sat down across the table from her.

All her anxious thoughts slipped back to grip her.

Even though they had agreed this was a non-date, it felt very much like a real date to her.

He had been such a considerate gentleman from the

time he picked her up at the beach house until now. His care for her, made this lunch feel even more like they were dating. Which they weren't.

Or so she continued to tell herself.

Looking out the window, she caught her breath.

The cafe he'd chosen for lunch had an incredible ocean view.

"Wow. Seeing the ocean touch the skyline, it seems like blue goes on forever. It's beautiful."

Jonathan grinned. "I'm glad you like it. This is one of my favorite places to eat."

"I can understand why." Lizzie loved looking at the wide expanse of blue sky and ocean.

It was peaceful and relaxing.

After tossing and turning most of the night from worry over last night's decision from the board, the beautiful view was a sliver of sunshine on an otherwise miserable day.

"I'm glad you accepted my invitation to lunch." Jonathan's low voice caused Lizzie to turn her head.

His gaze was intense as he assessed her frankly.

He was so handsome. Today he wore a royal blue t-shirt that matched his eyes.

Her heart hammered in her ears at the sight of him.

"Thanks for inviting me, Jonathan." Her voice sounded shaky to her own ears.

Lizzie shifted uneasily in her chair.

Nervously, she rubbed her clammy hands on the black capri pants she wore. It was a sure sign she was flustered.

Her close fitting, sleeveless top was brown with hints

of red. Tess had told her the colors highlighted her auburn hair.

Guilt plagued her for wanting to look her best for Jonathan.

She reminded herself that their lunch together was not a date. She wanted to be friends only with him.

It was safer that way. She had been hurt years ago and didn't want to go through that again.

"I'm happy you decided to move back to the island." His low voice washed over her like a refreshing rain.

Lizzie was strangely flattered that he was happy that she came back.

"Well, that's because of Grams' inheritance. The beach house was just what I needed, especially after my husband's death." Awkwardly, Lizzie cleared her throat.

"Of course. You moved back because of your inheritance." A look of disappointment passed quickly over his features, before it quickly went away.

Despite his closed expression, she sensed his vulnerability.

Lizzie questioned what his look was about.

He had always been a deep thinker, but she told herself his reaction wasn't for her to worry about.

Her cheeks colored under the heat of his gaze.

"Yes. I was quite surprised Grams left her beach house to me. It's a wonderful gift that couldn't have come at a better time. As an added bonus, my beloved Grandmother paid the annual property taxes the month before she passed away. So, that was truly helpful. I have a lot to be grateful for."

Jonathan leaned back in his chair, his gaze probing for

answers. "I am happy for you. However, I feel like I'm hearing a *but* in there somewhere."

He saw too much. Then again, he always had where she was concerned.

The waitresses brought the food they ordered.

Lizzie was too distracted as she thought of her own response.

Without warning, last night's worries poured out of her. "Yeah, there is. With last night's decision not to approve my business license, I am seriously thinking of giving up on the idea of an inn. Maybe both Ava and Madison are right after all. Maybe I should sell the beach house."

A crease formed between Jonathan's brows. "I don't think you should give up on the idea of turning your grandmother's house into an inn."

"Why not?"

"Just because the board of selectmen didn't approve your business license this time, doesn't mean they won't approve it the next time you apply," Jonathan stated. "I've seen it before when a business application takes up to three months to be approved."

"It just doesn't make sense to wait so long." Lizzie sighed. She fidgeted with the cutlery beside the plate.

"I know it doesn't." Jonathan's soothing voice calmed her. "But I really believe if you keep making renovations to the house and you move forward to get the parking space ready, you'll be approved."

Lizzie sighed, discouraged. "It's just that it will be costly to fix all of that. I don't know if I have it in my budget."

"Let's start on the most important fixes first and see where that gets us." Jonathan suggested.

"I suppose." Lizzie offered, still feeling very unsure.

"And I also know a guy who will get your driveway expansion finished at a reduced price."

"You do?"

Jonathan nodded with a grin. "I do. He'll give you a great deal. Do you want me to ask him to call you?"

"Yes, please. That way I'll know what to expect."

Jonathan smiled. "I'll do that." He looked at her, his blue eyes intense. "Now, tell me you won't think about selling the house to Ava."

"If I have a plan to move forward, that's within my budget, then I won't be selling the house."

"Good. Then let's map out what we'll be working on this month." Jonathan smiled.

Lizzie sighed. "There is a lot to fix in Grams' old house. Sometimes it seems overwhelming."

"No need to stress or worry. We'll simply do our best to solve each obstacle as they come. We'll do it together." Jonathan's calm voice soothed her misgivings.

"It might not be as easy as that, but I understand your meaning. And thank you." She appreciated that he was trying to encourage her.

"So, tell me what are the problem areas that need fixing?" Jonathan repeated.

"Well, all the bathrooms need to be fixed. And there are a few items that need to be fixed in the kitchen. I would really like to add an island in the kitchen. Recently, I've discovered I need more room for baking. That will be really helpful when more guests come to the inn." Lizzie said thoughtfully.

"That can be done. And I believe it can be done within a reasonable budget." Jonathan mentioned a cost that was surprisingly low.

"Good. Then I'm ready to finish up these renovations. I want this old beach house to be restored well enough so the board will approve my opening this inn," So many doubts filled Lizzie's mind.

As Jonathan drove her home, so many questions flooded her thoughts.

Would they get the necessary renovations finished in good time? And even if they did, would the board approve her request for a business license?

"Try not to worry. Remember, we'll tackle each obstacle as it shows up. We'll do that together, all right?" Jonathan's whispered words as he walked her to the door, soothed her.

Lizzie nodded. "All right. Thank you, Jonathan. This lunch was just what I needed."

"Good. Then maybe you'd be willing to come with me to the Cantrell festival later this month?" Jonathan's words melted the ice around her heart a little more.

His invitation was hard to resist.

Forgetting her resolve to keep her distance, Lizzie nodded. "I would."

"I'm glad." His hand stayed longer than necessary on the small of her back as they stopped at the front door. "I'll see you tomorrow, Lizzie."

A brief shiver rippled through her at the warmth of his touch.

All she did was nod. As he turned and walked away, she stared after him.

It looked like she had more obstacles to face than turning Grams' beach house into an inn.

The other hurdle that faced her was Jonathan himself.

Over the past couple of weeks, her defenses lowered whenever she was with him.

Her weakness when it came to Jonathan, is what worried her most.

CHAPTER EIGHT

In a letter to his brother, Captain Henry Stafford penned these words.
"Dear brother, I hope you and your family are well. Since, my ship is being refitted, I have been working at the house.

I promised my Mary, I would build more rooms to our house. Since we are expecting a baby in a few months, I have been hard at work. I even built a small secret room in the den — a place to keep important documents you might say.

Our oldest son William and youngest daughter Charlotte are looking forward to their new brother or sister. My hope is that I will have returned from my next sea voyage before the new baby is born. I will write again soon with more news. Your brother, Henry."
The Vineyard Historical Letters

A week later, a lot of work had been done on the house.

The bathrooms had been renovated and the dining room was expanded, now boasting new French doors.

After giving directions to the guy who worked hard to expand her driveway, Lizzie picked up some weeds in front of her house.

Turning the corner to go up the front steps, she stopped suddenly.

Ava Cantrell-Worth walked towards the house.

Lizzie's back stiffened.

Why was Ava at her house again?

Forcing herself to smile, Lizzie called out, "Hello, Ava."

Ava strutted towards her, as if on a mission.

The woman held out her hand for a handshake and Lizzie reached for it out of politeness.

"Hello, Lizzie." Ava's smile didn't reach her eyes. "I wanted to stop by to ask if you thought more about my offer to buy this old house? In all honesty, most likely you'll receive less than the expected real estate value. The house is so old and run down, you see. But I'm still prepared to offer you a fair price."

"I'm surprised you still want to make an offer on this house if you view its value in such a dim light," Lizzie finally said what was on her mind.

"Well, I believe in speaking the truth. In real estate it's best to say it how it is," Ava's voice was firm. "Considering the state of the house and land, my offer is quite generous."

Ava wrote down her offer on the back of her business card and handed it to Lizzie.

"I see." Lizzie looked at the number and swallowed. It was in the low millions.

There was a lot she would be able to do with that kind of money. Help her children or even move far away to start a new life.

The thought occurred to her that she could save herself the trouble of trying to fix up Grams' old home and just sell the place now.

However, as soon as the thought entered her mind, it was like she could hear Jonathan's words churning in her mind.

There's no need to stress or worry. We'll simply do our best to solve each obstacle as they come our way. You have people willing to help you. All of us will fix up this house together.

Feeling a spark of hope, she blurted out, "Thank you for offering to buy my house, but at this time I'm not interested."

Lizzie started to move up the steps towards the front door, when Ava's voice stopped her.

"Wait. You're seriously declining my offer to buy your house?"

"I am."

Ava sputtered in disbelief. "This is a very generous offer. You would be a fool to turn it down."

Lizzie sighed heavily, doing her best to keep her voice from wavering. "Still, that is what I'm doing."

Ava shook her head in disbelief. Her lips thinned in anger. "You will find that trying to make a living as someone who has never operated an inn before, very difficult. This is a hard business with no mercy. But you'll learn that soon enough. Besides, I believe there might be other ways to get you to change your mind. Good day, Lizzie."

Abruptly, Ava spun on her black dress shoes and hurried back to her car.

Lizzie stood on the steps staring wide-eyed as Ava drove her car away.

The nagging in the back of her mind refused to be stilled. What did Ava mean by saying there are other ways to get her to change her mind about selling the house?

Her face clouded with uneasiness as she walked up the front steps. An unsettled feeling overcame her. Maybe Annie had been right in her concern.

The problem was, she didn't know if it was Violet and Madison or Vera and Ava that her daughter overheard in the grocery store a few weeks ago?

As she opened the door to go into the house, she caught herself glancing uneasily over her shoulder.

Hastily, she turned back, doing her best to get rid of the dark thoughts that plagued her.

HOURS LATER, Lizzie took the muffins out of the oven just as the doorbell rang.

Setting them on the cutting board, she hurried down the hallway to the front door.

Annie was expected to arrive at any time. She was coming for the weekend and she had some news to share.

Her daughter's arrival was the reason she made muffins.

Lizzie jerked back, startled at the loud ringing tone of the doorbell.

The house was very quiet when she was alone, so the ringing echo surprised her.

Her son Jake had gone with Jonathan to look at lumber to build the large island for the kitchen. Jake had decided he was going to build the countertop himself.

Lizzie was thrilled her son wanted to help with the house. It meant a lot that her children supported this unexpected change in her life.

Hurrying to the door, she opened it.

Her eyes grew wide when she saw the women standing there.

"Hello, Lizzie, my dear." Mrs. O'Connor stood there. By her side was her granddaughter Sarah. On her other side stood another woman who looked vaguely familiar.

"Hello, Mrs. O'Connor. It's nice to see you again." Lizzie hugged the older woman. "Good to see you too, Sarah."

"Oh, Lizzie, this is Debbie McVay. I wanted to introduce you two." Mrs. O'Connor looked warmly at Debbie. "I helped Debbie get her bed and breakfast up and running a few years ago."

Debbie shook Lizzie's hand. "Hello, Lizzie. You might remember me from high school? We were in the same graduating class. I was Debbie Bennet back then."

A soft gasp escaped Lizzie. "Of course. That explains why you look so familiar to me. I'm sorry that I didn't remember your name. It's good to see you again, Debbie."

"It's good to see you too, Lizzie." Debbie grinned, her brown eyes lighting up her face. "I was sorry to hear about your husband's passing."

"Thanks for that. It was a shock to all of us. With the help of my family, I've been able to find my way." Lizzie replied.

"I'm glad." Debbie's gentle smile was comforting. "When I lost my husband to cancer a couple years ago, it was my two daughters, my mom, and Mrs. O'Connor who helped me get through that difficult time."

Immediately, Lizzie felt a surge of compassion. "I'm so sorry for your loss."

"Thank you. I'm doing all right now, thanks to my family and the support from Mrs. O'Connor here." Debbie looked over at the older woman with a big smile.

"I'm happy for you." It encouraged Lizzie to hear that another woman who had dealt with loss, yet had somehow moved on and been successful. "Where is your bed and breakfast located?"

"On the other southern side of the island," Debbie replied. "It's an older home that I renovated into a bed and breakfast."

"That's similar to what I'm trying to do with my grandmother's old home," Lizzie commented.

"Debbie has done well for herself, despite her loss." Her mentor nodded. "You will too, Lizzie."

"Thanks, Mrs. O'Connor. I hope so." Lizzie waved for the women to come inside. "Let's go to the dining room, where we can sit down at the table."

"Lizzie, you've made some wonderful changes here." Mrs. O'Connor looked around at the new renovations.

Sarah nodded. "There's more room for guests in here now."

Lizzie nodded. She loved the new French doors and the wall they removed to enlarge the space. "I'm glad we made the changes."

Debbie commented, "It looks good. The kitchen must be nearby. I can smell something wonderful baking."

Lizzie nodded. "Yes, the kitchen is just through that door. I just took the blueberry muffins out of the oven. Do you all have time for some tea?"

"That would be lovely." Mrs. O'Connor smiled and sat down at the large dining room table.

"I'll bring the food in a jiffy." Lizzie hurried to the kitchen, thinking it was so nice to have guests to stop in and visit. Hopefully soon, she would have folks stopping by all the time.

Before long, she carried the muffins and tea cups along with hot tea on a tray and set them on the table.

"Yum." Debbie took her first bite. "You won't have any problems having repeat guests. They will love your food."

Heat flew up Lizzie's cheeks. "Thanks. I hope that's true."

Mrs. O'Connor took a bite of the fresh muffin. "Your food is wonderful Lizzie. But that's not the only thing to think about when you have guests coming to stay at your inn."

The grandmotherly woman went on, "You need to think about what feeling you want guests to have when they first come to visit and what do you want them to leave with?"

"Hmm. I don't think I've ever really thought about that."

Mrs. O'Connor finished eating and took a sip of tea. "I believe your answer will help you create an atmosphere that will bring customers to your place year-round."

Lizzie took a few minutes to think about it. Memories wafted over her of Grams' warm hugs that made her feel loved and like she belonged.

A lightheartedness came over her as she remembered feeling accepted and welcomed. It was the kind of feeling that made one's worries all disappear.

"I guess, I would like guests to feel like they have come home. That they are accepted, that they belong and that they can be themselves here." Lizzie sighed as she pictured it.

"What colors would give that feeling?"

Lizzie took a sip of her tea, picturing Grams working at quilting another blanket to give away.

"Light blues, pinks, light browns, and light greens come to mind. You know, soft colors. Gentle colors." A crease formed between her brows as she continued to consider how to answer that question.

"Light colors have always reminded me of spring. The light blue sky, the pink and red sunrises, and the light brown wooden rocking chair that Gramps made that is out on the outside deck."

A warmth flooded her at the thought of family. "It reminds me of the freshness of spring. It's filled with the possibilities of new beginnings and restoring your life, with the mistakes of the old wiped clean. That's something I long for myself, so for guests that stay at the inn, I want them to feel those emotions too."

Sarah spoke softly, "That's a beautiful thought."

"I agree. I think you might be onto something there." Mrs. O'Connor stood to her feet. "Lizzie, you should come with us shopping. I know just what you need."

Her eyes widened in surprise. But she went along with the advice of the lady who had been Grams' friend. She'd known Mrs. O'Connor all her life and trusted her to steer her in the right direction.

Lizzie had just put the dishes in the kitchen, when her daughter arrived.

"Annie, you're here. Just in time too." Lizzie hugged her daughter smiling at the look of surprise on her face.

"What am I in time for?" Curiosity shone in Annie's eyes.

"Come with us shopping." Lizzie introduced her daughter to the three women.

"Sure, I'd love to go. Let me put my suitcase in my bedroom, and I'll be right back." It didn't take long before Annie was back and they were on their way.

They drove together to the clothing stores along the busiest streets of Martha's Vineyard.

"Mom, I wanted to tell you that I was let go at my job this week," Annie whispered in her ear as they walked into one of the clothing stores.

"What? I'm so sorry. What happened?"

"My boss just said they needed to make cutbacks to the budget. I lost my job." Annie sighed heavily.

"I'm so sorry. Will you come home for a while?" Lizzie wanted to help in whatever way she could.

"If you don't mind, I would like to come home. Just until I can figure out another job or something," Her daughter questioned.

"Of course, you can stay. Take as long as you need." Lizzie reached over and grabbed Annie's hand. "Let's talk more about this later."

Annie nodded, sighing with contentment.

As they walked through the aisles of women's clothing, Lizzie looked over at Mrs. O'Connor.

She needed an answer to the question that was uppermost in her mind. "Why did you bring us here?"

"I was thinking. A great first step is to decorate your house with the soft colors you love. But what about the clothes you wear?" Mrs. O'Connor asked.

"What about my clothes?" Lizzie's eyes looked down at her navy-blue sweater and brown designer pants. She couldn't see a problem.

"Well, they are very smart looking. But if you want a more warm and homey type of atmosphere, I think you might consider wearing clothes with lighter colors that feel more relaxed. A simple blouse or even a plain cotton t-shirt and a skirt or some jeans, wouldn't be amiss."

"I can't even remember the last time I wore jeans." Lizzie commented. It wasn't the type of clothes that her late husband liked at all.

Therefore, she never bought or wore them.

"Well, then it's time you did." Mrs. O'Connor stated emphatically.

Annie was all excited. "Mom, you'll look great in jeans."

"You think so? I wore jeans when I was in high school, but that was ages ago," She muttered uneasily. Change had never been easy for her. Switching the style of clothing she had worn for years, brought all her insecurities to the surface.

"Will people think I'm going through a midlife crisis if I suddenly start wearing jeans?" Lizzie wondered out loud.

"Who cares what people think, Mom. Do this because you believe this change will be good for you and for your inn." Annie's words struck a chord inside her.

"You're right. I do believe this will be a positive change for me. Hopefully it will reflect well on the vision I have for The Vineyard Inn." Lizzie nodded, feeling more settled inside.

Everyone started looking around the store.

"What do you think of these?" Debbie handed Lizzie a pair of jeans that were on sale.

Annie found her a couple of light-green and pink cotton t-shirts. The shirts were high quality, but had a relaxed feeling to them.

Lizzie tried on all the clothes. They fit perfectly.

When she came out of the change room, she twirled.

"You look amazing, Mom," Annie said.

"You're a new woman, Lizzie," Mrs. O'Connor declared. "Now you are ready to welcome your guests."

Lizzie stared at herself in the mirror for a long while. The light pink she wore, gave her a softer look somehow.

All the way home, Lizzie thought of the change she saw in herself. It felt like she was changing from a woman who had survived the harsh realities of life to a woman who was stretching out of her cocoon to fly her wings.

This was her transformation. She could feel it.

Since moving here she'd already had to make changes. She'd faced some of her insecurities and fears.

She had chosen to move to Grams' house.

She had faced the board of selectmen and the community of Sweet Beach Cove.

She had taken the risk to renovate the old beach house, even though she didn't know if she would get her business license.

Lizzie didn't doubt there were more changes to come.

But, in some strange way, today she'd been given more confidence that she could face whatever lay ahead.

IT WAS the last Saturday of September, when Jonathan picked her up to attend the annual Cantrell Family Festival.

Nervously, she opened the door to greet him.

Reluctantly, Lizzie admitted she wanted his approval of the recent changes she'd made to her wardrobe.

Her pulse quickened as his compelling gaze riveted her to the spot.

"Wow." Jonathan's eyes took in the new shirt and blue jeans she wore. "I must tell you that light blue color makes your lovely green eyes even bigger. And those jeans… well let's just say you look real good. You're beautiful, Lizzie."

Heat stained her neck and rose up to her cheeks at his look of appreciation.

As a widowed older woman with three full grown children, it was a wonderful feeling to have a man compliment her.

A smile hovered over her lips as he drove.

Jonathan spoke softly, "If you don't mind, I need to make a quick stop at my home. I spilled coffee on my shirt earlier when I hurried out the door. It won't take me long."

"Of course." Lizzie nodded, smiling a little. She hadn't noticed the stain on his shirt, but Jonathan had always liked to wear clean clothes.

Soon Jonathan turned the car onto a small acreage. A beautiful, large, two-story house was the first thing she saw. It had a ranch house appearance with a wrap-around deck.

"What a beautiful house you have, Jonathan," Lizzie said as she got out of the car.

Jonathan smiled. "Thanks, I designed it myself. One of my favorite designs has been the country look, even though I design many styles of homes for clients."

"It's lovely." Lizzie walked with him to the front deck. "I can wait here on your deck while you change."

"Sure. I'll just be a second." Jonathan was only gone five minutes before he appeared again.

Suddenly, a woman's voice called his name.

"Jonathan, are you home?"

It sounded like an older woman's voice.

Jonathan smiled. "Want to come and say hello to my mom?"

"Sure." Nervously, Lizzie walked beside Jonathan. They walked behind the big house to a smaller guest cottage.

A gray-haired woman sat on a rocker on the deck.

"Hi, Mom. How are you feeling today?" Jonathan leaned over and kissed her weathered cheek.

"I'm well." Mrs. Brookes looked over at Lizzie and smiled. "Who do you have with you, Son?"

"This is Lizzie Stafford Wentworth. Do you remember Lizzie?" Jonathan spoke gently to his mother.

"Of course, I remember Lizzie. How are you, my dear?" Mrs. Brookes took her hand, squeezing it gently.

"I'm doing well. It's good to see you, Mrs. Brookes." Lizzie's voice shook slightly, revealing her nervousness.

The older lady smiled warmly. "Well, I'm glad to see my son has brought home a lovely girl at long last."

Jonathan's cheeks turned to a ruddy red at his mother's comment.

There was something warm and enchanting about his reaction that touched her heart.

"Mom, we can't stay. We're just about to leave for the Cantrell Festival." Jonathan explained.

"Well, I hope you two have a fun time." Mrs. Brookes stood unsteadily to her feet. "I hope you come back again soon, Lizzie. It was wonderful to see you."

"It was good to see you again too, Mrs. Brookes."

As Jonathan and Lizzie drove away, he turned to her and whispered, "I think my mom really likes you."

Heat flooded her cheeks.

A self-conscious smile formed on her lips. "I'm glad. I like your mom too."

Lizzie didn't miss the look of satisfaction on Jonathan's face as he drove them to the Cantrell Festival.

Parking the car, he got out and hurried around to open her door.

When he held out his hand, Lizzie placed a shaky hand in his and stepped out of the car.

As her feet touched the ground, Jonathan gently pulled her closer. He gently gripped her hands.

His gaze was as soft as a caress as he searched her eyes.

She did her best to throttle the dizzying current racing through her.

Jonathan unsettled her. He made her want more than what she believed was possible.

Each time she was with Jonathan, the pull was stronger.

At the loud bark of a nearby dog, reason returned and she cleared her throat. "Thanks."

Jonathan took his time letting go of her hands.

Lizzie forced herself to talk about a different topic to ease the tension between them.

"I remember coming to visit Ida Cantrell with my grandmother when I was a child. It was only the one time. I remember the house was large and a little bit like a cold mausoleum." Lizzie shivered as she began to walk on the freshly cut lawn.

Jonathan walked beside her, his hands in his pockets. "I had a similar feeling when I walked through the Cantrell house years ago. Ida had asked me to give her an idea of the cost for restoring the old house. In the end, she chose a different architect firm."

Lizzie turned to him. "That's too bad. She missed out on some great restoration ideas. I speak from experience, having seen your work first hand."

Jonathan grinned. "Thanks, Lizzie. That's kind of you to say so."

Lizzie shrugged. "Just speaking the truth."

They continued walking towards where the crowd of people were gathered.

Lizzie was very aware of him as walked side by side.

The budding attraction she had for Jonathan, made her want to shake herself.

You are not going to let yourself fall for this man, Lizzie. Don't you remember what happened last time?

The voice in her head was a constant reminder to not let herself get too involved with Jonathan.

She was thankful that they were at the festival where there was a large crowd and plenty of distractions.

Some fun events for the children like pin the tail on the donkey and face painting, caught her eye.

There were snacks and drinks and many other events for people to try.

"Someone is playing jazz music. I've always loved the soft gentle rhythm of jazz," Lizzie commented.

"Every year the Cantrell's bring in jazz and blues musicians to play for the crowds at the festival," Jonathan explained.

"It's really nice. My sisters also like jazz music. Alex, Jane, Charlie, and Katie said they were coming today. And all three of my children were going to join me today too." Lizzie looked around. "However, I haven't seen them yet."

"I'm sure they'll arrive soon. It's good to have family here. My Mom and sisters are somewhere around here too. We'll catch up with them later." Jonathan smiled. "But first, maybe we should try some of the games. What do you say?"

"I'm in. But, fair warning, I haven't played outdoor games for years." Lizzie grimaced.

"Then it's time you got back into it." Jonathan led her to one of the lawn games. Folks had just finished, so nobody was playing.

"Remember how to play Horseshoes?" Jonathan picked up one of the colored ring-toss horseshoes and threw it towards the bright yellow peg.

"I think so. But my aim isn't very good," Lizzie commented. Jonathan threw the horseshoe to hit the peg dead center.

"You can do this. Throw another one, Lizzie." Jonathan handed her the horseshoe.

"Okay." Lizzie gripped a red horseshoe in her hand. "I'm glad these are made of rubber. I hadn't expected that. It feels lighter in my hand than the metal ones."

Eyeballing the yellow peg that was about fifteen feet away, she took aim and threw the horseshoe.

She sighed when it fell two feet away from the target.

"It's okay. You'll hit it the next time you try," Jonathan whispered.

Lizzie tried three more throws and each time, she missed the target. "Maybe I'm a slow learner." She turned to him, her lips turned up in wry amusement.

Jonathan's mouth quirked with humor. "Somehow, I doubt that. Here let me help."

He moved to stand behind her.

Lizzie inhaled a quick breath as Jonathan placed his large hand on her left shoulder. Then with his right hand he held her hand that gripped the red horseshoe.

"Let's try this again. If you relax your arm, I think it will help," his whispered words tickled her ear.

"I'll try." She shivered at his closeness.

It worried her that she had no desire to back out of his warm embrace.

The simple touch of his hand holding hers, made her heart pound faster.

Forcing herself to relax, she did her best to follow Jonathan's cues.

"Now, steady, aim and let it fly," He gently squeezed her hand and released the horseshoe.

Lizzie grew wide-eyed as the red horseshoe hit the target. She turned and threw her arms around his neck in response, excited that she finally hit the target.

Her reaction was spontaneous.

But not without unintended consequences.

Jonathan's strong arms reached around her waist, holding her there.

As she began to loosen her arms from around his neck, she found herself face to face with him.

His blue eyes stared boldly into hers with an intensity that shook her.

Instead of releasing his arms from around her waist, he pulled her closer.

His gaze moved down to her lips, and he began to lower his head.

Her emotions whirled in anticipation of his kiss.

Unexpectedly, a voice called out, "Lizzie, is that you? I've been looking everywhere for you." Her sister Charlie's voice was unmistakable.

She quickly backed out of Jonathan's embrace and ran shaky fingers through her hair. "That's my sister."

Jonathan leaned close and whispered, "Too bad we were interrupted. We will finish this later, I promise."

Heat rose to her cheeks and her pulse skittered alarmingly at his words.

CHAPTER NINE

One year after Ike Cantrell lost his land in a game of chance, he
returned with a new ship and plenty of money.
This is what he wrote in a letter to his brother George.
"My luck has finally turned. I have finally found some treasure.
I have bought a large house on ten acres of land and I've found
myself a new ship. I've decided my son Eli, will learn the
shipping business. I will teach him my methods of making
money and searching for treasure. I'm determined that all I've
learned will be passed down to my grandchildren. I'll tell you
more news in my next letter. Your brother, Ike."
The Vineyard Historical Letters

"Hello, Charlie, it's good to see you. I'm happy to see my sisters here today." She hugged Charlie, Alex, Jane, and Katie, doing her best to delay their questions.

From past experience, Lizzie knew her sisters were very curious about the details of her life. If there was a new romantic interest, her sisters were even more eager to pepper her with questions.

"Let's walk to the drink tables, shall we? Suddenly, I'm quite thirsty." Lizzie walked between her sisters, towards the tables that had been set up for soda, juice, coffee, and tea.

"I'll bet you are. You were quite cozy with Jonathan when we found you." Charlie leaned over, whispering in her ear.

She turned her head and spotted Jonathan walking toward them. He was chatting with her neighbor Jeb Whetstone.

"We're simply two friends who enjoyed a game of horseshoes together." Lizzie did her best to convince Charlie, but her sister was having none of it.

"Yeah, sure. I think the lady doth protest too much." Charlie usually had a quote for every situation — even though she often forgot a word or two in the retelling.

Lizzie sighed at Charlie's teasing. She was relieved when they reached the drink tables, maybe her sister would stop the verbal torture.

Pouring herself a strong coffee, she took a sip as she waited for her sisters.

There were empty picnic tables for people to sit down behind the drink tables.

Lizzie walked towards an empty table and sat down, sipping her coffee.

Her sisters joined her.

She asked, "I'm glad you all came today. Are you

staying overnight? There's plenty of room at the house. You'd be more than welcome."

Jane nodded. "That would be nice, Lizzie, thanks."

"Of course." She was glad to welcome her sisters to the rambling beach house. There were more than enough bedrooms for everyone.

"Katie, it's good that you're here this weekend. How's it going at the museum?" Lizzie asked.

"It's going all right. But my mind's mostly been thinking of Grams' will. I've thought a lot about moving back here. I've been missing you all." Katie sighed as she looked at her sisters.

"Ah, that's nice to hear. Just so you know, I've been thinking about doing the same thing," Jane commented.

Alex nodded. "I've thought about moving back to Martha's Vineyard too. However, I still need to figure out the details and what it would take to set up my medical practice on the island." Alex sighed. "It all seems a little overwhelming."

"I know that feeling," Lizzie responded. "It's what I've been facing as we've been renovating Grams' old house and also trying to get the business approved. When I started, I didn't understand all the red tape I would need to sort through."

"But you're doing it," Alex replied.

"Yes, I am." Lizzie looked up and saw Ava Cantrell-Worth had stopped at the drink table. Not far from her was Madison Hayes pouring a cup of coffee. "I've definitely had a few islanders try to hinder my progress."

"I'm not surprised. Folks don't like change." Alex stated in her usual matter-of-fact way.

Lizzie sighed. "I guess."

Although she wasn't convinced fear of change was the reason for Ava or Madison's chilliness towards her.

Walking across the lawn, Lizzie spotted a familiar face.

She waved, and the man walked over with his young daughter.

"Samuel Chadsworth, is that you?" Lizzie stood to her feet and shook his hand.

"It's me." Sam looked down at the little girl holding his hand. She looked to be eight years old.

Alex stood to her feet as she saw him. "Sam, this is a surprise. How are you?"

Lizzie had often wondered if Alex still thought of the man she once dated.

"Hello, Alex." Sam's voice seemed to be filled with a deep weariness. The shadows under his eyes, reflecting loss of sleep.

"It's good to see you again. I was sorry to hear about the loss of your wife." Alex swallowed.

Alex shifted uncomfortably.

Lizzie recalled Sam hanging around the Grams' house with Alex almost every weekend when they were teenagers. They had been quite close friends.

Sam even went to visit Alex during her first year of college, but then everything changed. They no longer saw each other.

"I see you have someone very cute with you." Alex quickly changed the subject to the little girl.

"Yes, this is my daughter Zoe. She loves to be where all the people are." The pride in Sam's voice was unmistakable.

"Hello, Zoe." The little girl's cheeks turned a beautiful rosy red upon hearing her name.

"Hello." The little girl's smile grew wide as Alex talked to her.

"Have you had fun today?"

"Yeth." The lisp in the little girl's, made her all the more adorable.

Samuel explained. "We've checked out a few of the events here today. It's been fun, hasn't it, Zoe?"

The little girl nodded with a happy smile.

He turned to Alex. "I'm surprised to see you at the festival."

"I wanted to come to the island to check on Lizzie and to see how the renovations are coming along." Alex grinned.

"Renovations? That sounds interesting."

Lizzie explained, "I moved back to Martha's Vineyard after inheriting my grandmother's house."

"That's good news. It's good to have you back." Sam replied. "Renovations are a big job."

"Yes. But I have some help, thankfully. We're trying to fix Grams' old house to get it ready for approval with the board of selectmen. I hope to have guests book their stay at our inn soon. Hopefully, in the next couple of months." A crease formed between Lizzie's brows.

Each day she struggled with worry about how long it would take for the board to approve her business license.

"I'm sure it won't take long." Sam tapped a finger on his chin. "I seem to remember my friend Jonathan mentioning that he was helping with a house rebuild on the island. Is that your house, Lizzie?"

Lizzie nodded. "Jonathan has been an amazing help. I'm happy to see you and he are still good friends."

"We are. I help him with computer software and he gives me tips on house renovations. It's been good." Sam grinned.

Lizzie smiled warmly, when she heard his daughter yawning. Samuel turned to his daughter, watching her rub her eyes tiredly. "It looks like we need to be going. Zoe is very tired from our busy day."

"Of course. It was nice to meet you, Zoe. And it's good to see you again, Sam." Alex smiled warmly as she looked at both of them.

As Lizzie watched father and daughter walk away, she couldn't help but wonder if Alex moved back to the island would Sam come back into her life once again?

She didn't know what the future would bring, but she hoped the two of them would find a new friendship and perhaps something more.

"It was good to see Sam again," Lizzie commented as she turned to her sister.

Alex nodded, sighing heavily. "It was."

Her sister had a crease between her brows, that meant she was deep in thought.

"Do you miss your old friendship with him?" Lizzie could see the sadness in her sister's eyes.

Alex nodded and shook her head regretfully. "I do. But it's all been lost. It's my own fault."

Lizzie squeezed her sister's hand. "I don't think it's completely lost. You just need time to have an honest conversation."

"Well, I don't know when that's going to happen. Both

of us lead busy lives." Alex sighed. "But it was good to see him again."

They stood together in silence for a long while. Lizzie wanted to encourage her sister, but was unsure of what to say.

Abruptly, Alex turned to her. "Do you want something to drink? I think I'm going to grab another coffee."

"No, thanks. I'm good."

As her sister walked away to the drink table, Lizzie wondered if there was a way she could invite Alex and Sam to the same event where they could talk.

Lizzie was still thinking about that, when she spotted Annie walking towards her, with Jake and Will on either side. "Mom, I'm glad we found you."

"I'm glad you all came today." Lizzie stood to her feet and hugged her daughter and two sons.

Jake chuckled. "Well, we wanted to show you our support, didn't we brother?"

"Yeah, I guess," Will replied, his tone, his stand-offish attitude towards her.

Lizzie didn't miss her oldest son's lack of enthusiasm.

His attitude towards her had been chilly ever since the day he learned that she hadn't been aware of how his dad's addictions had drained their finances.

She hoped that her and Will's relationship would return to being loving again, like how it used to be between them.

It was because of the shock from the debts her late husband left behind that she'd been pushing herself. She needed to learn all she could about how to handle finances, including starting a business.

In the past couple of weeks, she had appointments with Grams' lawyer and with an accountant Jonathan recommended. She was determined to learn all she could.

Now, everything was set up to begin the inn. All she needed to do was be approved by the board of selectmen.

Everything had been a steep learning curve, but she was resolved to no longer be in the dark when it came to her finances.

"I'm grateful to see my children today, no matter the reason." Lizzie hugged each of them.

"Mom, look over there." Annie nodded her head towards the crowd of people walking away from the teddy bear booth. "The artist whose dad created that painting of Grams' beach house is here." Annie nodded her head in his direction.

Lizzie turned to see him walking their way.

"Lucca, what a nice surprise to see you here." Lizzie shook the man's hand.

"Thanks. It's good to be back on the island. Lizzie, is that correct?" Lucca's Italian accent was unmistakable.

"Yes." She introduced Lucca to her children.

Then turning to her sisters, she re-introduced them to the artist. "Do you all remember years ago when Grams held a dinner and invited Lucca and his dad? Lucca's dad was the artist who created the original painting of the beach house that's in the den. At the time Lucca was a young boy. Lucca is now a well known artist too."

"I do remember. It's been years, but it's great to see you again, Lucca," Jane replied, shaking his hand. Her other sisters followed suit.

"I remember that day. Grams was excited to host the

talented artist who did the beautiful painting of her home. I love that painting. Your dad was the artist who painted the artwork, but you were by his side," Her sister Katie gushed. "Come sit down. Tell me more about your work."

Katie pulled out the empty chair next to her and soon Lucca and she were talking nonstop. It wasn't surprising that Katie's love for historical artifacts and artwork would spill over as she connected with a real artist.

Lizzie smiled happily at the instant connection between them. She walked back to her children.

She waved at Sheriff Jerry Hart and his wife Linda walking towards the crowd where the music played. They waved back. Walking with them were their twin adult sons, Ryan and Dylan Hart.

It looked like Dylan Hart had finally joined his family and didn't object to being seen in public. He was the younger of the Hart's twin sons and had lived like a hermit — isolated from the rest of the islanders for many years. It was good to see him out and about again.

It was wonderful to see friendly faces at this Festival.

Turning she saw Sarah and Mrs. O'Connor walking towards her.

"Mrs. O'Connor, it's good to see you and Sarah. Are you enjoying the festival?" Lizzie asked as the two women walked towards her.

"Yes, we are. It's always nice to see folks in the community enjoying themselves together," The older woman commented. "There are lots of activities here. Sarah saw the face painting booth and wanted to drag me over there."

Sarah grinned. "Grandmother isn't sure she wants to

have that makeup on her face. But I've been reminding her, it's only for one day. Besides, it's fun."

Lizzie grinned. "True enough. My daughter, Annie, was thinking of doing the same thing."

Quickly realizing she hadn't introduced her sons, Lizzie asked, "Have both of you met my sons, Will and Jake?"

"I've seen Jake in passing, fixing up your house. But I haven't had the privilege of meeting Will," Mrs. O'Connor replied and shook their hands. "It's nice to meet you both."

Sarah smiled and spoke softly, "It's nice to meet you both, Jake and Will."

Will talked with Sarah, getting to know her.

Lizzie noticed there seemed to be an instant connection between her oldest son and Sarah.

Her smile broadened with approval. She had always hoped for a nice girl for her oldest son.

Mrs. O'Connor's voice interrupted her musings, "Have you boys come home to stay with your Mom?"

"No. I will be going back to my job at a law firm in Boston," Will replied. "I plan to come back for visits like this weekend, however."

Mrs. O'Connor nodded her approval. Sarah's cheeks formed a rosy blush as Will's gaze shifted to her.

Jake responded, "I have been living with my Mom. I've been busy working on renovations to the house."

"That's good that you are helping your Mom, Jake. It will be wonderful to see that old beach house fully restored." The older lady turned to Lizzie. "You have fine sons, Lizzie."

Lizzie beamed. "Thank you. I agree. My daughter is

also a treasure. They've all been a big help to me, especially these past few months."

Will looked uncomfortable at her compliment, but Jake smiled brightly.

"Hey, Lizzie."

Lizzie turned to see Debbie McVay and her two daughters.

"Hello, Debbie. These must be your daughters." Lizzie smiled as the three women joined them.

The older girl Emma had blond hair with blue eyes and looked to be Jake's age. The younger girl had auburn hair with brown eyes and looked like she just finished high school.

"Yes, this is Emma and this is Sophia." Debbie replied. "They've been helping me run our bed and breakfast. Emma works the front counter answering phone calls and checking our website for new registrations. Sophia loves to bake. So, we have a lot of delicious food to offer guests."

"Looks like you have ready-made help," Lizzie commented. "I'm grateful for the help my three of my children have given me. I should introduce you to them."

Lizzie introduced her children to Debbie, Emma, and Sophia.

Soon they were all busy talking, getting along famously.

"Mom, it looks like we're all going to the face painting booth," Annie announced.

"Sounds like fun. I can't wait to see what you look like later." Lizzie grinned as she waved them off.

She grinned. A delightful image of Mrs. O'Connor

with rosy cheeks from the bright pink paint surfaced in her thoughts.

It would be fun to see how everybody looked with their faces all made up.

***

SHE POURED another cup of coffee at the drink table with the intention of joining her sisters.

However, right at that moment, Jonathan walked away from the crowded area. Cecily walked close beside him, looking up at him laughing.

Jonathan pulled the woman's hand off his arm.

Cecily seemed to keep her distance after that. Lizzie didn't know what it was about the woman that irritated her.

Its simple jealousy, Lizzie. The voice in her head snuck past her excuses and hit on the truth.

Jonathan was trying to keep his distance from Cecily, so that was something she supposed.

She sighed.

As soon as Cecily was caught up talking with some girlfriends, Jonathan started walking in her direction.

She carried her drink towards the table where her sisters sat.

Jonathan met up with two men and they were walking her way.

"Lizzie, I was just congratulating your neighbor on his win in the island's fish derby," Jonathan said as he stood beside her.

Her gaze swung from Jonathan to the older man. "Jeb,

I didn't realize you won the grand prize. How exciting. Did you receive any sort of prize?"

"Yep. I won a twenty-two foot hard top fishing boat. It'll make the fishing trips that much easier." Jeb turned to the man next to him. "I didn't do it alone though. My son Zach and a few friends helped me."

Lizzie grinned at the camaraderie between the two men. "That's amazing. Zach, it's good to see you again. I remember seeing the two of you fishing together when I was a teenager."

"Nice to see you again too, Lizzie." Zach chuckled as he turned to her. "Dad and I have caught a lot of fish over the years, that's for sure."

"What size fish did you catch this time?" Jonathan questioned.

"We caught a shore bluefish that was just over sixteen pounds." Jeb straightened his shoulders, proud as a peacock.

"That's a large one. Amazing." Jonathan grinned. "Good for you."

"Yeah, hopefully soon I'll have more time for fishing," Zach commented.

"Why is that?" Lizzie's curiosity got the better of her.

"I am retiring from the Coast Guard next month. Dad asked if I would move back to Martha's Vineyard. It'll be good to be back again." Zach shrugged his wide shoulders.

He was a tall man with broad shoulders and muscled arms. She could tell he was very fit, which was probably something that was important in his job.

"It would be good to have you back here on the island again." Lizzie beamed. "A few of my sisters are considering moving back here too. Must be something in the air."

Zach grinned. "Maybe."

"Why don't you say hello? It's been a long time and I'm sure they'd like to chat with you." At Zach's nod, Lizzie turned to where her sisters were sitting and talking around the table.

Lizzie spoke up, "Girls, here's a familiar face. Do you remember Jeb's son, Zach?"

"Of course, we do. Good to see you again, Zach." Alex shook his hand.

Jane was busy talking with another familiar face that Lizzie remembered from years ago.

Ward Hampton He had been interested in Jane back then. The two of them had hit it off. She didn't know what happened. Ward and Jane were busy talking, and she didn't want to interrupt.

Charlie peered over at Zach, lifting her neck to see the tall man. Her green eyes brightened noticeably as she looked at him. "Zach, it's been a long time. Are you still working in the Coast Guard?"

"Yeah. I only have one month left though, then I'll be officially retired from service. I plan to move back to Martha's Vineyard then." Zach's tone of voice changed and became softer when he spoke to Charlie.

Lizzie couldn't help but wonder at that.

Memories swirled in Lizzie's thoughts of how Zach would often stop by Grams' house to talk to Charlie. Sometimes on the weekends they went fishing together.

The two of them had been thick as thieves until something happened. Lizzie didn't know what went wrong between them. All she knew was they didn't hang out together after that.

It was good to see the roses blooming in her sister's cheeks again.

Jonathan leaned over and whispered in her ear, "Can I get you anything to drink?"

Lizzie shook her head. "I've had too much to drink already." She looked at the clouds gathering in the sky. "It's been a long day. I wouldn't mind heading home soon."

"Same here. I can drive you back, if you're ready?" Jonathan offered.

"I would like that, but it looks like we'll need to wait. We're about to have company." Lizzie paused to catch her breath as she saw the Cantrell family walking towards them.

An uneasiness stirred within her as they approached.

"HELLO, Lizzie. Jonathan, it's good to see you." Ted Cantrell's booming voice rang out.

Ted turned to look at her sisters at the table beside them. Turning back, he looked at Lizzie and commented, "It's really good to see some of the Stafford sisters back together again."

Those words were so familiar coming from Ted. He'd been a constant presence in all their lives since she was a small girl. Ted had been one of Dad's good friends.

Ted's wife Lola stood by his side.

"Hello, Ted and Lola. Nice to see you again," Lizzie responded.

"Lizzie, your Dad and Mom would have loved to see you sisters back together again on the Island. I should have encouraged you girls to come back home sooner. I think that's one of my duties as your Godfather isn't it?"

Lizzie smiled. "Maybe it is. But you're right. I think Dad and Mom would have loved to see all of us back here again."

Ted Cantrell's charm had always helped him quickly get on the good side of people, for as long as she could remember.

She had always been surprised that Ted had been good friends with her dad. They were two very different men.

Her dad had been a quiet man. He had been a marine biologist who enjoyed his simple life.

Ted Cantrell had always been more talkative, always being the most charming when around a group of people. Maybe that's why he was so popular as a politician.

"At last, you've come home to stay. Have I heard correctly that you are opening an inn at your grandmother's old place, Lizzie?" Ted asked.

As Ted was speaking, Ida Cantrell, Ted's mother, joined them, followed by Vera and Ava.

Ida's youngest daughter, Nettie, stood by her mother. Nettie, now in her late forties, had always stayed away from the spotlight — like the quiet mouse of the family.

Some islanders said Nettie had a simple mind and couldn't understand when they spoke to her. But, to Lizzie, she thought Nettie understood a lot more than she was letting on.

In some ways it was strange to see the Cantrell family again. She couldn't help but feel intimidated at being surrounded by one of the most powerful and wealthy families on Martha's Vineyard.

Grams' words swirled in her memory. You are a Stafford with all the respect, honesty and hard-working values that go along with that name. So, stand tall and be confident in who you are.

Lizzie straightened her shoulders and nodded. "Yes, that's right. We're working on renovations to the house right now."

"That's good to hear, isn't it, Mother?" Ted turned to Ida Cantrell. The older woman wore a crease between her brows.

"You know I always appreciate someone who takes charge and gets things done. Yet, it does make me wonder if we need another inn on this island," Ida commented.

"Mother, of course we do. There's always a need for unique businesses here. After all, we do get a lot of visitors each summer." Ted chuckled.

Turning to Vera, he said. "What do you think of Lizzie's new inn?"

Vera shook her head. "Well, I worry for her, of course. I know you have good intentions, Lizzie. But I wonder if it will be too much for you, since you haven't been in the hospitality industry before. It will be a very difficult learning curve. Since I bought a bed and breakfast years ago, I can tell you there is a lot to learn."

"I understand it won't be easy. That's why I'm grateful to have the help of my daughter and sons. Of course, there are others like Mrs. O'Connor who are helping me as well," Lizzie replied.

"Yes, Mrs. O'Connor. She seems to have her hands in a

lot of things these days." A crease formed between Vera's brows. "Well, who knows if the support you're getting will be enough for you. I guess we'll have to see."

Ida Cantrell, the grand old lady, stepped closer to Lizzie, peering at her through thick glasses.

"As I look at you, Lizzie, I can't help but be reminded of your great-grandmother. She always had people coming and going in that old beach house, with her husband being a sea captain and all. She often seemed overwhelmed by it all."

Vera nodded in agreement.

Ted huffed, turning to his mother. "People get over-whelmed all the time, Mother."

"Yes, but it was worse for Lizzie's great-grandmother. For the last ten years of her life, many times folks on the Island said she didn't seem to be in her right mind because of the stress." Ida paused for a few seconds her dark eyes fixed on Lizzie. "It makes me wonder about you, Lizzie. They say eventually what's in the genes will show up."

Ava smirked. "I, for one, really hope Lizzie hasn't inherited her great-grandmother's inability to cope with stress. Maybe she should quit trying to set up the inn, before things get too out of control."

"I don't need to quit. I believe with the support I have we'll be able to figure it out just fine." Lizzie's temper flared at the hint that she wouldn't be able to cope with running an inn.

Ida paused, looking her over critically. "Well, you never know. These things tend to be passed down from one generation to another. We'll just have to wait and see."

Ava smirked, sending Lizzie an unfriendly glare.

Lizzie couldn't believe she was on the receiving end of so much criticism.

Ted Cantrell jumped into the conversation, glancing in her direction. "Well, I believe Lizzie will be fine."

Jonathan sighed in exasperation. "There's no question Lizzie will be able to figure out the start-up of her business just fine. I'm shocked to hear a hint of anything else."

Ida Cantrell thumped her wooden cane on the ground twice. Her gray eyes threw flames at Jonathan.

The matriarch of the island had never been a woman who was daunted by opposite opinions. She always stood firm to her opinions, whether right or wrong.

"Well, I haven't changed my mind. I still believe Lizzie might be in way over her head starting up that inn. I wouldn't be surprised if the extra stress causes problems for her mental health," Ida repeated, showing no sign of relenting.

"Mrs. Cantrell, you are, of course, entitled to your opinion. But I don't agree. I am confident Lizzie will be successful at this. Not only because Lizzie is a strong, intelligent woman, but because she has help. I am one of those people, who has offered Lizzie all the resources I have available to me to get this project off the ground," Jonathan spoke with quiet firmness.

The older woman bristled with indignation. "Well, there's no accounting for fools in this world."

The tick in Jonathan's jaw was noticeable, but he didn't say a word.

Lizzie couldn't help but notice a mixture of anger and an uneasiness flickering far back in the eyes of the three Cantrell women.

Why were they concerned about her and the changes she was making to her grandmother's beach house?

The more she pondered what was going on, the more frustrated she became.

"Take me home, Son. I'm tired of this rabble-rousing crowd." With one last glare at Jonathan and Lizzie, the old woman turned around and began walking away, leaning on her cane.

Ted turned and whispered to Lizzie, "Looks like I've been summoned. Don't worry about my mother. She gets a bee in her bonnet sometimes about some things. Anyway, I need to get going. It was nice seeing you both again."

Lizzie nodded, instantly relieved they were leaving.

As the Cantrell family walked away, Lizzie closed her eyes feeling utterly miserable.

She turned to Jonathan, with a heavy feeling in her stomach. "That did not go well."

"Yeah, I agree," He spoke in a solemn whisper. "Let's walk. I'll drive you home and we can talk on the way."

Lizzie waved goodbye to her sisters and sent a quick text to her children, to let them know she was leaving.

Jonathan continued talking as they walked. "All the years I've known Ida Cantrell, she has always had definite opinions about one thing or the other. It's nothing for you to worry about."

Lizzie bit her lip until it throbbed. "I don't know about that. Those hints that I might be losing my mind like my great-grandmother, were not very subtle."

"I don't quite understand why she chose to attack you

like that. But I did notice that Vera and Ava jumped on the same bandwagon immediately afterwards."

He shook his head and ran a hand through his hair.

"Thankfully their opinions don't matter," Jonathan declared.

Lizzie pondered his words.

Jonathan parked his car in her driveway. The dark clouds in the sky above, seemed like a storm warning.

She turned to him. "I think it does matter. Vera is on the board of selectman. She might refuse to give me a business license again."

"I don't believe Vera can refuse you forever, not when you have done all they've asked you to do." Jonathan shrugged.

Lizzie shifted uncomfortably. "Maybe. I just don't know."

She couldn't help but feel discouraged about the conversation with the Cantrell family.

"Let me walk you to your door." Jonathan helped her out of the car. It felt strange that he brought her home.

Lizzie added, "The Cantrell women aren't the only ones who have been trying to get me to sell Grams' house. Remember Violet and Madison Hayes? They stopped by recently to let me know they want to buy the house."

Jonathan sighed. "I don't think their interest in your house is going to be a problem. Yes, the Hayes are also a wealthy family around here, but they can't force you to sell."

Lizzie nodded. "I guess that's true."

She thought about what he said earlier and knew she needed to thank him. "Jonathan, it was kind of you to come to my defense earlier when Mrs. Cantrell was attacking my mental health. She was angry with you for disagreeing with her."

Lizzie walked up the steps to her front door and turned to him. "I'm sorry if she decides to cause more problems for you."

Jonathan placed his hands gently on her shoulders. "You don't need to apologize. I'm not worried about them. Just so you know, I will stand up for you in a heartbeat. I'm on your side, not theirs."

Her heart melted at his words.

Jonathan's hands on her shoulders sent an involuntary chill through her body. Her cheeks colored under the heat of his gaze.

"Thank you for saying that," she whispered.

As his fingers gently caressed her arms, she felt blood coursing through her veins like an awakened river.

The look of tenderness in his blue eyes was her undoing.

She didn't resist when he slowly pulled her close.

Lowering his head, his lips brushed hers like a gentle whisper.

The moment his lips touched hers, she felt transported on a soft cloud, so light it seemed like she was floating.

He pulled her closer to deepen his kiss.

A crack of thunder split the night air.

Without warning, all of Lizzie's memories began to swirl around in her thoughts. Fears of falling in love and getting close to Jonathan resurfaced.

She remembered what happened years ago, and was

reminded of seeing Cecily hanging onto Jonathan's arm earlier today.

As the dark thoughts circled around in her mind, she jerked out of Jonathan's arms.

Reluctantly, he loosened his embrace.

Looking up, she saw the surprise etched on his features. Confusion was evident in his blue eyes.

Rain began to pour down as the storm clouds unloaded their bounty from the sky above.

"I'm sorry, Jonathan. I don't know about this." Lizzie blurted out, unsure how to explain her feelings. "I've got to go. I'm sorry."

With one last look at him, she opened the door and hurried inside her house.

Leaning back against the door, she swallowed back emotion. Fears and worries continued to flood her.

Would she ever be healed so she could love again?

CHAPTER TEN

*To his cousin Evangeline, Captain Henry Stafford wrote this
sad letter.*
*"Mary lost the baby. It was necessary to postpone my trip out to
sea, because my wife is having a very difficult time. Dear sister,
will you come and stay with Mary until she recovers? I leave
with my ship and crew in two months and I worry for her.
Please let me know. Love your cousin, Henry."*
The Vineyard Historical Letters

Lizzie took a sip of her tea and walked over to the painting of the beach house.

Her sister's chatter filled the room from where they were talking together on the sofa nearby.

She couldn't help but remember Jonathan's kiss last night. Her toes curled just thinking about it.

But fear had caused her to leave abruptly. She shifted uneasily, as she wondered what she would say to Jonathan the next time she saw him.

Her daughter, Annie, had gone with Will and Jake to get more wood to finish building the kitchen counter. Jonathan was planning to meet them at the store and would help them with the project.

Uncertainty and misgivings flooded her. She wasn't looking forward to seeing Jonathan again.

Switching her thoughts, she focused on the painting in front of her. Memories of a childhood spent with her sisters here in Grams' house swirled around in her mind.

Her grandparents' home had been her safe place.

"Lucca Lommbardi is a very talented artist," Alex whispered as she walked over to stand near her. "It was good to see him at the festival."

"Yes, it was good to see him again. Grams knew he had a lot of talent, which was why she asked him to paint the house." Lizzie sighed.

Alex turned to her, a puzzled look on her face. "I've seen you look at this painting many times. What fascinates you about this painting, that you are so drawn to it? I don't get it."

"It's a very compelling picture in how this beach house was painted with the water in the front and the beach house behind it. There's something captivating about the blue water that is very peaceful." Lizzie sighed.

Alex nodded. "I suppose."

She went on, "Of course, that's only a tiny fraction of what really moves my emotions when I see this painting."

"Tell me," Her sister insisted, leaning closer.

Lizzie smiled secretly. "You know I never told anyone this before. But as a young girl, I always had a secret longing to live in our grandparents' home when I became an adult." She sighed. "Grams' home was a safe house for me. It's where I felt secure and where I felt loved."

Alex's keen, probing eyes stared at her as if seeing her for the first time.

"I can't help it." Lizzie blinked back tears that pricked at the back of her eyelids. "I remember the seven of us young girls, coming to live here right after our parents died."

Lizzie swallowed at the memories that for years had caused many sleepless nights. "Each of us felt so forlorn, abandoned, and scared. I never told you this, but I also felt a terrible sense of guilt and failure."

"Why would you feel that way?" Her sister's eyes widened with curiosity.

Her fingers shook as she ran them through her hair. Lizzie whispered in a hoarse voice. "Because, on the night of the storm, just as Dad was hurrying out the door, he told me to make sure I stopped Mom from following him. Dad said he didn't want her out on the boat alongside him in the bad weather. That's all he said before he hurried out the door."

Alex swallowed. "But then mom came home."

"Yes. Mom came home in a hurry looking for Dad. I started to tell her what Dad said, but she told me she didn't have time. She had to find Dad and talk to him. She said it was urgent. Then she left the house." Lizzie rigidly held her tears in check.

"So, you see, it was my fault that Mom died. I was supposed to stop her from following Dad, but I didn't. I failed Dad, Mom and all of you, my sisters."

Alex sucked in a breath. "No Lizzie, it wasn't your

fault. I remember how determined Mom was that night to find Dad. There wouldn't have been anything you could've done to stop her."

Lizzie's eyes bordered with tears as she released a heavy sigh. "Do you really think so?"

"I really do. Mom could be fairly stubborn at times, and that night was one of those moments." Alex assured her.

All of a sudden, it felt like a heavy weight was removed from her shoulders. "Thanks for telling me, Alex. All these years, I've experienced deep feelings of failure and guilt because of that night."

"The failure ran so deep, that self-doubt hindered me from making many choices for myself. I think that's why I didn't interfere when my late husband made decisions about our finances. I didn't trust myself to take on that responsibility."

Alex shook her head in disbelief. "Oh Lizzie. That is so sad. We should've had this conversation years ago. I didn't realize how deeply that night affected you."

Lizzie nodded, still reeling over the fact that maybe her mother's death all those years ago wasn't her fault after all.

Turning to look at the familiar beach house in the painting again, Lizzie whispered. "One of the big reasons why I love this painting is because Grams made this house into a peaceful sanctuary. It was just what all us girls needed at the time. To me, this painting represents the warmth of family and a safe refuge from the sea of life's storms."

Alex turned, moisture in her eyes. She nodded. "I

understand and agree. Grams and Gramps made this into a place of refuge just when we needed it most."

She nodded, giving Alex a wobbly smile.

"You know, Lizzie, I'm very grateful we talked. I never fully understood how our parent's death affected you until today. I think it's helped me understand you better. Thank you for sharing your heart." Alex slipped an arm around her shoulders.

Lizzie stood beside her sister for a long time, simply staring at the painting together. She was grateful for her family.

"Hey you two. I thought we were going to have tea and talk." Charlie's blustering voice reached Lizzie's ears.

"I guess that's our cue."

Lizzie turned around and Alex followed.

"We got caught up in the painting, Charlie," Lizzie whispered in her sister's ear as she sat down beside her.

Charlie turned. "I love that painting too, but we only have today to chat with each other before we all go back to our jobs."

"I'm sorry." Lizzie smiled and turned to everyone. "It's so nice that most of us sisters can be together. It's too bad Torrie and Jules couldn't make it, but hopefully they'll be here next time."

In their comfy sofas near the fireplace, her sisters nodded their agreement.

"This is really nice, Lizzie," Jane commented, then sipped her tea. "There's more room in this house than my small condo in California."

"Thanks, Jane. The renovations have taken some

money and time, but we're slowly improving the place." Lizzie sighed.

Katie gushed, "I saw the changes to the dining room. It's so much bigger now that you removed that wall. And the French doors were a real nice touch. I think guests are going to love that."

Lizzie grinned at her youngest sister's enthusiasm. "I really hope so, Katie. I am trying to make this into an inn that feels like home for visitors."

"It's working, Lizzie," Charlie commented as she looked around the room.

She grinned, happy with her sister's encouragement on this large project.

"When will you open your place for visitors?" Jane asked. She was a very talented event planner and had an eye for details to make each event appealing to guests.

"I first need to be approved by the board of selectmen. There's another meeting this coming week. Hopefully, I will be approved then, but there's no guarantee." Lizzie bit her lip and looked down at her clenched hands.

Her throat ached with a sense of discouragement from memories of the last board meeting.

"Hey, Lizzie. You will get approved. How can they not approve your business license when you've obviously done so much work to get it ready?" Jane lifted her tea cup in a salute. "Chin up. It's going to happen."

Lizzie smiled weakly. "Thanks, sisters. You've boosted my spirits just when I need it. And since we're on the topic of opening the inn to visitors, I wanted to run an idea by all of you."

"Sure, what's up?" Jane asked.

Lizzie gaze swept over each of them. "I was wondering if you would be willing to come stay here for a weekend, before I officially open it up to guests? It would be sort of like a test run for the inn."

"That's a good idea. What date did you have in mind for the test run?" Alex opened the app on her phone where she organized everything.

"If I get approved this week, I was hoping we could do a test run for the last weekend in October. I realize it's a lot to ask, so don't feel like you need to do this for me." Lizzie rushed to assure them.

To her surprise they all agreed.

"This will be such fun." Katie grinned.

Lizzie smiled. "It will be fun. But I hope you all will tell me what I need to fix so that your place will be ready for paying guests."

"You can count on us, Lizzie." Charlie grinned. "We'll be tough as nails on you."

Lizzie chuckled. "All right, sounds good."

Alex picked up a large notebook that was on the side table next to Lizzie and handed it to her. "Why don't you tell us what you've been reading lately in Grams' journals? We're dying to find out what else she had to tell us."

"Good idea," Charlie said. "Last time, I read your text about what you read in our grandmother's journal. Thanks for keeping us in the loop."

Lizzie nodded. "Of course. I think she would have liked for all of us to read her words together.'

Her sisters leaned back as Lizzie began to read.

"Today marks one year since we lost our son John and his

wife Anne. Our seven granddaughters have lived with us for one year now.

Ever since the boating accident, they've cried many tears over the deaths of their parents. I feel sad that we haven't been able to answer their questions over how or why it happened. I hope someday those questions will be answered, but not today.

Those seven girls are orphans at such a young age.

With Lizzie only eleven years of age, Alex just ten and Jane only nine, these three oldest girls have been a steadying influence and comfort for their four younger sisters.

The four youngest girls are missing their parents. With Charlie only seven years of age, Jules just five and the twin girls Katie and Torrie barely four years old, this loss has been really difficult for them.

It breaks my heart. Yet, our granddaughters are slowly healing. They light up our lives, even on the gloomiest of days like today.

Another interesting thing happened today. We had unexpected visitors to the house. Ida Cantrell stopped by with her grown children Vera, Nettie and Ted. Ida said they wanted to let William and I know they were thinking of us on this anniversary of the tragedy.

Ted seemed unusually shaken when we talked of John's death. They were close friends, so that's understandable. Nettie, their youngest daughter who some folks say is a slower learner, seemed really agitated when she saw photos of John and Ted together. I wonder what that was all about?

During their visit, Ida mentioned that someone else needed to take charge of the popular island newspaper, The Vineyard Bulletin. She went on to say that it was our duty as citizens to be aware of what stories were newsworthy.

Ida was convinced it was that reporter Sean O'Connor who asked so many questions and made folks on the island think too independently. People need guidance on the opinions they form when they read articles.

She told me it was time that somebody else took the reins of that newspaper.

I didn't say much at the time, but it sounds like Ida Cantrell wants to decide for folks around here what they should believe. It doesn't seem like she's too interested in the news — but more interested in guiding people's opinions.

Ida is always up to something, it seems. Her daughter Vera has started in the real estate business. The old saying is proven true once more: the apple doesn't fall far from the tree.

Many times, I have questioned the true motives of some of the people we know here on the island. Perhaps, only time will tell what the truth is.

Well, enough going on about all that. I'll write some more tomorrow about the new artist who has agreed to paint our beach house. I am looking forward to that."

Lizzie stopped reading and looked around at her sisters. Some of them like Katie and Jane were dabbing tears from their cheeks.

"Grams sure loved us." Another tear trailed down Katie's cheek and she quickly wiped it away. "It can't have been easy to take all seven of us in to raise as her own. And I love how she mentions having the artist come to paint the house. That must have been Lucca she was talking about."

Alex nodded. "I remember that painting was done after the one-year anniversary of Mom and Dad's death."

"Maybe Grams hoped we would look at the painting

and it would bring us joy after so much sorrow." Katie offered a shaky smile.

Lizzie spoke softly, "I think that's true, Katie."

They all sat in silence pondering their grandmother's words.

"Grams didn't seem to have much respect for Ida Cantrell, did she?" Jane looked at Lizzie.

Lizzie shrugged. "It sounded like Grams struggled to understand what Ida's motives were as to why she did certain things."

"I can relate. I struggle with that too." Jane nodded.

Alex's lips thinned in irritation. "I didn't know Ida Cantrell had an interest in the newspapers in town."

Lizzie shook her head. "I didn't either. But I'm not surprised. She has a lot of interests and seems to be involved in a lot of things."

"Hmmm." A shadow of annoyance crossed Alex's features as she pondered that.

Her sister's expression was so similar to the feeling she had at the festival when she had spoken with Ida Cantrell and her family.

Lizzie didn't understand what was going on. It was so strange and confusing to hear Ida hinting that Lizzie might not be able to handle running the inn.

Maybe that was why it had been comforting to read Grandmother's journal. It seemed she wasn't the only one who doubted the motives of others.

"WE'LL SLIP the last board here." Jake held one end of the wide piece of wood.

Jonathan held it in place while Jake hammered the nails into each of the four corners.

Annie, Will, Lizzie, and her sisters watched the two of them finish this newest project.

"Good job, Jake. You're a natural." Will raised his hand up in the air and gave his brother a high five.

"Thanks bro. I think it's because I love working with wood. I always have." Jake smiled as he looked at his newest creation.

"It looks really good. I adore this new kitchen island." Lizzie turned to Jake and hugged him. "Thank you, Son."

"You're welcome, Mom. We still need someone to come and install the countertop, but the rest of it is done now." Jake loved working on this project, she could tell by his wide smile. "Don't forget, Jonathan did a lot of work on this project too."

"Of course." Lizzie turned to Jonathan with a wobbly smile. "Thank you for helping Jake build the kitchen island, Jonathan. It's perfect."

Loud chatter from the rest of the family could be heard in the background so she stepped closer to Jonathan to speak to him.

Being near him brought on more nervousness. His kiss the other night had awakened feelings she thought long since dead.

These new feelings scared her.

A satisfied light came into his blue eyes. "Anytime, Lizzie. I am always happy to help you."

Heat rose to her cheeks at the intensity of his look.

Jonathan leaned closer and whispered. "Are you all right?" He reached out and squeezed her hand gently. "You left quickly the other night and I didn't get a chance to ask if you were okay."

Awkwardly, she cleared her throat. Just being near him aroused old fears and uncertainties.

Her heart ached under her breast at the tenderness in his voice.

"I'm fine." A shudder passed through Lizzie and her voice cracked with emotion.

He stared at her for a long time as if unsure if she was truly all right. "I'm glad you're alright. But I think we really need to plan a time when we can talk."

A knot rose in her throat at his words. She had a feeling he wanted a serious conversation and Lizzie wasn't sure if she was ready.

"Now?" Lizzie was already feeling the pressure of the day with her sisters leaving the next day.

"No, not today. In fact, I'll be leaving for two weeks to work on another architectural design project, but I was hoping we could talk when I get back." There was a gentle coaxing in his tone that softened Lizzie's heart.

"Yes, we can talk." Her heart took a perilous leap as their eyes locked. A mixture of emotions ran through her.

Jonathan whispered, "Would it be all right if I called you when I'm gone? It would reassure me that you're okay."

"Sure." She didn't trust her voice not to squeak or crack with emotion. Lizzie found his concern for her touching.

"Thanks," Jonathan whispered.

Annie called out, "Mom, I'll check to see who has arrived."

Lizzie turned to her daughter. "Thanks."

Turning to Jonathan she said, "I better go."

He whispered, "I'll talk with you later."

Lizzie blushed and her heart thumped uncomfortably at his compelling look.

She nodded quickly and hurried to get away from the man who disturbed her more every day.

❦

"How are you, Mrs. O'Connor and Sarah?" Annie had opened the door for the dear old lady and her granddaughter.

Lizzie sent a warm smile to the woman who had done so much to help her understand how to turn her grandmother's old house into an inn.

"So, tell me, Lizzie, how are all the renovations coming along?" Mrs. O'Connor slid her arms out of the light fall jacket she wore.

"Good. There have been quite a few improvements made." Lizzie sighed. "I'm happy about how it's coming along."

"Tell me, my dear." Mrs. O'Connor grabbed her hand and they started to walk around the house.

"Well, we updated the bedrooms, so each room now has a theme. And the bathrooms have all been fixed so they are in good working order." Lizzie explained.

"Good, good." The older lady stopped when they

reached the dining room. "And this dining room is now quite large with room on the deck for visitors too."

"Yes. We've also enlarged the parking area, so there is more room for guests."

"My son Jake, just finished building a kitchen island for me. Now baking will be so much easier." Lizzie's smile widened at the changes that were improving the beach house. "My daughter, Annie, has started taking photos in preparation for when we can set up the website for the inn."

"Oh, that's wonderful. Then it seems like you have almost everything ready to go." Mrs. O'Connor's face brightened at the news.

Her face clouded with uneasiness. Memories of her business not being approved last time, still worried her.

"I'm afraid I'm not out of the woods yet." Lizzie paused to catch her breath her fears stronger than ever. "We still need to be approved by the board of selectmen for Sweet Beach Cove. Lately, I've had serious doubts that it will ever happen."

"I understand that kind of uncertainty. In my years of running my bed and breakfast I noticed that some people were determined to stop me from going forward with my goals. I wonder if that is what you're facing, Lizzie." Mrs. O'Connor sighed heavily, shaking her head.

"In fact, you might want to read an article from today's newspaper. I'm afraid there is someone who is deter-mined to stop you from moving forward with the inn."

The older lady turned to her granddaughter. "Sarah, would you find that newspaper we brought over? I think Lizzie should see it."

An unwelcome tension stretched ever tighter in Lizzie's belly. Her hands shook as she took the newspaper out of Sarah's hand.

It was *The Vineyard Bulletin* newspaper.

Fear knotted inside her belly as she opened the newspaper. "On what page is the article?"

"The front page."

Icy fear twisted around her heart, as she turned to the front page.

As Lizzie's gaze travelled down the page, she came to an abrupt stop.

She gasped out loud.

Her heart jumped in her chest.

Staring up at her from the page was a photo of her standing in front of her beach house with her daughter, Annie, by her side.

Her shaky hands shook the newspaper as she started to read. She was so consumed by reading the article, that she didn't even notice that Jonathan stood beside her, reading over her shoulder.

The title of the article seemed to cast doubt on Lizzie's abilities.

"Is this a do-or-die moment for a middle-aged widow as she struggles to turn a run-down house into an inn?

After inheriting an old beach house from her late grandmother, Lizzie Stafford Wentworth moved to Martha's Vineyard.

A few short months ago, Elizabeth Stafford, long-time resident of the island, passed away leaving her granddaughters each a substantial inheritance.

Lizzie was bequeathed what most islanders for years have nicknamed, The Stafford beach house.

The house, originally built in the early 1900s, is very old. Despite having a few minor renovations over the years, this large house is still quite run-down. Some folks would say, it needs renovating from the ground up.

Yet, despite all the problems, the new owner seems to think that turning this old house into an inn is a good idea.

Lizzie has steadily worked on renovations since she took over her grandmother's house. But will all those hours of hard work be enough to give that house the face lift it needs to transform it into a house that will be available for paying guests?

The other concern this writer has is in regards to Lizzie's mental readiness to run an inn. At the last board of selectmen meeting, the widow admitted she had no experience in the hospitality industry. Not only that, but she hasn't worked outside the home for twenty-five years.

This lack of experience should be a big red flag to Mrs. Wentworth and to the business community of our island.

However, there is still one last warning sign to consider. This reporter has been told that Lizzie's great-grandmother suffered from depression and mental illness.

Is mental illness something we can expect from the owner of our island's newest inn? This reporter can only see danger signs on the path ahead for Lizzie Stafford Wentworth if she continues to pursue this reckless path.

Perhaps, people in the business community at Sweet Beach Cove would be wise to urge the widow to stop this obsession before either herself or folks in the community suffer greater loss from this ill-conceived decision."

Lizzie breathed in shallow, quick gasps and her chest felt as if it would burst.

CHAPTER ELEVEN

Another family that we discovered as early settlers on Martha's Vineyard was the Whetstone family. Captain Abe Whetstone and his wife Maria settled in the Sweet Beach Cove community.
His wife Maria, wrote her cousin a letter during a time when many folks were struggling to make ends meet.
"Dear Edith, I hope you are well. Our son Jeb and our daughter Lilly miss their dad.
He's been gone with his ship for four weeks now. We are working hard and doing our best to put food on the table. Abe hopes to bring home a good load of fish. We really need it. Please write and tell me your news, dear sister. Love Maria."
The Vineyard Historical Letters

"I can't believe they wrote such a horrible article about me in the newspaper." Lizzie's thoughts fluttered with anxiety as the hurtful words sank all the way down to her bones.

Mrs. O'Connor shook her head sadly. "This is what they do. And it happens more than you think."

Lizzie's hands shook as she gripped the newspaper with a white knuckled grip.

"I'm in shock. How can they get away with writing such... lies about me?" She sputtered, desperately trying to understand why someone would write such terrible things about her.

"I don't know. And I definitely don't know why. This is what my son Sean faced when he was a reporter. They attacked him viciously." The older lady walked towards Lizzie and gripped both of her hands gently, looking her in the eyes. "But you can't let them win, my dear."

Panic rioted within her. She tried to swallow back the fear.

Annie stepped close to her mom. "Whoever wrote that article isn't right about you, Mom. They don't know you. You are smart, capable, and very intelligent. Don't let their words make you doubt yourself or your ability to make this house into an inn."

Her daughter's words helped her to refocus.

Lizzie nodded, blinking back tears. She swallowed, pressing a hand to her throat.

"I... I don't know how to respond to this." She bit her lip until it throbbed like her pulse. "When folks around here read this article, they will believe that I struggle with mental illness."

Her shoulders slumped in despair and ran a shaky hand through her hair.

Unexpectedly, she felt a warm hand squeeze her shoulder.

Turning, her eyes widened in surprise.

Jonathan spoke to all, but gazed only at her. With a low, resolved tone of voice he said, "Your business license will get approved, Lizzie. I don't know why this reporter attacked you, but this has gone far enough. This needs to end. Somehow the truth must come out."

Squeezing her shoulder one last time, his gaze lingered on hers, blue eyes filled with concern.

With a quick wave to everyone in the room, he spun around and was gone.

As Lizzie watched Jonathan go, his words swirled around in her thoughts.

He was right. It was time for the truth to come out.

The hurtful words from the newspaper continued to roll around in her head.

The writer of the article condemned her for having no experience.

Well, when she cooked and hosted all those dinners for her late husband's law firm, she did learn more about cooking, hosting, and serving meals to guests.

To her way of thinking, she had gained some experience that would be helpful as a host of her own inn.

As she thought back to that time, the face of her friend Reagan Tosby came to mind. She had been involved in media relations for her late husband's law firm.

Through the many Benefit Galas the law firm hosted, Lizzie had been able to get to know Reagan well.

Perhaps, she should call her friend and ask for advice.

LIZZIE SHIFTED NERVOUSLY on her feet as she waited for the interview to begin.

She stood next to the TV reporter on the front porch of Grams' beach house. The morning sun shone on them, giving warmth despite the chilly breeze.

This had all started when she called her friend Reagan Tosby. The media relations professional told Lizzie that islanders needed to hear what happened to her.

Within a few hours, Reagan called a TV reporter friend, and it didn't take long before Lizzie was asked for an interview.

So, that's why she stood in front of the camera today.

The reporter cleared his throat and began.

"Recently, Lizzie Stafford Wentworth inherited her grandmother's house on Martha's Vineyard. Her goal is to transform the beach house into an inn." Ian Nanton shifted so they stood in front of the house. "Tell us how it's going with the renovations."

"It's going well. We have managed to get the renovations done inside the house that we needed to finish for now. We have also expanded the parking area to hold more vehicles. So, we are ready for guests." Lizzie smiled nervously as the camera zoomed closer.

"That's good to hear." Ian stepped closer. "Tell us. Have you faced any opposition or red tape to try to hinder your progress in getting your business license?"

Lizzie nodded. "Yes. I was not approved the first time I applied. They asked me to improve the house and increase the available parking. Those details are now completed." Lizzie sighed.

"Have there been other problems you've faced?" Ian looked at her and then at the camera.

Lizzie nodded. "Yes. Just yesterday, I was shocked to read an article in a local newspaper — The Vineyard Bulletin — that smeared my character. They discredited my ability to run the inn and besmirched my mental capabilities."

Ian shook his head. "It makes a person question whether someone is purposely trying to hinder your efforts from moving forward with that inn?"

Lizzie nodded. "I've started to ask myself the same thing."

Ian Nanton faced the camera. "There you have it, folks. We've uncovered some questionable practices from a local newspaper. We'll keep a close eye on Lizzie in the weeks to come and see how her quest to set up the inn plays out. Thanks for watching and have a good night."

She sighed in relief as the TV reporter and camera crew drove away.

Would telling her story make any difference?

Annie sat beside Sarah on the chairs at *The Vineyard Bulletin.*

Sarah was writing an advertisement in the newspaper for the crochet and knitting club at her grandmother's house.

This newspaper was a hot topic around her mom's house lately because of that horrible article.

However, she thought her mom did a great job in the

recent tv interview. If folks had formed negative opinions about her mom from the article, her interview would help change their minds.

In her opinion this newspaper was a waste of paper.

She wouldn't have come here at all, except that Sarah was her friend.

As Sarah re-wrote the advertisement for the third time, Annie leaned over to her friend and whispered. "I'm going to use the washroom."

"Of course. I'm almost finished here, I promise." Sarah smiled warmly.

Annie nodded. "Be right back."

She remembered where to find the washroom, from other times she had been here.

As she walked along hallway, she couldn't help but hear loud voices coming from a nearby office.

Without thinking, she stopped to listen.

"You shouldn't have printed the article, mom. That was going too far." The woman's angry voice reached through the walls.

"Ava my dear, you have no idea how far I can go when I want something." The other woman's tone was lethal and determined.

Annie's eyebrows flew up, as she realized the two women speaking were Ava and Vera Cantrell.

Ava sighed. "Mom, you need to stop this obsession. There are other houses you can buy."

"No." Vera said emphatically. "There is no other property like this one on the island. I can assure you. I must have it."

Ava persisted. "Not like this mom."

"Daughter, where is your loyalty? To that Stafford woman or to your own flesh and blood?"

Something loud slammed against the table.

Ava words shook. "I am loyal to you, mom. But, there is a line that shouldn't be crossed. And I think you've gone too far this time. Now, Lizzie has done this new interview, labeling this newspaper as liars. Grandmother won't like that one bit."

"Oh my mother will just have to put up with it." Vera insisted. "For once, I get to have my way, instead of doing every-thing for the approval of the grand old matriarch, Ida Cantrell."

Annie heard a loud sigh of frustration.

The same voice spoke again in a resolute tone. "And I don't need your approval either, Ava. All my life, I've done everything to please my mother."

"I've done the same thing with you, mom. All my life I've tried in vain to gain your approval. But, so far I've failed." Ava's words were stuttered and cracked.

"Well, today you certainly don't have it. You're not on my side." There was a harshness in the older woman's tone.

"I can't help how I feel." A heavy sigh resounded through the thin walls. "But if you're determined to keep pushing then I wish you luck. I have a feeling you're going to need it."

Annie heard footsteps walking to the door. She hurried into the washroom.

The door clicked open and shut twice before Annie knew it was safe to get back to Sarah.

As they left the newspaper office, Annie told her friend. "I've got to get home. It's important."

She needed to tell her mom about this conversation. For some reason Vera really wanted her mom's house and seemed determined to do almost anything to get her hands on it.

CHAPTER TWELVE

One family that settled on Martha's Vineyard in those early years is the Frank and Estelle Hart family.
Captain Frank Hart ran a bootlegging business on his ship at that time.
His wife Estelle, wrote to her sister a very interesting letter.
"Dear Rebecca, I hope you are well. We are healthy here. Our son Jerry and daughter Leah miss their dad. Frank is gone a lot. My husband tells me he is selling barrels of beer to those can't buy their own. It's the new prohibition laws. I worry Frank might get into big trouble. Please write back and tell me your news, dear sister. Love Estelle."
The Vineyard Historical Letters

*L*izzie rubbed her clammy hands along the front of her jeans.

It was a new month and time for another board meeting.

She sat among the front row chairs, the crease between her brows deepening.

Would her application for a business license be rejected again?

"Mom, stop worrying." Annie squeezed her hand gently.

Lizzie turned to her daughter, managing a small, tentative smile.

"You're right. I shouldn't worry." Suddenly, her face went grim. "Besides, after yesterday's interview, who knows what will happen?"

Her son Jake turned to her with a bemused glance. "Mom, I watched your interview. I think you did great. You were brave to say what you did."

"Thanks for telling me, Jake." A warm glow flowed through her at his encouraging words.

Before long the board took their seats at the front of the room and the lawyer walked to the microphone.

"Welcome, everyone, to this month's Board of Selectmen Meeting for Sweet Beach Cove." Mr. McTavish introduced the board members.

The board members began to talk about issues from previous meetings that were unresolved.

Finally, Mr. McTavish turned to the crowd. "Now we will turn to the topic of requests for approval. There are two requests tonight."

"We'll start with Ellie Thorne's request for approval of her new coffee shop. The suggested location is in a renovated older home near the Sweet Beach Cove business area.

Mr. McTavish, began to give details of the request. "The coffee shop will be near the heart of the business area. It is unique in that it is a 1940s style coffee shop. Is there anyone who would like to comment on this application?"

No one raised their hand to comment or to object.

After a short discussion among the board, Ellie's request was approved.

At last, it was Lizzie's turn.

"Finally, the last request. This one is from Lizzie Stafford Wentworth. She applied last month for business license approval but was denied. The board recommended improvements to the house and the parking space."

"There are photos here to show that's been done. Lizzie would like to run an inn out of her home. Most of you know of the old Stafford beach house on the waterfront," Mr. McTavish explained.

He continued, "Lizzie would like to call her new place, *The Vineyard Inn.* There are fourteen rooms for guests available to rent on a daily, weekly or monthly basis throughout the year. Lizzie doesn't have any experience in the hospitality industry. And it looks like this inn would be the first of its kind in the Sweet Beach Cove area."

Mr. McTavish looked at the crowd. "Would anyone like to comment on this request?"

Lizzie held her breath.

Surprisingly, no one raised their hands.

"Since there are no comments or objections, we will let the board discuss."

Only a couple minutes later, the board came to a decision.

"The board has unanimously approved Lizzie's application. This concludes tonight's meeting." Mr. McTavish's words faded into the background, as Lizzie's excitement grew.

"I can't believe my business is finally approved." She hugged her children, a big smile on her face.

The crowd began to leave the building. Lizzie noticed Madison and her mother and Ava and Cecily walking in their direction.

"Congratulations, Lizzie." Madison chirped. "If your new business doesn't work out like you planned, let me know. We can talk about buying your place."

Lizzie pressed her lips pressed in a firm line. "Thanks for letting me know." It was tiring to be approached constantly about the sale of Gram's home.

As soon as Madison and her mother walked away, Ava approached.

Raising her fine, arched eyebrow, Ava spoke with a syrupy sweetness. "Lizzie, I must say I'm surprised your business license was approved. I hope you realize that the hard work is just beginning. If the day comes when you fail at your new venture — and I believe that day will come — you can call me. I might just buy that old beach house off your hands."

Lizzie's jaw tightened at her words. "I'll keep that in mind, Ava."

She finally relaxed, when the two women walk away.

Lizzie knew in her heart that she would never sell Gram's house to Madison or to Ava and Vera.

Those women had spoken words loaded with criticism ever since she moved to the Island.

"I say good riddance," Debbie McVay whispered as she

stepped closer to Lizzie. "I hope you never have a reason to sell your beach house to that woman, Lizzie."

She turned to her friend. "I don't believe I will, Debbie. I can't help but wonder at Ava's boldness in declaring that I'll fail at running the inn."

"Her opinion isn't important. What's important is, do you believe you can do this?" Debbie turned her brown eyes intense.

Lizzie nodded. "I do believe I can do this. It'll take hard work, but I can work hard and continue to learn what I need to in order to make this inn a success."

"There you have it. You'll be fine." Debbie grinned. "I think many folks — the board included — believe you'll succeed. I couldn't help but notice you were approved immediately at tonight's meeting."

Lizzie released a long audible breath. "I know. I'm still shocked."

Debbie whispered in a low voice, "I'm not surprised. I watched the video interview you did with the Boston TV station. You did a good job telling your story. Between you and me, I think whoever was behind that horrible article, got scared. They got the message that you wouldn't be intimidated, loud and clear."

Lizzie sighed with relief. "Well, I'm grateful that the board finally approved my business license."

Mrs. O'Connor and Sarah joined them. "Congratulations, Lizzie. We are so happy for you. "I'm glad to know the board finally saw common sense in your application."

Her lips grew wide with happiness. "Thanks, Mrs. O'Connor. You have helped me so much to get started. I'm grateful to you."

The older woman smiled warmly. "It's what I do. Maybe sometime in the future you'll be able to help someone else get started."

Lizzie nodded. "What a nice thought. I would love that."

It really would be wonderful to help someone else get their start. However, first there was still so much she needed to learn.

"What do you have left to get done before you're ready to open the inn to guests?" Debbie asked.

Lizzie thought about the long list she had written down last night.

"Quite a few things need to get done yet. But the most important thing is to get *The Vineyard Inn* website finished. My daughter, Annie, is working hard to get that done. The renovations that we needed to do are complete. But I expect there will always be something that needs to be fixed," Lizzie stated.

Mrs. O'Connor nodded. "That's a fact. When my husband and I started our bed and breakfast, we were always fixing something. But, that's just part of running an inn, my dear."

Lizzie nodded. "I'm beginning to understand that."

Debbie chuckled. "It's true. But it sounds like you've almost ready to receive guests."

"I think so." Lizzie tapped her chin. "That reminds me of something I was meaning to ask you all. Debbie, would you and your girls want to come to a test run for the inn for the last weekend of October? Mrs. O'Connor would you and Sarah like to come too?"

Mrs. O'Connor nodded. "That would be wonderful.

We'd love to join you for the test run, wouldn't we, Sarah?"

The quiet girl nodded and smiled.

Debbie was thoughtful. "If I can get my parents to take over the running of my bed and breakfast for that weekend, then yes, we would love to join you."

"Just let me know if it works. We have enough room for everyone." Lizzie smiled.

Debbie nodded. "I'll let you know."

"Well, I need to be going. I still have a few things left to do." Lizzie hugged each woman before walking with her children outside.

"Annie and Jake, I'll come inside in a few minutes." Lizzie waved at them and reached for her phone.

AS HER CHILDREN HURRIED INSIDE, she dialed her friend's number.

"Hey, Lizzie, what's up?" Tess's cheery voice answered.

Lizzie grinned and hurried out of the car. "Tess, you're not going to believe this. My business license was approved."

She heard Tess's quick intake of breath.

"Oh, my goodness. You're approved! That means you can start taking in guests for the Inn!" Tess laughed out loud. "I'm so excited for you, Lizzie!"

Lizzie strode up the stairs and hurried inside the house.

"Thanks. I am excited too."

Tess cheered on the other end of the phone line.

It was so loud Lizzie pulled the phone away from her ear.

She giggled at her friend's enthusiasm.

"So, when can I come join you to celebrate?" Tess probed for answers.

Lizzie stopped in her tracks. "That's so funny, because I was about to ask if you wanted to join a bunch of us for a test run at the Inn?"

"Of course, I do. When?"

Lizzie grinned. "The last weekend in October. Will that work?"

"I'll be there."

They said their goodbyes and Lizzie hung up her phone.

Her heart was happy and content.

Now that one of the biggest roadblocks was out of the way, hopefully the rest of the details would flow easier from here on out.

❧

Two weeks later, Lizzie was working hard to clean the bedrooms and bathrooms.

There was only one day left before guests would arrive.

"Mom, can you come take a look at the website when you have a minute?" Annie called from downstairs.

Lizzie quickly folded the clean blanket on the bed and hurried downstairs.

As she walked into the den, Annie waved her over.

"Come take a look at what we have so far."

Lizzie went over to stand behind the large desk.

Leaning close, she could see the beautiful blue ocean and a photo of the beach cottage.

Soft pink, blues and greens were scattered tastefully along each side of the website.

At the top in a lovely script, was the name of the inn.

"Oh my, Annie. This website design is gorgeous." Lizzie leaned closer to get a better view.

"I'll show you some of the webpages." Annie opened a different menu at the top of the website. She saw photos of the beautifully decorated bedrooms and the large dining room and the deck. Photos of their private beach looking out onto the ocean, added beauty to the page.

Lizzie hugged her daughter.

"This is so beautiful. You're a wonder, Annie." Lizzie hadn't quite realized how talented her daughter was with design.

"Thanks, Mom." Annie grinned. "But I haven't shown you the best part yet.

Her daughter opened a new page and scrolled down the page. "See here are photos of the food you've made."

"I see photos of beef Wellington, Clam Chowder soup, Quiche, Chicken Fettuccine Alfredo, and Chicken and Dumplings. And I love the assortment of salads you've added as well. It's so lovely. Thank you, Annie."

"Ah, Mom. I'm happy to help. I want you to know, I think you're brave to start this new venture of opening up your own inn." Annie's wide smile of approval was the encouragement Lizzie needed.

Unexpected tears pricked the back of her eyelids and she blinked them away. "You're going to make me cry."

Lizzie leaned over and kissed her daughter's cheek. "From the bottom of my heart, thank you."

Annie grinned. "But it's not quite done yet. I need to add the checkout pages so visitors can schedule and pay for their stay at the inn. I'll work on that this morning."

Lizzie nodded happily. "Well, I'll let you get to it then. I'm off to get groceries for all the guests that will arrive for the weekend."

"All right. See you later." Annie waved and quickly went back to work.

Lizzie shook her head.

She was grateful for her daughter. What a big help Annie continued to be in her life.

She was also happy that preparations for the arrival of guests were going smoothly. Was it too much to hope that this weekend would go by without too many obstacles?

LIZZIE'S CART was full by the time she reached the checkout line at the grocery store.

Her thoughts were so busy with all the meals she would be preparing for the weekend that she didn't even notice the person in front of her.

"Lizzie, how are you?"

She looked up to see Linda Hart in the line in front of her. Linda was the wife of the island's sheriff.

"Hello, Linda. I'm doing well. How have you been?" Lizzie looked up to see a middle-aged woman with dark brown hair, wearing the latest fashion.

"I'm well." Linda glanced over, noticing her full

grocery cart. "Looks like you'll be cooking a lot of meals. Or did you hire a cook?"

Lizzie grinned. "Yes. I agree my cart is quite full. But I didn't hire a cook as I plan to prepare these meals myself. This weekend will be a test run for my new inn. So, it will definitely be a busy one."

Linda lifted her eyebrows in surprise.

"Oh yes, I remember you recently were approved. Congratulations." Linda smiled graciously.

"Thanks."

"Well, with all the cooking you are doing, it looks like you could use some help. Have you thought of hiring someone to help serve your meals?" Linda asked.

Lizzie shrugged. "That would be helpful. I would have to see how well the inn does, before I could commit to hiring full time. But I could start someone part-time, I suppose."

"Of course." Linda wrote something down on the back of her business card. "Call Maeve Bletchley. She has served at large gatherings before and does a good job. She needs the work."

Lizzie reached for the business card and saw the name and number of the woman Mrs. Hart suggested she hire.

"Thanks for passing along her name, I appreciate it." Lizzie tucked the card inside her purse.

"Of course, anytime." Mrs. Hart hurried to pay for her groceries and waved at Lizzie as she left the store.

Lizzie thought about the idea of hiring someone part-time as she drove home.

Maybe it was a good idea.

❧

WHEN THE DOORBELL rang later that afternoon, Lizzie hurried to answer it.

Opening the door, she saw a thin woman with short, wavy, black hair who looked to be in her early thirties.

There were holes in her tennis shoes and jeans.

Lizzie wondered how long it had been since the woman had a proper meal.

The woman spoke hastily. "I'm Maeve Bletchley."

Lizzie extended her hand to shake hers. "Of course. Welcome, Maeve. I'm Lizzie."

"Come on in." Lizzie led the way to the kitchen.

Maeve followed quickly behind.

"So, Linda Hart told me you have helped serve at large events in the past."

Maeve nodded. "Yes, I've helped serve at large restaurants on the island as well as events for Ted Cantrell as he has campaigned for governor. I've also worked for large catering events around here."

"Good. That's just what I need help with." To Lizzie, this woman seemed like the perfect solution to help her for the weekend.

"If you could help me this weekend and then if that works out for both of us, then we can talk about a more permanent position here at the inn. Does that sound good to you?" Lizzie asked.

Maeve nodded. "Sure. That sounds fair. When do you want me to start?"

"If you could stop by tomorrow morning and be ready

to help cut the vegetables and prepare some desserts, that would be helpful."

When Maeve agreed, she gave her a tour of the house before her new employee left for the day.

She now had a part-time employee.

Lizzie paused to catch her breath her fears stronger than ever.

Last night she had checked her bank account, and there was only enough money there to last for three more weeks.

She was in desperate need to have paying guests soon.

Which was why she needed to have this test run of The Vineyard Inn, so she could quickly see what needed to be fixed before paying guests arrived.

To her surprise, all the friends she had invited said yes.

Lizzie was grateful to them.

She hoped it would be a good weekend for everybody.

Lizzie sat up in bed, paging through her grandmother's journal. She wanted to read the next entry.

She had a feeling reading more of Grams' words would help her to unravel more of the mystery that needed to be solved.

Today, I had a nice long talk with my husband, William. I was so curious about the story I heard long ago about his father Captain Henry Stafford.

I asked him: "Is the story of your father saving the young princesses life — really true?"

William nodded. "It is true, but it's difficult to prove with the tiara and pink diamond now missing."

I urged him to tell me the whole story.

He said, "I'll tell you just how my father told me. My father said he had taken his ship and crew to islands in the South Pacific Ocean. They finally ended up in Australia.

He and his crew went ashore and Dad said he went to visit an old military friend, who had been a general before he retired.

While staying there at the general's spacious house, a prestigious guest arrived along with his wife and young daughter.

King Stefan DeWither, his wife Queen Maria and his daughter Princess Beatrice.

The general knew many important people, but Dad said he was surprised to meet the king and queen and the princess.

The next day, they all went for a walk. The general's property was ten acres that connected to the shoreline.

Guards walked in front of them and behind them, but still Dad said he knew the area could be dangerous.

They nearly made it to shore, when suddenly out from the trees came a snake. It swirled right in front of the young princess.

Acting on reflex, Henry Stafford drew his gun and shot the head of the snake clean off.

Dad said the king was very extravagant in his praise. Since he knew Henry Stafford had a young daughter, the king told him as thanks for saving his only daughter's life, he was going to give him a beautiful tiara with a rare pink diamond.

My father said he knew better than to decline a gift from the king, so he graciously accepted.

Dad brought the tiara home with him.

My parents both died without telling anyone where they had hidden the tiara."

I told William, "That is so strange that your father didn't tell you where he hid the tiara."

William said, "It wasn't really that strange. My dad never did get over losing his youngest daughter to fever. It was like the gift from the king was forgotten, the same day my sister died."

Lizzie wiped away a tear.

It was very interesting that at one time there was a tiara with a pink diamond gifted to her great-grandfather. Where did Henry Stafford hide it?

She was trying to think of possible places, when she was startled by the loud ringing tone of her phone.

Quickly, she picked up her phone on the nightstand.

"Hello?" Out of breath, she sat down on the bed.

"Hello, Lizzie." Hearing Jonathan's low voice on the other end of the phone line, sent tingles up her arms. "You sound out of breath. I must have caught you at a bad time."

His voice lulled her into a relaxed mood.

"I'm… it's fine. I mean, I'm not busy," Lizzie replied, her words tripping over each other. She was always a little nervous talking to Jonathan.

"Good. I'm glad to hear it. So, how is everything going?" His tone held a degree of warmth and concern.

"It's going well. I don't think I told you, but the board approved my business license. Needless to say, that's a big relief," She whispered, her hand on her heart.

"Finally. That is good news. I'm happy for you, Lizzie." He had a wonderful, low voice, soft and clear.

Lizzie shifted to a more comfortable position, leaning against the headboard on her bed.

"Thanks. But I believe now the real test will be to see if everything goes as planned this weekend." Her voice sounded shakier then she would've liked.

"Lizzie, it's going to go well. You've got this." Jonathan encouraged in a soothing voice.

Lizzie smiled. He always seemed to be on her side, which was something that still surprised her.

"I appreciate your confidence in me, Jonathan," She spoke softly. "Do you think you'll have time to join us this weekend?"

There was a hint of laughter in his voice as he replied, "I wouldn't miss it. In fact, the manager of this project asked if I could stay, but I told him I had another commitment this weekend."

"Thanks, Jonathan. It'll be really good to have you here," Lizzie whispered. "You'll be able to point out where the problems are and what needs to be fixed before I begin to accept paying guests to stay at the Inn."

He chuckled. "Somehow, I doubt there will be many problems. But I hope you know I will help you however I can."

"I do know that. Thank you." Lizzie felt a warm glow flow through her at his words.

Jonathan had been one of her biggest supporters ever since she began this journey.

"I'm glad." There was a faint tremor in his voice as though some emotion had touched him. "I look forward to seeing you again, Lizzie."

"Tomorrow." Lizzie smiled, sighing.

When he spoke again, his voice was tender, almost a murmur. "Tomorrow, Lizzie. Goodnight."

Hanging up the phone, Lizzie leaned her head against the headboard of her bed, and released a long sigh.

Lately, whenever she thought about Jonathan, her heart turned over in response. Her traitorous heart was opening up to him in a new way that she could have never imagined.

It was an awakening experience that left her reeling.

Yet, fear still crowded into her heart every time she thought of him.

Very soon, they would need to have a serious talk.

They had reached the point in their relationship that it had to be resolved — one way or the other.

CHAPTER THIRTEEN

From a letter written by Henry Stafford to his cousin.
"I have returned from my latest shipping business in East India,
New Zealand and Australia.
While on my trip, I stayed at General Miles's home in Australia.
I was surprised when a visiting King and Queen and their
daughter who were touring the nation, stayed a few nights at the
general's large home. When we went for a walk near the river, a
snake attacked the young Princess. I shot its head off.
The King was so grateful that I saved the Princess's life that he
gave me a gift of a tiara with a large pink diamond — he said it
was for my daughter. I am eager to give this gift to Charlotte. I
will write more news soon. love your cousin, Henry."
The Vineyard Historical Letters

"We've arrived for the weekend." Mrs. O'Connor stopped in the front entryway of Lizzie's house to catch her breath.

Lizzie turned her head from talking with Annie, to see

the older lady standing near the door. Sarah set down the small suitcases and helped remove her grandmother's fall jacket.

"I'm happy to see both of you ladies." Lizzie walked over to them. Reaching for their hands, she gave them each a warm smile. "Thanks so much for coming to our weekend of fun."

The older grandmother squeezed her hands and, with a faint twinkle in her gray eyes, said, "We wouldn't miss it my dear. This trial run of your new inn promises to be enjoyable with many stories we can laugh about later."

Lizzie grinned. "That might be truer than you know." She turned to Sarah. "Sarah, thank you for being here."

She waved them over to where Annie stood by the tall counter. Jake had been busy building the counter for the reception area this past week and finally completed it.

"Of course, this weekend is free for everyone, but we wanted to register everybody that arrives today. That way, we'll be able to test the new software to double check it is working properly." Lizzie turned to her daughter. "Annie will type your names into the computer and she'll also give you a room number."

"Sounds good, Lizzie. My goodness, you are very organized." Mrs. O'Connor smiled. She leaned over the counter and told Annie all the necessary details.

"You two will share a room on the first floor. Room one hundred and six." Annie handed Sarah the key.

"How wonderful. We'll go and rest for a little while. Will we all meet up later on?"

Lizzie nodded. "We thought for this first night we would have homemade pizza. We'll meet together in the great room at six thirty. We can all watch a movie together there, or you have the option to eat pizza on the deck or even take it back to your room. Whatever you want."

Sarah grinned. "Oh, that sounds good. Grandmother, this will be a pleasant weekend."

The older lady's smile was wide as she and Sarah followed Annie down the hallway.

Lizzie had planned the assignment of the rooms carefully for the weekend. She planned for Mrs. O'Connor and Sarah to share a room on the first floor.

The older lady might appreciate that she didn't need to climb the stairs and might like to have her granddaughter nearby.

Moments after Mrs. O'Connor and Sarah walked away, her sisters arrived.

"You are all here. It's so good to see you all." Lizzie exclaimed as she hugged each one.

"We weren't about to miss this big event, Lizzie." Alex grinned.

Jane nodded. "This is so much fun. I noticed you have a fresh coat of paint, a couple of couches, and a reception counter in the entryway, Lizzie. It's beginning to look like an inn. I love what you've done."

Lizzie smiled. "Coming from you — the professional event planner — that means a lot. Thanks, Jane."

Jane beamed at the compliment. "I hope you remember me for future events you have at the inn."

"I will, dear sister." As her gaze turned from Jane to each of her sisters, she couldn't help but grin at their enthusiasm. "Annie will register you and give you a key to your rooms. Then we'll all meet in the great room at six thirty for homemade pizza."

"Ooo… I love Lizzie's pizza. I can't wait." Charlie swung her key around on a finger as she followed her sisters to their rooms.

All her sisters, she'd placed on the top floor. They would be two to a room so there would be enough bedrooms available for everyone.

Lizzie couldn't help the misgivings that increased by the minute as she thought about what her sisters' reactions would be when they discovered the single men she'd invited for the weekend.

During the next few hours, everyone that she invited had arrived.

The fun was about to begin.

MAEVE HELPED Lizzie carry the pizzas into the great room.

Since this room was the largest in the house, it made sense to have everybody meet here.

They made a few trips until all the pizzas had been placed on warming mats along the two side tables.

People were seated on the sofas next to people they knew. Mrs. O'Connor was talking with Debbie McVay. Debbie's daughters, Emma and Sophia were seated next to Sarah.

Lizzie smiled as she noticed Jake and Will join the girls' conversation. She was pleased with both her sons' interest in these young ladies.

Annie was talking about something serious with Chris. Lizzie couldn't help but wonder if something was amiss in their relationship.

Her friend Tess was explaining something and talking with her hands like she usually did — with her neighbor Jeb. Jeb's son Zach was seated near Charlie, Alex was asking Sam questions and Jane was renewing her acquaintance with Ward Hampton.

Her three other sisters, Jules, Katie, and Torrie were talking and laughing about something.

It was so good to see family and friends here for the weekend.

Lizzie turned her head to see Jonathan. He stood motionless, leaning one shoulder against the doorpost.

His blue eyes traveled over her face and searched her eyes.

A rush of pink stained her cheeks. Her heart hammered foolishly in her chest at his look of approval.

He must have just returned from his business trip, arriving at the door just as she began to talk.

A nervous flutter began in her belly and moved up to her throat.

She turned to face her guests, coughing lightly trying to clear her throat. It was an effort to bring a sense of calm to her traitorous body. "Everybody, welcome to a weekend at *The Vineyard Inn.*"

Her heart sang with happiness when they cheered and clapped. "I truly appreciate you all coming for this test run of the inn. If you could each do me a favor and make a short list of things that need to be improved while you're here, I would be grateful. I want to make this place a wonderful experience for visitors."

"Of course, Lizzie. We will help however we can." Mrs. O'Connor looked around the room. It seemed the grandmotherly lady had influence on the others, as everyone nodded in agreement.

"Thanks, everyone. For tonight, we thought it would be fun to start with homemade pizza and to watch a newly released, family friendly movie. We prepared many different toppings and there is also gluten-free pizza, so find your favorites." Lizzie turned to her son with a smile. "Jake will be in charge of getting the movie started."

People stood to their feet and walked to the table, filling their plates with their choices of pizza. She was thankful Grams had left behind all her furniture, including the four large sofas and six cushioned lounge chairs, so there was enough room for everyone.

Lizzie had decided to keep her large television from their Boston home and was grateful that she brought it here when they moved. Jake and Will had set it up on the far wall of the great room. The large screen was perfect for watching movies with a large crowd of people.

Jane stepped out of the crowd walking towards the food and strolled towards her with long, purposeful strides.

Her sister's blue eyes snapped at her with a little more fire than usual.

Lizzie tensed.

She'd been expecting one of her sisters to reproach her about the surprise guests.

"Dear sister, I have a bone to pick with you." Jane's

quiet voice sputtered with indignation. "Why in the world did you invite single men that three of us used to date — to this weekend event?"

Awkwardly, Lizzie cleared her throat. "When we met up with them at the Cantrell Festival, it looked to me like you were all talking and getting along so well. So, I thought, why not invite them to our fun weekend? Don't you enjoy talking with Ward?"

To her surprise, she spotted a blush on her sister's cheeks. "Well, I am surprised that I enjoy talking with Ward very much." Jane began, but suddenly turned flashing blue eyes back to Lizzie. "But that's not the point. You went behind our backs and invited the same men we were in love with years ago. Those days are over, Lizzie. We can't bring them back."

Lizzie replied softly, "I know we can't bring those days back, Jane. But, the thought occurred to me, at the very least, we might be able to clear the air and have a second chance to forgive the hurts that happened in those relationships years ago." Lizzie spotted Jonathan talking with her son Jake. "Healing hurt from relationships in the past, has been on my mind a lot lately."

Jane sighed, studying her thoughtfully. "Well, when you put it like that, I suppose your idea has some strong points."

The beginning of a smile tipped the corners of her mouth upwards. "I'm glad you see it that way, Jane. And I really do think we can make this a good weekend."

"I hope that's true." Jane sighed, turning to glance at Ward. The man's bold gaze was riveted on her.

A thoughtful smile tipped up the corner's of Lizzie's mouth.

"It is true, Jane. Now, go have some fun." Lizzie grinned. Jane smiled reluctantly before she walked away.

Lizzie was pleased that things were going okay between her sisters and their unexpected male guests.

Now that the movie was beginning to play, Lizzie thought she'd take a few minutes to check on Maeve. She needed to check how the food preparation was coming along in the kitchen.

With quiet footsteps, she hurried away.

As she walked down the hallway towards the kitchen, Lizzie's thoughts were on the meals she would be preparing for the next day.

It was important to double check all was in order before she would be able to enjoy herself with the rest of the guests.

As she got closer to the kitchen, she heard loud voices.

Suddenly, she stopped.

It was her daughter, Annie, and her son Will. It sounded like they were in the middle of an argument.

"Will, you've been angry at Mom ever since Dad died." There was an intensity in Annie's lowered voice. "I don't understand it. What's going on with you?"

Will responded with a voice that had a cold steely edge to it. "I *am* angry at Mom. I think it was her responsibility to have known about Dad's addictions. They were married. Mom should have known Dad spent money uncontrollably when he was drunk."

"So, you're angry about Dad losing all that money?" Annie questioned.

Will's strong voice was insistent. "It's not just about Dad losing the money. I'm also angry that Mom didn't know and didn't stop him — when she should've known and stopped — Dad's uncontrollable spending."

Lizzie bit her lip. She knew her oldest son had trouble forgiving her, but she didn't know Will still clung to such a deep anger towards her.

She swallowed hard and bit back tears.

It was quiet in the room for a little while before Annie spoke again.

"You want to know what I think?"

"I'm sure you'll tell me." Will's low voice was edged with anger.

Annie sighed heavily. "I believe that deep down, you are really angry at Dad, but you feel guilty about it because he passed away. You feel guilty about being angry with Dad now that he's dead. After all, the truth is that it was Dad's fault for spending all our family's money in the first place."

Lizzie could hear the shuffling of feet in the otherwise silent room.

Annie continued in a low intense voice, "I think that rather than being angry at Dad, instead what you've done — maybe subconsciously — is that you've seen Mom as an extension of Dad. So, all your anger has now landed on her. But she's not the one who spent the money. Dad did."

"I suppose that's true," Will replied.

Lizzie detected a thawing in his tone.

"But I still don't understand. Why didn't Mom know about what was going on with Dad?" There was a confusion in her son's voice that made Lizzie's heart ache.

"I think it's because, in the past few years, Dad was home less often and when he was home, he didn't tell Mom much. Dad handled the finances all their married life, so Mom didn't know what was going on." Annie's voice was soothing. "But Mom is really working hard now to get her finances and everything else together. I mean, look at what she's done with Grams' house."

Will stammered, but his voice still held an angry edge, "Yeah… I can see that she's been making changes. I just don't know anymore."

"Give her the benefit of the doubt, Will. She's your mother and loves you very much." Annie coaxed. "That's all I have to say. I guess we'd better start heading back to the party. They'll have missed us by now."

The sudden clanging of pots and pans caused Lizzie to remember where she was. She didn't want her children finding her here.

Tears trailed down Lizzie's cheek. Her heart ached at how angry her son was with her.

Turning quickly, she ran smack into a solid chest.

Looking up, her gaze met Jonathan's blue eyes.

"Lizzie, what's wrong?" Gentle hands gripped her shoulders, and a crease formed between his brows.

Smothering a sob, she fled to the one place where she'd always felt safe.

❧

"LIZZIE, I'M COMING IN." Jonathan's low voice spoke from the other side of the door.

In the past, he'd seemed to find a way to learn her whereabouts whenever she was in trouble.

Jonathan opened the door to the den, quickly closing it behind him.

The tenderness in his blue eyes was nearly her undoing.

She had curled up on the old sofa near the fireplace.

With a shaky hand, she wiped the tears from her cheeks.

Steadily, he walked towards her.

Sitting beside her, he put his arm around her shoulder and pulled her close.

"Lizzie, talk to me," He whispered into her ear. "Tell me what's happened."

Her voice shook with emotion. "It's my son, Will."

She explained about what happened with her husband's drinking problem and his uncontrollable spending.

"That's the reason my budget is so limited. Ever since Gray passed away, Will has been angry with me because I didn't know what was going on with our finances. It's my fault that he's so angry. I should've been aware of everything that was going on. I don't know if he'll ever forgive me or we'll have a close mother-son relationship ever again."

Jonathan pulled her closer, kissing the top of her head. With a low murmur he said, "I am sorry to hear that. But I don't understand how your son could blame you, when it was your late husband's fault."

Lizzie swallowed back emotion. "Because, I should have been aware of the state of our finances."

She released a shaky breath. "I didn't know how Gray was handling our money. I'm partly to blame because I should've been assertive asking my husband about our bank accounts. But I felt I wasn't very smart when it came to making decisions about finances. Self-doubt and fear held me back."

"Oh Lizzie. I'm sorry you've felt that way." With one hand Jonathan gently pushed a stray curl away from her forehead.

A familiar shiver of awareness jolted through her as his touch.

She bit her lip and shrugged. "I have felt that way for years. Yet, even though I am partly to blame, I still feel angry at Gray for putting me in this horrible position of debt in the first place."

"That's understandable."

Lizzie turned in his arms to look into Jonathan's eyes. "Is it? I feel so guilty that I've been angry at him. Gray is now gone. I shouldn't be feeling angry at him."

She stopped, closing her eyes as she released a shaky breath.

"Oh, Lizzie. I think your feelings are normal. Even after someone we love has passed away, there can still be the emotions that go along with the memories of them — whether they are good or bad." Jonathan sighed.

He hesitated, deep in thought.

"I remember, when my dad passed away twelve years ago, I was angry at him for all the traumatic drunken rages he'd put Mom and my sisters — his entire family, through for years."

Lizzie reached for his hand, holding it gently.

"It was during my sophomore year in high school — when you and I began to date — that I had the worst fight with my dad." His expression was one of anguish.

She questioned in a low, tormented voice, "What happened?"

"My dad came home one night drunker then usual. He was angry at his boss and angry that Mom hadn't saved any extra money for booze." Jonathan closed his eyes at the memories that still haunted him.

"Dad flew at my mother as soon as he got home from work. He managed to hit her twice. I heard my mother's screams from my back bedroom. I ran to the front of the house and we fought until I managed to pin him down. But not before he punched me and he gave me a deep cut near my eye. I still have that scar now."

Lizzie reached up and, with a gentle finger, traced the jagged edges of the scar. "I'm so sorry you had to live through all that pain."

Jonathan grabbed her hand and kissed her finger, smile lines appearing by his big blue eyes.

He peered at her intently.

A tremor rippled through her body and she continued to talk, nervous by his nearness. "I remember that day you came to class with a large bandage by your eye. I didn't realize everything that had happened to you."

Jonathan nodded. "Yeah. I was fairly quiet about my home life. That was more to protect my Mom and my sisters, than for any other reason."

Lizzie nodded, feeling the misery of the young boy who needed to protect his mom and sisters from his abusive father all his life.

Her memories of him when he first moved to the Sweet Beach Cove community, were vivid.

The first day she met him at the beach, Jonathan had helped her rebuild her sandcastle. Her heart had filled with joy at his kind gesture and she'd been sad to see him go when his sisters came to get him.

His sisters had seemed scared that day, saying they were worried their dad might come home before they got there.

"I'm so sorry, Jonathan." Lizzie saw the pain of the past still flickered in his eyes.

Jonathan squeezed her hand. "The past is over now, Lizzie. I'm all right. In the first few years after my dad passed away, I saw a therapist. She helped me understand that I needed to forgive my dad and let the anger go, because the only person all that bottled up anger was hurting — was me."

Pensively, she looked across the room pondering his words. Lizzie realized she needed to forgive her late husband. Even though the debt had been Gray's fault, the problem was that unforgiveness and anger were festering inside her like a raw wound that wouldn't heal.

The anger was hurting her, she could see that now.

"Thanks for sharing the pain you've gone through. It's difficult to forgive someone when you feel so wronged, isn't it?" Tears pricked the back of her eyelids as she looked over at him.

"Without a doubt." Jonathan caressed her hand softly.

"But, for me, it freed me from the heavy anger that had been crushing my spirit for a very long time."

They sat together in silence for a long while.

Jonathan whispered. "Maybe your son still feels anger at his dad — but is taking it out on you, simply because you are the parent who is still living."

Lizzie's mouth dropped open. "That's what my daughter said. Maybe that is what's going on with Will."

The heartache of her son's anger weighed heavy on her. "I pray that someday he will forgive me and that our relationship will be restored."

Jonathan breathed softly. "Somehow, I believe that will happen sooner than you think. "

"I hope so." And she did, with all her heart. "Thank you, Jonathan. The way you've listened and shared your own heart has really helped me."

Jonathan turned to face her. Placing both hands on the sides of her face he held it gently. The heart-rending tenderness in his gaze was her undoing.

"Aww… Lizzie," He whispered. "You must know by now I'd do anything for you."

He leaned down and pressed his lips against hers, then gently covered her mouth.

His slow, drugging kiss was as sweet as a summer breeze.

It was a kiss for her tired soul to melt into.

Gathering her into his arms, he held her snugly.

For the first time in a very long time, she felt cherished.

CHAPTER FOURTEEN

While her husband Ike Cantrell was finding more treasure,
Clara wrote letters to her sister Helen.
"Dear sister, I miss you. I am struggling with loneliness because
Ike is gone a lot. He tells me he is determined to become richer
than Henry Stafford.
To be honest, I think my husband is still upset that he lost that
waterfront property in that game of chance. So, he spends a lot
of time away from home. He takes our son Eli with him too. I
feel like I'm losing my family. Please come visit when you can.
Love, Clara."
The Vineyard Historical Letters

"This is a lovely table filled with delicious food," Maeve commented as she set the plates on the table in preparation for the big dinner gathering that evening.

"Yes, it is. My Grandmother insisted on hosting many dinner parties during the years that she and my grandfather lived here." Lizzie smiled as she arranged fresh-cut flowers for the table's centerpiece. "As a teenager I remember sitting at this table across from famous authors, actresses, painters, and two different governors."

"Wow." Maeve's eyebrows lifted in surprise. "That must have been a fascinating experience as a teenager."

Lizzie nodded with a smile. "It was. Those experiences gave me an appreciation for art, politics, and really helped me learn more about culture and people."

With one last adjustment, the pink and red flowers were just about right.

Lizzie stepped back to get a good view of the table.

"It looks good," Maeve commented.

She smiled. "I think so too. Now, I'll let you finish setting the table while I go check on the food. I can smell the turkey from here."

With a smile, Lizzie hurried back to the kitchen.

As she checked on the meat and started peeling potatoes, she remembered the recent weekend with so many of her family and friends.

Her two sons, Will and Jake, had enjoyed their time with Sarah and Emma. She would need to wait and see what happened with those relationships.

She couldn't help but be a little worried about Annie. Her daughter said Christopher and her broke up on the weekend.

Her daughter said that she and Chris had argued. He wanted her to move back to Boston, but Annie wanted to stay on Martha's Vineyard. Their fight brought up questions of whether they truly were committed to each other.

Annie said they decided to take a break in their relationship for now. They needed this time of separation from each other to help them understand if they were meant to be together.

Lizzie felt her daughter's heartache. She hoped that in some small way, she would be able to encourage her daughter during this difficult time.

As her thoughts drifted to her other friends who had joined them for the test weekend for *The Vineyard Inn.*

Mrs. O'Connor, Debbie McVay, and her friend Tess had spent much of the time talking and having fun together.

A smile formed on her lips as she thought of her sisters spending time with the men they loved years ago.

Perhaps it was silly, thinking she could play match-maker. But there were many times she caught her sisters talking and laughing with the men that weekend.

It was uncertain if her efforts would mend any rela-tionships. Lizzie was certain her sisters would let her know one way or the other.

As she thought of relationships, Jonathan's smiling face popped into her thoughts.

A shiver ran through her body as she recalled his arms around her holding her close. He had listened to her worries and had shared some of his heart.

Her lips tingled in remembrance of his kiss.

Lizzie knew her feelings for him were intensifying.

Every time she saw him, the pull toward him was stronger.

Yet, there was a part of her that held back.

Maybe it was because the vivid picture of watching Jonathan kiss Cecily years ago, still burned in her memory. She didn't understand her own emotions sometimes.

But the truth was, they still hadn't developed trust in their relationship. She knew first-hand how lack of trust affected a marriage.

Sighing, she continued to work getting dinner ready.

Lizzie was happy to be following in her grandmother's footsteps and having dinner with a lot of guests.

Hosting a dinner was a step in the right direction.

The dinner was to be celebrate the grand opening of the inn.

Much to Lizzie's surprise, guests from a couple of places in the country had signed-up to book their stay at her inn.

Annie's beautiful website design for the inn, along with the ads she'd placed in different blogs, newspapers, and social media sites were helping to get the word out.

Most of her friends who came for the trial weekend for her new inn, had written a short list of improvements.

A few things on the list were easy to fix. A couple of doors squeaked and in a couple of rooms the drawers on the dressers were broken. Jake had already fixed those problems.

The more difficult item to fix on the list would be to install a bathroom in every bedroom. But that would need to come later.

Lizzie planned to talk with Jonathan and her children about ideas on the best way to handle that problem.

At some point down the road, she would need to hire a cook. But, for now, she was happy to make the meals. It was helpful to have Maeve's help with food preparation.

For tonight's dinner, she felt ready.

It was important to her to invite some of Martha's Vineyard's important citizens like the Cantrell family and Hart's. Along with friends and family.

She hoped everything went smoothly.

In all honesty, she hadn't really wanted to invite Ida, Vera or Ava Cantrell. Those women had really discouraged her efforts to get the Inn started.

Yet, somehow Lizzie felt she needed to ask the Cantrell family if they would come to this dinner. Her grandmother had always invited the Cantrell family to important dinners.

She had also followed in Grams' footsteps and invited her dad's long-time friends: Ted Cantrell and his wife Lola, Jerry Hart and his wife Linda, and Bobby Sutton and his wife Susan.

A part of her hoped that people would see the invitation as a gesture of goodwill.

In her mind, this was a significant dinner, marking a new start in her life here in Sweet Beach Cove.

&

"YUM. THE DINNER IS SUPERB, LIZZIE." Lola Cantrell sat next to her husband Ted, across from Lizzie.

Everyone had arrived on time for dinner. It felt good to have so many people that her grandmother used to know at the beach house once again.

Lizzie had seated Ida Cantrell next to her son Ted. Ida's daughter Nettie sat on her other side.

"Thanks, Lola." Lizzie glanced around the table

looking at all the people who joined her. "I thought this celebration could be an early Thanksgiving dinner."

Lizzie nodded at Maeve as she cut more slices of the large turkey on the dinner table. "This is Maeve. She's helping to serve dinner tonight."

Maeve nodded with a small smile to the guests around the table before hurrying back to the kitchen.

"Well, we appreciate your invitation to dinner." Ted grinned as he took a sip of his juice. "I remember sitting around this very table many times when your grandmother made her delicious dinners. It was always an honor to be included among her distinguished guest list."

A thoughtful smile curved her mouth. "Yes. Grams' guests intimidated me every time she had one of her big dinners. Yet, I have fond memories of learning so much about art, culture, and people every time."

"Did your grandmother ever tell you what inspired her to host these dinners?" Lola's gaze rested on her with questioning eyes.

Lizzie's mouth twitched with amusement. "Yes, she did. My grandmother said her father, who served as governor years ago, would tell her that she should always learn from people in all walks of life. He'd say, there's a little bit of wisdom all around you, you just need to look for it. Gram told me that's why she brought people from all professions and backgrounds into her home."

"Your grandmother was a wise woman," Lola commented.

Lizzie nodded. "She was."

She turned back to her meal, enjoying the meal along

with the rest of her guests. It pleased her that the turkey, mashed potatoes, and side dishes had all turned out well.

"It's very delicious, Lizzie. But then I suppose you've always enjoyed cooking, haven't you?" Mrs. Linda Hart commented. "My husband only gets homemade meals on very special occasions."

Linda's husband was Jerry Hart, the sheriff of Sweet Beach Cove. They had twin adult sons, Ryan and Dylan. Ryan was a police officer and Dylan worked as a handyman.

The meal was a little awkward between Cecily and Ryan because of their divorce a little over a year ago.

That was the reason Lizzie had seated Cecily at the opposite end of the table, beside her friend Ava.

Jonathan was seated beside Cecily and Lizzie was on his other side. At the time it had seemed to be the only way to get everybody seated at the dinner table.

Seeing Jonathan leaning towards Cecily, in close conversation with her, made her feel irritable and unhappy.

Lizzie quickly turned back to focus on her other guests.

Jerry Hart's gaze met hers from across the table.

"Home cooked meals like this happen only on rare occasions. I do miss this, Lizzie. It's delicious," Jerry commented, earning a sigh of exasperation from his wife.

Lizzie smiled. "Thanks."

Ida Cantrell sighed. "In my day, women were expected to cook meals, do the gardening, raise the children, and also help with whatever their husband was doing."

Ava commented, "Times have changed, Grandmother.

Women sometimes work long hours, outside the home now."

Ida huffed. "There's been too much change, if you ask me."

Vera added. "Mom, if there hadn't been changes, women wouldn't have had a chance to be a real estate agent like myself, or run an inn, like Lizzie here."

Ida Cantrell sighed. "I suppose."

A deep crease formed between the old matriarch's brows as she peered over at Lizzie. "Your grandmother could handle many tasks at once. But your great-grandmother struggled in her mental health. I was a young girl back then, but I remember seeing it with my own eyes."

"Lizzie, like I said before, I really hope you didn't get your great-grandmother's sensitivity to easily feeling stressed and overwhelmed. That won't do you any good, especially when you're trying to run this inn."

Ted sighed, shaking his head. "Mom, didn't you watch Lizzie's recent interview with that Boston TV reporter?"

Ida Cantrell huffed. "No, I didn't watch the interview. I don't keep up with the news all the time, Son."

"Well, that's too bad. You missed Lizzie telling her story. Apparently, a journalist from our own newspaper, The Vineyard Bulletin, smeared her character. They discredited her ability to run the inn and tainted her mental capabilities. Lizzie wasn't impressed with their name-calling. I don't know who was behind that article, but they need to be called out for their lies."

The glass of water shook in Vera's hand as she took a drink.

Ida gave Ted a black layered look. "Well, I just say it how I see things."

Ted sighed. "Mom, I must say, this time, how you see things isn't right. Not this time. Lizzie has done a wonderful thing opening The Vineyard Inn. And I believe she deserves our encouragement and support."

Mrs. Ida Cantrell harrumphed, miffed with her son.

It was clear the old matriarch wasn't happy with her son's support of her. Lizzie could only hope that would change at some point.

Vera's expression was unreadable, "Mom, I suppose we need to know when we've been beat. It's time we support Lizzie in her new project."

Vera's lips formed a thin line as she turned to Lizzie.

A shudder ran up her spine.

The atmosphere suddenly became unfriendly. She couldn't wait for this dinner to be over.

Susan Sutton turned to Lizzie from where she sat on the other side of the table beside her husband Bobby.

"Thank you for giving us a quick tour of your new inn, Lizzie. I had forgotten how many bedrooms were in your grandmother's old house. It looks like you've made a few renovations too."

Lizzie breathed a sigh of relief that Susan had changed the subject. "Yes, we've done a few renovations. My sons helped and so did Jonathan. Mrs. O'Connor, her granddaughter Sarah, and Mrs. Debbie McVay all gave me advice on how to make improvements to this house."

"My daughter, Annie, did the website design. My friend Tess and my six sisters have been a constant support during this whole process." Lizzie sent a warm smile to all the people she named. "I am very grateful for everybody's help."

"Lizzie is an inspiration to all of us," Mrs. O'Connor spoke from the far end of the table.

"Yes, she is. Lizzie is just like her beloved grandmother" Miss Sadie smiled widely as she spoke from the other end of the table. "It has been encouraging to watch Lizzie continue to work hard to finish restoring this old house into an inn. It's amazing what a little hard work, and support from friends and family can accomplish."

"Hear. Hear." Ted lifted his glass. "A toast to Lizzie."

Pink stained her cheeks as everyone clinked their glasses.

Afterwards Lizzie raised her glass and said, "And here's to everyone who helped to restore this old house."

"Our dear sister certainly has surprised us with how she's turned our grandmother's house around so quickly." Alex turned to her. "We're proud of you."

"Thanks, sis. It means a lot to have your support." Lizzie grinned, turning to all her sisters.

Jonathan turned. "You've hosted a wonderful dinner, Lizzie. It's good to see so many friends here tonight."

"Yes, many are friends. Although, with some folks, I'm not quite sure where I stand with them." Lizzie muttered, her face clouding with uneasiness as her gaze met his.

Jonathan hesitated, measuring her for a moment. He was about to say something when Maeve walked into the dining room.

She was carrying plates filled with dessert.

After Maeve had set peach pie on everybody's plate, she returned to the kitchen.

Each of them had just started eating dessert when Lizzie thought she could smell something strange.

"Does anyone else smell smoke?" Lizzie's gaze turned to Jonathan.

He nodded. "Now that you mention it, I do."

Alex also nodded. "I smell smoke too."

No sooner had she spoken, than they could hear the high-pitched sounds of the house fire alarm.

"Excuse me, everyone. I need to find out what's going on." Jumping to her feet, Lizzie hurried out of the dining room.

"Where's the fire?" Lizzie hurried to the kitchen which was the room next to the dining room.

She thought this would be the first place that a fire would likely be. "And where is Maeve? I thought she was in the kitchen."

Jonathan followed behind her. "I'm not sure."

Alex met them in the kitchen. "I can't see smoke in here, but I can smell it coming from somewhere. I'll call the emergency number to reach the fire department."

"Thanks, Alex." Lizzie was grateful her sister knew how to stay calm and that she took charge during emergency situations.

"We need to keep looking for the source." Panic was beginning to riot inside her. The thought came to mind, where there was smoke, there was fire. So, where was the fire?

Jonathan grabbed the fire extinguisher from the wall in the kitchen.

Lizzie hurried out of the kitchen into the hallway. "Let's go this way."

As she walked down the long hallway, smoke became so thick they could hardly see their way.

Lizzie coughed, finding it difficult to breathe.

"It'll help you breathe if you cover your mouth and nose with my hankie, Lizzie." Jonathan reached into his pocket and pulled out a white handkerchief that he always kept handy.

"Thanks." Lizzie placed the hankie over her nose and mouth, breathing easier with the covering.

The piercing sound of the fire truck's siren could be heard in the background.

A loud thump could be heard. Something had fallen.

Stark fear swept through Lizzie.

Grams' house that she worked so hard to restore, was now crumbling down before her eyes.

How did this happen? Just where was the fire?

Jonathan spoke loudly, "I think the fire might be coming from the den."

They reached the door to the den, barely able to see through the haze of smoke.

"I can see a bright light flickering through the crack at the bottom of the door." A deep crease of worry formed between Jonathan's brows.

Lizzie's wide-eyed gaze stared at the light.

Icy fear twisted around her heart.

No. Not the den.

The den was the place where she had the best memories with Gramps and Grams from years ago.

"The door is already open a little bit. I'm going to push it open. Stand behind me, Lizzie." With one arm, Jonathan protectively moved her body, so she stood behind him.

Anxiety spurted through her, wondering what they would find when they opened the door.

Gripping the fire extinguisher in one hand, Jonathan slowly opened the door.

Hot air blasted towards them.

They could see the fire raging. The fire raced up two walls and already two of the sofas in the room were on fire.

Immediately, Jonathan held up the fire extinguisher and began spraying where the fire was the heaviest.

Her stomach churned with fear and dreams at the sight. Her beloved house was burning down before her eyes.

Would they get the fire out in time, before it ruined the entire house?

As if in answer to her silent prayers, she heard footsteps running down the hallway.

Lizzie turned, hurrying out of the room.

She saw four firefighters rushing towards her.

Two of the men carried a long, thick water hose.

"The fire's in there." Lizzie pointed to the den.

Alex came to stand beside her.

Without a word, they hurried into the den and began spraying water.

Jonathan was soon escorted out of the room by one of the firefighters. "You're not wearing safety gear. The only place you'll be truly out of danger is outside. You should both get to safety."

Lizzie's heart jumped in her chest when she saw Jonathan's soot blackened face, chest, and hands.

"You look awful. Are you alright?" Lizzie rushed towards him. She looked at him, closely checking to see if there were burns on his body.

"Lizzie, I'm okay," Jonathan whispered in a hoarse voice. He coughed, still trying to catch his breath.

"I hope so." Lizzie sighed in relief.

"We can be grateful the firefighters arrived so quickly. I hope they can get the fire out quickly."

Jonathan turned to her. "Stop worrying. Help is here now and they are working as quickly as possible."

"I know." Lizzie gave an anxious cough. Turning to look down the hallway, she thought of her guests. "We need to leave. And I need to tell everyone what's happened."

Lizzie hurried down the hallway, without waiting. She headed towards the dining room.

However, she only got as far as the entryway.

There was a yellow ribbon across the hallway and on the outside door with the words: *fire line, do not cross.*

As she hurried outside, she spotted her children and sisters.

"Mom, are you alright?" Annie hurried over.

Lizzie nodded. "I'm fine. The firefighters are putting out the fire in the den now. Where is everyone?"

"Since the fire started, everybody left quickly." Annie replied. "The firefighters told us not to come down the hallway. We were forced to wait outside until you came to us."

Jake grabbed her in a big hug. "I've been so worried about you."

Lizzie smiled, pleased by the affection from her children. "I'm fine."

Will hugged her. "I'm glad you're alright, Mom." He swallowed back emotion. "And, I want to say I'm sorry for being angry at you since Dad passed away. I was scared of all the changes and blamed you. I'm sorry. Will you forgive me?"

"Of course, I forgive you Will." Lizzie embraced close to her heart.

After a long while, Will loosened his grip on her.

Lizzie stepped back, surprised to see moisture in his eyes. "I love you, Son."

"I love you too, Mom." Will whispered, swallowing back turbulent emotions.

Lizzie's smile widened and she squeezed his arm. "We'll be okay. Everything will be fine. We're a family and we stick together."

Will nodded, swallowing hard. "We will stick together. Thanks, Mom."

Annie walked over and touched her arm. "Mom, the firefighters were worried about us breathing in too much smoke."

"Of course. We were there very long, so hopefully we'll be alright." Lizzie sighed as they began walking out the front door. "I just hope they get the fire out in time."

All her sisters walked over to her.

"Looks like you love to have dramatic dinner parties.

The way you ended tonight with a fire, was a nice touch." Jane quipped. "I'll need to remember that in the future."

Lizzie's mouth quirked. "Jane, sometimes you are funny with your dark humor."

Jane chuckled.

"Good thing people left as soon as they knew there was a fire." Charlie shrugged. "I think they were worried that the entire house might soon be engulfed in flames."

Lizzie nodded, as fear clenched her stomach in knots again. "I know the feeling."

"It's going to be alright, Mom." Annie slipped an arm around her shoulders.

"Thanks, Annie. I really hope so."

All of a sudden, Jonathan appeared in the entryway. He was still covered in black soot but he had a smile on his face.

"I just spoke with one of the firefighters. They said they got the fire out. There is a lot of damage in the den, but at least the fire is out." Jonathan's voice was resigned as he looked over at her.

Lizzie nodded and swallowed emotion. "At least the fire is out. That's the good news."

"It looks like we'll all need to stay a few nights in a hotel." Jane looked at everyone. "Let's go see what's available."

Everyone started to walk to their vehicles.

Lizzie followed her family.

She swallowed back fear and worry that continued to run rampant through her trembling body.

"I'm not sure. But I suppose I'll get through this. I

must." Lizzie could manage no more than a hoarse whisper.

Jonathan stepped closer. "You will, Lizzie. The house will be restored again."

Would it? She thought of all the work they had done on the house already. Now there would be another room that they would need rebuild.

He paused before asking, "Are things all right between the two of us?"

Thoughts of Jonathan and Cecily with their heads close together at tonight's dinner, sifted through her thoughts.

Memories came back. The bad back-up in high school had haunted her for years.

Was it her fears from their shared past that held her back?

"I'm not sure, Jonathan. For a while, I thought things were good. But lately I've been noticing that Cecily keeps getting in between us. I don't know what to believe anymore."

Jonathan sighed and ran a hand through his hair. "We need to talk, Lizzie. I should've talked to you far sooner, but I have so many things to say to you. I know you'll want to take care of what's going on with the investigation of your house fire for the next couple days. But I want to ask, would you meet me on the beach, one week from today at sunset?"

Deep inside, she wanted to tell him no.

However, she was reminded of how much he'd done for her since she moved here. Not only how he'd offered to help renovate the house for free, but how he helped to save the house from burning to the ground.

Unbidden, her thoughts filtered back to the day she'd met him.

He had patiently helped her re-build her sandcastle on the beach. He helped her yet again with her real house today.

Still, Lizzie hesitated. Dare she risk her heart again?

"Please, Lizzie?" She surrendered to the entreaty in his low voice.

She nodded slightly. "I will meet you on the beach then."

Turning, she walked out the door.

Uncertainty rose up inside her. Lizzie hoped their talk would finally bring clarity and understanding between them.

She was desperate for both.

A WEEK later she arrived back at the house.

Sheriff Hart was waiting for her. A man from the fire department was just leaving as they arrived.

"Hello, sheriff." Lizzie's eyes widened in surprise. "I was told we could come back to the house, as the fire damage was limited to one room."

"Yes, that's true. And the cleanup crew has come and gone, so that's good." The sheriff walked beside her into the house. Her children followed behind them. "There was a lot of damage to the den. I just want to prepare you."

Her stomach clenched tight. What would she find?

When they reached the den, Sheriff Hart opened the door.

Lizzie gasped at the sight.

The walls still looked soot-streaked and blackened in some areas.

"The sofas have been removed."

"Yes, furniture or wall hangings that had a lot of fire damage have been removed." Sheriff Hart nodded.

Lizzie swallowed. "Wall hangings — my painting — is gone."

"The painting was far too damaged to keep. I'm sorry, Lizzie."

Tears blinded her eyes.

Lizzie nodded, swallowing hard. She didn't trust herself to speak. Biting her lip, she did her best not to give into tears.

The painting had been one of her best memories. That beautiful piece of art had been a constant reminder of how Grams made this house into a peaceful sanctuary when she and her sisters arrived, scared, just after their parents' death.

The painting of the beach house, with the peaceful blue water surrounding it, served as a reminder of the warmth of family — a safe refuge from a sea of life's storms.

But now all that had been destroyed.

All that was left behind were charred remains.

Her eyes bordered with tears, but refused to let the tears run rampant down her cheeks.

Jane slipped one arm around her waist, standing with her, lending comfort.

She was so angry that a fire had started in the first place.

"Did you ever find out how the fire started?" Lizzie had no idea how a fire would have begun in the Den.

She'd always been careful to pour water on the ashes if they had used the wood burning fireplace.

"We looked for clues and swabbed for fingerprints. We didn't really learn anything until a woman came into the police department." The sheriff adjusted his hat and shook his head. "It's the first time in a long time that I've had someone come and confess to wrongdoing."

"Who was it?" The silence grew tight with tension as she waited.

Sheriff Hart grimaced. "It was Maeve that started that fire."

Her body stiffened in shock. "I hired her, knowing that she needed the money. I can't believe she would do this to me."

The sheriff held up his hand, doing his best to stop her tirade. "But, for what it's worth, Maeve was paid to set that fire. She showed us the texts. There was a paper trail left by the woman who paid her off."

Jane sighed. "This is beginning to sound worse than one of those mystery movies."

Lizzie expelled a breath. "I agree. I'm at a loss for words."

She shook her head in disbelief and finally asked. "Who was the woman that paid Maeve to start that fire?"

"I'm disappointed to have to tell you, it was Vera Cantrell." Sheriff Hart scratched the top of his head. "I don't understand it myself. But we have the evidence we need. Vera is undergoing rigorous questioning as we speak."

Lizzie shook her head. "I don't understand why Vera would want to do this to me? She has more friends, influence and money than most people. What possible reason could she have for wanting to start a fire in my home?"

"Those are questions we hope to have answers to very soon." Sheriff Hart nodded, his mind clearly on the case. "But, until then, it looks like you can move back home." His phone beeped and he glanced down at the message. "I've got to go. Take care of yourself, Lizzie."

Lizzie nodded at him and watched him leave.

As her gaze roamed the desolate, soot-blackened den the pain in her heart gave way to despair.

With so many people and circumstances tearing her down, she felt hopeless.

She had lost so much… too much.

Lizzie didn't think she would ever recover.

She covered her face with trembling hands and let herself give in to the agony of her loss.

CHAPTER FIFTEEN

A fever swept through Martha's Vineyard in some homes some
family members didn't survive.
In a letter Henry Stafford wrote to his cousin he shares what
happened.
"Dear Evangeline. Thank you for staying with my wife. She is
still mourning the loss of the baby. But there is more news. Since
I arrived home with my ship and crew, a fever ravaged some
families on the island.
We were one of them. I am saddened to tell you that our
youngest daughter, Charlotte has died.
Our grief has been so difficult that I don't believe it will ever
leave. So, I have put away the tiara — the gift for Charlotte
from the king. I can't look at it anymore.
This lovely gift, lost all its beauty when my daughter died. This
is a difficult time for all of is. I will write again, when I can.
Love your cousin, Henry."
The Vineyard Historical Letters

*J*onathan stared out at the orange-red glow of the sunset as it hovered just above the calm blue water.

He had been nervous all day, thinking about all the things he needed to say to Lizzie.

An unusual nervousness had fluttered through his veins all day. He wanted share his heart with Lizzie when she met him on the beach this evening.

He loved her, but fear held him back from telling her the truth.

He could tell she was upset at him. He would need to try to overcome her doubts and fears. He would do everything possible, so Lizzie would trust him again.

Looking down, with one hand he smoothed the last edge of the sandcastle he had just built.

Memories of the first time he met Lizzie on this beach as a young girl were pure and clear.

His mind burned with the memory of Lizzie's tears after the sandcastle she'd built had been ground into dust.

His heart swelled with emotion as he remembered her tear-filled smile when he ran down the hill that day to help her rebuild her sandcastle.

Jonathan would never forget a single detail of her face — from years ago or from today.

All he'd ever wanted, was to be with Lizzie.

Since the day he first met her years ago, she had been the only woman for him.

It had devastated him when he learned Lizzie had married.

After a few years, he dated other women, but none of them truly interested him.

The truth was, he could never marry any other woman because his heart had long ago been captured by this beautiful, auburn-haired woman with soft green eyes.

She had left a burning imprint on his heart.

He wasn't about to lose her… *he couldn't.*

Soft footsteps sounded softly on the sand behind him.

Turning, he saw Lizzie walking towards him.

His heart lurched madly at the sight of her.

Her shoulder-length, auburn hair fell in thick waves against her light blue t-shirt. Somehow, making her green eyes shine like polished jade.

Jonathan was pleased to see her wearing lighter colors. To him, it felt like awakening to sunshine whenever Lizzie was nearby.

"Hello, Lizzie." Holding out his hand, he helped her to sit beside him in the sand.

She turned to him, a pensive shiver in the shadow of her eyes. "Hello, Jonathan."

His gaze traveled over her face and searched her eyes.

"I'm glad you decided to meet me here today," Jonathan whispered.

Lizzie nodded. "To be honest, I was debating up until the very last second whether to join you today."

"I understand." And he really did understand. For too long, lack of trust had come between them. "But I'm glad you came, anyway."

She merely nodded, waiting for him.

"I wanted for us to finally have a chance to talk about what happened years ago."

Lizzie sighed. "I know. I'm not sure it will help, but I'll listen."

"Thanks." Uncertainty made him hesitate.

But he knew in his heart it was time she knew everything.

Forcing himself to speak, he began.

"I still remember seeing you on this beach outside your grandmother's cottage when you were twelve years old." Jonathan whispered.

A ghost of a smile appeared on Lizzie's face. "I remember. Those teenagers were playing a game and one of them fell and wrecked my sandcastle. You decided to rebuild what I'd lost."

He continued. "I needed to fix it. Your happy smile when we finished was all the reward that I needed that day."

She turned to him, a small smile on her lips.

Encouraged, Jonathan went on. "After that day, we began to see each other when school started and we became good friends."

She nodded, listening in silence.

"I was so amazed that you, Lizzie, would choose to be my friend." Jonathan filtered sand through his fingers nervously. "You see, for years before we moved to the Island, with every school I went to I was treated as an outcast. Whenever we moved to a new town, folks soon found out that my dad was an angry drunk. When they learned about my family problems, I was rejected by my friends."

A crease formed between Lizzie's brows as she turned to him. "If they rejected you because of family problems, then it wasn't you that had the problem, it was them."

Jonathan chuckled. "You see? I was safe with you because I knew you would always stick up for me."

She smiled at him, recognizing the truth of his words.

Jonathan swallowed and continued his tale. "It was incredible to me to have a friend who stood by me through thick and thin. My mom said she noticed I smiled a lot more after we moved to Martha's Vineyard. Even having a drunk dad who hit us regularly and called us good-for-nothing kids, wasn't so hard to deal with when I had at least one friend."

He turned to Lizzie and saw her eyes misting. "I'm sorry you went through all that pain."

Jonathan shrugged in resignation. "It was all I knew."

Silence stretched between them until Jonathan spoke again.

"I think my experiences with the ugly side of life made me yearn to find more beauty around me." He stuttered a little, still feeling the emotional effects of his troubled childhood.

"I longed to bring beauty to the world. I always saw beauty in how buildings were designed. So, I started to look at magazines to find photos of beautiful houses."

Lizzie nodded. "That must have been the reason you chose architectural design."

"It was." Jonathan's gaze swept over the beauty of the sunset. "I loved designing beautiful houses right from the start. But even doing what I loved wasn't enough to make me truly happy."

She regarded him with a somber curiosity.

"It was you I was missing in my life all along, Lizzie."

Lizzie swallowed and heaved a sigh. "If you remember, we were starting to become very serious with each other in high school, Jonathan. In fact, I had even dreamed of marrying you after graduation. That's why I was shocked to find you behind the bleachers holding Cecily in your arms and kissing her."

He could hear the hurt in her voice even after all these years.

"And I've regretted that every day since then." The misery of that day still haunted him. "I'm so sorry, Lizzie."

"I am too." She whispered, her voice sounding strained.

Jonathan turned to her, desperate to tell her the truth.

"I need to tell you what happened that day, Lizzie."

She nodded without saying a word.

"I had just gotten off the football field. I started walking behind the bleachers on my way to find you, when Cecily came running up to me." Jonathan shook his head in dismay as he remembered.

"She threw her arms around my neck and started kissing me, telling me she knew we would win the game. That was the exact moment you found me."

Lizzie sighed. "So, Cecily was the one who started that kiss. But I didn't see you trying to push her away."

"I don't know if you remember, but my hands were on her shoulders. I was trying to push her away from me. I finally managed to get her off of me, but you had already left." Jonathan shook his head in regret.

"Later that day, I found the note you wrote me. In that note you wrote you had decided to break up with me and leave for Boston."

She sighed, clasped her slender hands together, and stared at them. "Because I believed that you were fickle and unfaithful to me. And I couldn't stand the thought of your betrayal. It hurt far too much. So, I ran away."

Jonathan nodded. "I know and I'm so sorry. After you left, I missed you so much. The pain of losing you was so fierce that three days later I went to Boston to try to talk to you. One of your sisters gave me your aunt's address. I came to the door, but your aunt wouldn't let me see you."

Lizzie's eyes widened in surprise. "I wasn't aware you came to see me back then."

"I did. I tried a few times to see you. And I even wrote you letters, but I'm not sure if you got them." Jonathan shook his head regretfully.

"I didn't. It looks like I might need to have a talk with my aunt." Lizzie grimaced as she pondered his words.

He nodded and then continued his story. "A year after you left, you were married. Your sister Alex told me the news."

The misery of that time still haunted him.

"For the next few years, I pushed myself to work harder. I did the same thing later when I began college. I figured if I pushed myself hard enough, I wouldn't feel the aching pain of losing you." To his dismay, his voice broke slightly.

Quickly, he swallowed, forcing himself to regain control of his wayward emotions.

An uncertainty crept into his expression as he turned to face the woman he loved.

His eyes widened with surprise when he saw tears running down her cheeks.

Reaching over he squeezed her hand gently. "I'm so sorry, Lizzie. I have so many regrets about how I treated you. Can you ever forgive me?"

She bit her lip and sighed heavily. "I do forgive you, Jonathan. It looks like I got too many things wrong from the beginning."

Jonathan moved closer.

"It's all right. I did too."

Lizzie sighed her green eyes bright with tears. "I misjudged you for so many years. I truly regret that. I'm sorry. Can you forgive me?"

"Of course, I forgive you, my Lizzie." Jonathan sighed in contentment. "I love you. I have loved you ever since I first met you on the beach all those years ago."

Slipping his arms around her, he pulled her close to his side.

Since she moved back to the island, every day his love for her had intensified.

It was time to ask the question his heart had been longing for.

"Lizzie, do you think you'd be willing to give our relationship a second chance?" Jonathan whispered in her ear, eagerly waiting for her answer.

LIZZIE'S wildly beating heart was the only sound she could hear.

Being back in Jonathan's arms was where she wanted to be.

After Jonathan explained his story and what happened

years ago, she was aware she hadn't known all the details of what happened that day.

She did forgive him. And she also decided she would need to have a talk with her aunt. She wanted to know why her aunt stopped her from seeing Jonathan years ago.

It felt wonderful to be back in his arms once again.

Leaning her head against his chest, contentment flooded her soul.

"I'm ready to give our relationship a second chance, Jonathan." She pulled away slightly, so she could see his face.

The smoldering flame she saw in his eyes drew her.

He had unlocked her heart and soul.

She felt like a breathless girl of eighteen again.

His blue eyes darkened with emotion and his gaze moved downward to her lips.

Pulling her close to him, he moved his mouth over hers, devouring its softness.

The touch of his lips was a delicious sensation that sent shock waves through her body.

She drew his face to hers in a renewed embrace, kissing him back, lingering, and savoring every second.

By the time he finally lifted his mouth from hers, she was breathless.

"I love you. You, my Lizzie, are definitely worth the wait," Jonathan whispered.

A rush of pink stained her cheeks and her pulse beat and swelled as though her heart had risen from its usual place.

He had revived her dead heart and once again she felt blissfully happy, fully alive.

SHE HELD Jonathan's hand as they walked back to her home.

It was a wonderful feeling to be back together as a couple.

As they came around the bend near the beach cottage, her jaw dropped and heart sank at the sight of the woman who was her nemesis waiting for her.

Jonathan grip tightened on her hand. "Looks like Ava is waiting for you. Do you want to talk to her?"

Her stomach spun in circles at the protective tenderness in his voice.

Lizzie sighed. "It's alright. I'll talk with her and see what she wants."

Her heart beat faster. With Ava's mom being questioned by the police, she doubted this was a good idea.

"I'll be right around the corner." Jonathan walked around the side of the house.

She was grateful for his concern.

Straightening her shoulders, Lizzie walked up the steps. "Hello Ava. This is a surprise."

Ava's hands fidgeted with the hem of her shirt. Her brown eyes blinked twice. She swallowed repeatedly.

Nervous energy sucked the air out from around them.

"Hello Lizzie." Her voice rasped. She rushed on. "I realize I'm the last person you want to see right now. But I needed to talk to you."

She wanted to run away, but forced herself to remain rigid. Pent up anger rose to the surface.

"You're right. I don't want to see you. Especially, since

your mom is being questioned by the police right now about her involvement in setting fire to my home." The words poured out of Lizzie, like a damn that was suddenly discharged.

Ava jerked back as if physically struck.

"I know. And I'm so very sorry." This remorseful side of Ava, was a real shock to Lizzie.

The woman had been quick to question and criticize her ever since she moved to the island.

At her apology, Lizzie couldn't help feel a little skeptical at the change of heart.

"Why would you be sorry? I thought you wanted to see this project fail." Lizzie pressed for answers.

Ava sighed. "I doubted you Lizzie, but I never wanted this. If it turns out my mom is responsible, I want you to know I had no part in it."

She took a breath and rushed on. "My mom has always been determined to get her way. All my life I've done everything I could to please my mom. I've tried to win her approval and failed. Many times, she got me to do her dirty work. But not this time. I just wanted you to know that." Ava swallowed repeatedly.

Lizzie nodded. "Thanks for telling me. I'm glad you weren't part of your mother's terrible plan. But, that doesn't change the fact that the fire damaged some of my most precious heirlooms and memories."

"I'm truly sorry. And I mean it. That's all I have to say." Ava sent her a quick nod and hurried towards her car.

As she watched Ava walk away, she shook her head and sighed.

Someday, Lizzie hoped she'd be able to forgive her.

Jonathan's footsteps echoed behind her.

"Are you okay?" With gentle fingers, he touched her shoulder, his blue eyes filled with concern.

Lizzie released an angry breath. "I'm okay. Ava told me she's sorry and that she wasn't part of her mother's scheme to start the fire. But I can't but feel anger towards Ava and her mother."

"That's understandable."

Lizzie rubbed the back of her neck. "I hope I can forgive those women someday. At this moment, there's too much pain and anger inside me. But, I don't want to hang onto it."

She remembered her grandmother. "Grams told us girls often not to let bitterness fester inside of us. She said, it will only hurt you and not the person you're angry at. I guess all the anger inside me, is something I'll need to work through."

Jonathan nodded. "You're more generous than most people would be in similar circumstances. But, I believe your Grams is right. I was angry at my dad for years for how he treated his family. When I finally forgave him and let it go, I felt more peaceful."

"You're inspiring. I'll do my best to follow your example." Lizzie swallowed back emotion. "It won't be easy, though."

Jonathan grabbed her hand and squeezed. "Forgiving those who have hurt us is never easy. But, it's worth it in the end."

Lizzie stood motionless for a minute, pondering his words. The truth was, it would take every ounce of strength she had and extra prayers to be able to forgive Ava and her mother.

"I'm sure you're right, Jonathan. I think I just need some time." Lizzie said. Turning, she looked over at the house. "Should we go inside? I'll show you the fire damage in the den."

He nodded and they walked inside the house together.

Jonathan said. "I'm glad the fire didn't get to the entire house. Did they get all the damage cleaned up in the Den?"

"Yes, but the walls are still colored black and yellow." Lizzie turned to him. "Do you want to come see for yourself?"

Jonathan nodded. "I would."

Together they walked into the house and towards the den.

As she opened the door to the den, she heard Jonathan's intake of breath.

"Oh, Lizzie, the room looks awful, doesn't it?" His words were more of a statement than a question.

Lizzie nodded. She could only agree.

"It's truly a desolate room now. Even my painting was fire damaged and had to be thrown away." She swallowed the despair in her throat.

Jonathan pulled her close to his side. "I'm sorry, Lizzie, for all you've lost. But I promise we'll rebuild it again."

She could only manage a quick nod.

"Looks like the bricks near the mantle were bent out of shape from the heat of the fire." Jonathan walked towards the mantle.

Lizzie watched as he reached up and grabbed a couple of bricks trying to put them back in their places.

Without warning, a small portion of the brick wall caved in and the bricks went falling to the other side.

"What just happened?" Jonathan peered into the gaping hole in the wall. "Lizzie, you're not going to believe what I'm seeing."

Lizzie hurried over to where he stood.

"What?" She stepped closer to stand beside him. Standing on her tiptoes, she peered into the large hole.

Her eyes widened in surprise. "It's another room. Like a secret room."

Jonathan grinned. "It looks like it. Shall we see if we can find a way inside?"

"Let's do it." Lizzie and Jonathan began to remove the bricks that blocked the way into the room, one by one.

Finally, there was enough space to walk into the secret room.

Lizzie looked around the small rectangular shaped room. Her eyes widened when she saw shelves with rare books, a few knicks and knacks and some paintings leaning up against the wall.

"This is incredible." Jonathan ran a hand gently over some of the old books. "There are first edition books in this collection."

Lizzie walked over to look at the collection of paintings. "I can't believe there are paintings here by artists like Thomas Gainsborough and Sir Joshua Reynolds. These artists lived in the 1700s. Looks like my Great-Grandparents loved art."

"Truly amazing." Jonathan looked around the room, stopping when he saw a shiny object on the shelf. "What's this?"

Lizzie walked to stand beside him.

Jonathan whispered as he held the object in his hand. "It looks like a really old tiara. You know the kind that real princesses used to wear."

"A tiara?" Lizzie used one finger to wipe off the dust.

Jonathan nodded. "And it looks like it was made of real gold and silver too."

Lizzie shook her head amazed. Ceaseless inward questions began nagging at her.

"Wait a minute, my grandmother mentioned a tiara. I've been reading her journal in the past few weeks." Excitement began to build in Lizzie as she told the tale.

"Apparently, my Great-Grandfather Henry Stafford was on one of his trips with his ship near Australia. A visiting king was there with his young daughter. Grandmother said that the princess nearly died, but Great-Grandfather saved her life. The king was so grateful, that he gave Henry Stafford a tiara with a pink diamond to give to his daughter."

"Is she still living?"

She shook her head.

"Great-Grandfather's youngest daughter died from a fever when she was a child. My Grandfather, William Stafford, was the only one that lived." Lizzie hesitated for a moment, thinking about her grandmother's tale. "But if this is the same tiara, then where is the pink diamond?"

Jonathan turned the tiara over in his hands searching for any sort of gemstones.

"I see a few tiny white diamonds near the front of the tiara, but see here? It looks like there are six prongs here where there should be a gemstone. Could this be the spot where the pink diamond is supposed to be?" Jonathan questioned.

Lizzie nodded. "I think so."

She shook her head, still in shock. "I thought Grams was telling a tall tale. I would never have guessed that the story of Captain Henry Stafford being given a tiara with a pink diamond — was actually true."

"It is surprising." Jonathan pondered. "But now the question is: *Where is the missing pink diamond?"*

Lizzie's gaze met his. "Good question. We need to find the answers to that as well as this: *Did the pink diamond simply go missing or did someone steal it?"*

Jonathan shook his head. "I believe we've opened a bigger can of worms than we realize."

Lizzie nodded. "I think that might be true."

An alarming awareness washed over her.

She whispered, "It's unbelievable to think we wouldn't have found this secret room and the treasures inside — without the fire that ravaged the den."

At that moment, something clicked in her mind.

A flash of insight so powerful came to her from a place beyond logic and reason.

"The fire that destroyed the den — my safe place — turning it into ashes, has become a beautiful blessing." Lizzie pondered that for a moment.

"The tragic fire that ravaged this room — the place that held the best of my memories — has been turned around into treasure. This is a reflection of what's happened in my life over the past six months. It's a transformation that has brought me beauty for ashes."

As those deep thoughts swirled in her mind, a warm glow flowed through her.

A sense of strength came upon her and her despair lessened as she thought about all that had happened.

Turning to Jonathan, her heart sang with happiness.

Jonathan whispered, "Beauty for ashes. That's an inspiring thought."

He pulled her into his embrace. "We might have found treasure and beauty in this room today, but I believe the treasure and beauty my heart has been longing for is right here in my arms, my Lizzie."

She tingled as he said her name.

Lizzie looked into his burning blue eyes full of promises.

Cupping her chin, he searched her upturned face and placed a gentle kiss on her lips.

As she drank in the sweetness of his kiss, her thoughts spun.

Her heart leapt with happiness.

Their adventure together was just beginning.

EPILOGUE

 *even months later...*

A WARM BREEZE drifted through the air as Jonathan stood on the sandy beach.

His gaze drifted over the small crowd of guests. They were sitting not far from the archway where he stood.

Samuel stood beside him as his best man. Lizzie's sons had agreed to be groomsmen.

Alex had agreed to be Lizzie's maid of honor. Her bridesmaids were Jane and Annie.

The bridesmaids wore light colors of blue, pink, and purple — perfect for their beach wedding.

A smile lingered on his lips.

His heart beat faster as he waited for the woman he loved.

It was still hard to believe that today was his wedding day.

After they bared their souls to each other seven months ago, they had seen each other every day.

After months of waiting, he couldn't delay any longer.

He was going to marry the one woman he loved for years.

One evening in spring, as they walked along the beach in front of Lizzie's new inn, he asked her to be his wife.

He'd been worried she wouldn't want to be married again.

He'd been worried her children wouldn't accept him as part of their lives.

He'd been worried she would change her mind about loving him.

But his worries had been unwarranted.

She'd said yes.

When Lizzie told him June was a perfect month to get married, he was more than happy to agree.

She'd wanted a beach wedding.

So many of their best memories had happened on the beach.

Soft wedding music played in the background.

Jonathan looked up and smiled wide.

Lizzie wore a simple ivory-colored, cocktail-length dress. She had white pearls in her hair and over one arm carried a spray of red roses with white baby's breath.

Their old neighbor Jeb Whetstone had agreed to walk with Lizzie to the archway where Jonathan stood next to the minister. Jeb had known Lizzie's grandparents,

parents, and Lizzie since she was a little girl, so somehow it seemed appropriate.

Jonathan couldn't take his eyes off his bride.

He blinked back tears that pricked the back of his eyelids at the sight of her.

She was so beautiful.

At that moment, their eyes met.

Lizzie sent him a wide smile that made his heart beat faster.

Jonathan reached out his hand, with his palm up and, without hesitation, Lizzie placed her soft hand in his.

Even as the pastor spoke, their eyes connected.

Soon, it was his turn to speak his vows.

He'd never been more ready.

His gentle words were for her ears alone. "I am forever grateful to have this second chance at love with you, my Lizzie. Ours will be a forever love that will never end. I love you."

The vow he spoke was short, but it said everything in his heart on their wedding day. He slipped the ring on her finger.

Lizzie whispered her vow, "Jonathan, you have accepted me and loved me, flaws and all. It's been many years since we first met on the beach when we were children. I knew you would be important in my life back then. But today I'm happy you've become my forever love. I love you."

As Lizzie slipped the wedding band on his finger, Jonathan exhaled a long sigh of contentment.

Before the minister could say, you may kiss your bride,

Jonathan pulled her close and gently pressed his lips against hers.

&

LIZZIE QUIVERED at the sweet tenderness of his kiss.

She felt transported on a soft, dainty cloud and she slipped her arms around his neck.

Her thoughts spun in circles, dizzy with a new found happiness.

She was grateful for Jonathan and for their second chance at love.

The cheering of the wedding guests shattered the intimacy of their shared moment.

Pulling back, her smile widened as her gaze met his.

As soon as the minister announced them as husband and wife, Jonathan grabbed her hand.

They walked between the rows of people while the wedding guests clapped and cheered.

Lizzie was happy when Jonathan's mom was one of the first to congratulate them afterwards.

"Welcome to our family, Lizzie. I'm very thankful my son is finally wed to the one woman he's loved for so long." Mrs. Brookes stepped forward to give her a hug. "I look forward to getting to know you and your children better. Let's make sure we get together often."

"I'd like that, Mrs. Brookes."

The older lady squeezed her hand. "My dear, please call me Mom. I can't think of anything I'd like more."

Lizzie grinned. "All right I will. Thanks Mom."

Jonathan's sisters came to wish them well.

"I've always thought you would be the perfect wife for Jonathan. I'm happy you've joined our family now, Lizzie." Mary Beth grinned and gave her a quick hug.

Sue Ann gave a quick hug too and whispered in her ear, "I'm glad we're finally sisters."

A bright smile turned up the corners of Lizzie's mouth at the welcome she was given by Jonathan's family.

Later, many friends also stopped to wish them happiness.

"Lizzie, I am not surprised you married Jonathan, I saw this coming months ago. I'm only surprised it took so long." Tess grinned. "You deserve every happiness, Lizzie. I'm so happy for you."

A warm glow flooded her at her friend's support. "Thank you, Tess. Your words mean so much to me."

"I'm happy for you, my friend." Tess hugged her and hurried to hug Jonathan too.

Sheriff Hart walked up to them. "It's good to see you two married. My wife mentioned she thought the two of you made a good team, and I agree. As you know, your dad was a good friend of mine, Lizzie. We wanted to show our support."

Lizzie smiled. "Thanks, Sheriff. We're glad you came today."

With a furrowed brow, he asked, "I understand you went to visit Vera Cantrell after she was sentenced to jail-time, Lizzie."

She nodded, sighing heavily. "Since her conviction and the five-year jail sentence, I wanted to talk to her."

"And how did that go?" He questioned, filled with curiosity.

Lizzie sighed, shaking her head in regret. "Not good. Vera wasn't happy to see me. I asked her about why she hired Maeve to set my house on fire, in the first place."

"Vera told me she wanted the Stafford beach house all her life. And since I wasn't going to sell it, and her daughter Ava didn't have the courage to do it, she needed to take extreme measures to convince me to sell the house to her."

Sheriff Hart shook his head. "She was desperate. The good news is, you don't have to worry about her anymore."

"I hope that's true." A quiver shot up her spine as she recalled the hate in Vera's eyes. "She also was the one that asked that reporter to write those lies about me in that article in *The Vineyard Bulletin*. So, she really was scheming to get rid of me since I moved to Sweet Beach Cove."

"Sounds like Vera really was desperate. But that chapter in your life is over and done." Sheriff Hart promised.

Lizzie commented, "I'm glad you could use your connections to help Maeve get a job at that half-way house, Sheriff."

"It's only because you decided to speak up for her, Lizzie. She should be thankful every day that you didn't press further charges." Sheriff Hart commented.

"After talking with Maeve, I believe she was truly sorry and regretted her actions. As a single mom who has also struggled to make ends meet, I felt she deserved a second chance," Lizzie said.

"Not everyone would be so kind," The sheriff said, shaking his head. "But I'm glad you're satisfied."

"I am satisfied about that situation. However, there's another question that's been troubling me." Lizzie shifted her feet, questions going through her mind as her gaze met his. Now after the fire, she decided it wasn't too late after all to search for the truth of what happened years ago.

"What's that?"

"Since my grandmother passed away, I've been reading through her journals. Grams wrote that she wasn't convinced that someone didn't deliberately cause my parents' death in the boating accident years ago. Do you have any thoughts on that Sheriff?" Lizzie bit her lip, curious as to what he'd say.

Sheriff Hart hesitated, measuring her for a moment. "For starters, we closed that case years ago. Your parents' death was tragic, but we deemed it an accident, Lizzie."

Lizzie pushed forward, needing answers. "But, if there were people that wanted the case to be reopened because they had fresh evidence to bring forward, would that cause the police to reopen the case?"

"Well, if there was enough evidence and someone could prove that it wasn't a simple boating accident, then yes, I suppose they would reopen the case." The sheriff looked puzzled. "Do you have additional evidence, Lizzie?"

Lizzie shook her head. "Not yet. But I am concerned by what my grandmother wrote in her journal. That's why I wanted to ask."

"Well, I wouldn't worry about your grandmother's

ramblings, Lizzie. Maybe, she started to go out of her mind at her advanced age." Sheriff Hart's expression darkened with an unreadable emotion. "Besides, I don't think it would be wise to reopen that case. You might not like the consequences."

She swallowed hard, trying to manage a feeble answer. "Thanks, sheriff."

"I should be going. Again, congratulations on your marriage." Sheriff Hart nodded and put two fingers on his hat before walking away.

The nagging in the back of her mind refused to be stilled as she watched the sheriff walk away.

It continued even as they spoke to the rest of the wedding guests.

After talking with the last person, Jonathan took her by the hand.

"Let's walk along the beach for a little while before we head back to the house to be with our families." He whispered.

She happily agreed.

*

As Jonathan and her strolled along the water's edge, she turned to him a crease between her brows.

"What's this?" With his finger he touched the deep lines on her forehead. "You shouldn't be worrying on your wedding day."

"I found the sheriff's last remark very disturbing." Lizzie said. "It was almost like he was warning me. Telling me I shouldn't meddle and try to reopen that case regarding my parents' death. He said I might not like the consequences." Lizzie's misgivings increased by the minute. "What do you think he meant by that?"

Jonathan hesitated, worry etched in the lines of his face. "I'm not sure. But if I were to guess, it's possible you'll find out details about your parents' boating accident years ago that will shock you."

She chewed on her lower lip as fear gripped her. "I don't know. But the way he warned me to stay away from searching for answers worries me. Now, I am more determined than ever to uncover the truth."

"Then you should search for answers. Don't let the sheriff or anyone else stop you, Lizzie." Jonathan's calm words encouraged her.

"Thanks, Jonathan." She looked out at the ocean as they walked along the sand. "But now let's forget about troubling mysteries and focus on happier things… *like the two of us.*"

"I agree." Jonathan pulled her to his side.

As they walked along the beach, Lizzie thought of all that had happened.

The last year had flown by.

She had been so busy with setting up and getting The Vineyard Inn running, that time had flown by.

By Thanksgiving weekend, they had restored the den and the first guests were booked for their stay at The Vineyard Inn.

After that weekend, there had been a steady flow of visitors who scheduled their stay at the inn.

She exhaled a long sigh of contentment.

Annie was now working as a designer for many businesses in Sweet Beach Cove on a contract basis. She was doing well, but she was alone now. She hoped someday her daughter would meet a man who loved Annie like Jonathan loved her.

Will had begun to come regularly to the island.

The last time he visited, Will apologized again about being angry with her after her dad passed away. Her son assured her, he was happy about her move to Martha's Vineyard and believed starting the inn had been a great idea.

Sarah stopped by the inn more often too. Lizzie was curious to see if her oldest son and Sarah would get serious about each other. Time would tell.

Jake was seeing Emma more often as well. In between jobs for his skills at creating wood projects, he found time to date Emma.

Her smile broadened in approval as she thought of both her son's choices in women.

How would her new marriage affect her children?

"You're deep in thought." Jonathan whispered. "What's on your mind?"

"I was thinking about us. It will be a change for my children to get used to seeing us together." Lizzie grinned. "I want them to see you as the kind and thoughtful man I know you to be. To love you as I do."

Jonathan smiled, slipping an arm around her shoulders. "You are a wonderful woman, kind and generous. And I can't wait to get to know your children better. I hope they will grow to love me. I love you very much, Lizzie."

She saw the heart-rending tenderness of his gaze and her heart turned over in response.

"I love you too, Jonathan." She sighed. "You were a wonderful surprise in my life. When I first moved to my grandmother's house, I never thought I would marry again. But then I never counted on us rekindling our relationship."

"I'm told by my sisters that I can be surprising, at times." Jonathan winked. "Are you saying I swept you off your feet?"

Lizzie chuckled, loving their playful banter. "You certainly did. And I couldn't be happier."

"I'm happy too, my Lizzie," Jonathan spoke softly, his hand squeezing her shoulders.

She leaned her head on his shoulder and sighed with contentment.

For a long moment they stood side-by-side in the stillness, staring over at the horizon line, watching where the red-orange glow of the sunset met the deep blue waters.

Jonathan whispered into the stillness of the evening.

"I remember when I first met you on this beach. As a young boy, when I first saw you building your sandcastle, it was your radiant smile that drew me to you. I longed to experience a little of the happiness I saw on your face."

Her thoughts filtered back to the day she'd met him.

She remembered the skinny boy who stuttered his words like he was scared. Her heart ached at the memory.

Jonathan's voice broke with huskiness, "Then the teenager wrecked your sandcastle and you cried. I was so upset. I was determined to do whatever I could to help rebuild your sandcastle. Something deep inside me, yearned to see your beautiful smile again."

With gentle hands, turned her so she could look into his eyes.

"When the fire destroyed the den in your house — and I saw your tears and heartache at the loss — I was determined to help you rebuild that room to see the smile on your face once again," he whispered, his blue eyes earnestly seeking hers.

Managing no more than a hoarse whisper, Lizzie said, "And you rebuilt it. The den is now fully restored."

She fingered the collar of his white shirt. "You have always been the one who has helped me smile again, Jonathan. You first did it years ago, when you helped me rebuild my ruined sandcastle and later when you worked to rebuild and restore my den that the fire destroyed."

Lizzie's voice was an indistinct murmur. "Jonathan, you have brought me happiness, over and over again. And I'm so very grateful for you."

He leaned over and kissed her forehead and the tip of her nose.

Jonathan's throaty voice was low and smooth, "You must know by now I will do everything I can to make you happy. When the fire destroyed so much of what you love, I knew the wedding gift I wanted to give you."

Her eyes widened, and she turned to him. "What is it?"

Jonathan chuckled. "About six months ago, I asked Lucca Lommbardi to recreate the original painting of your grandmother's beach house that his dad painted. I wanted to give the painting to you as a gift, because I know how much it meant to you. It's waiting for you at the house."

A single tear made its way down her cheeks. "Oh, Jonathan. Thank you. That means so much to me. I will treasure it always."

Jonathan kissed her forehead. "You're welcome."

"My wedding gift for you is unexpected, but I hope you'll like it." Lizzie began. "I remember your dog died years ago. Well, I decided to give you a new puppy. We can pick her up after we're back from our trip in two weeks."

Jonathan raised his eyebrows, a big smile lighting up his face. "I can't wait. Thank you, Lizzie. It's perfect."

She saw the tenderness of his gaze and she sighed.

He whispered, "I have never loved any woman as much as I love you. You are the sunshine of my life, my Lizzie."

A passionate fluttering arose in her chest at the heated look in his eyes.

His lips came coaxingly down on hers.

She felt her knees weaken as his mouth descended.

She kissed him back, lingering, savoring every moment.

His arms tightened around her and shivers of delight followed his gentle touch.

This man who held her in his arms, was now her husband. He was her forever love.

Lizzie was wrapped in a silken cocoon of euphoria.

The sandcastle girl had been transformed.

What was once ashes in her life had become beautiful.

This, her wedding day, was a new beginning and her second chance for a forever-kind of love.

৯৯

THANK YOU FOR READING LIZZIE'S STORY!
READY TO READ ALEXANDRA'S LOVE STORY?
Get your copy of *The Vineyard Neighbors & Friends(Sweet Beach Cove Series Book #2)*.

When Dr. Alex Stafford is unexpectedly let go from her position as a children's doctor at Mercy Children's Hospital in Boston, she is forced to make a change.

When her grandmother died, she bequeathed to Alex an old house. In her Will, Grams asked if Alex would be willing come back and be a children's doctor on the island.

Alex doesn't want to return.
Fear still haunts her memories of when she was attacked by a man when she was 16 years old. Ever since that day, she's hasn't allowed herself to be in a relationship with a man.

As soon as she returns, she begins renovating Gram's old house which is located near the downtown of Sweet Beach Cove community.
She hires local construction workers with the work.

In between renovating the house and visiting her sisters, Alex runs into a past love... her boyfriend from years ago. Recently widowed, Samuel Chadsworth lives in the sweet beach cove community with his eight year old daughter Zoe.

But they begin to talk and Alex begins to see Sam as a friend and his daughter as an adorable little girl.
As she begins to settle into her place on the island, she is happy to see her six sisters more often. As she talks with her sisters about their parent's death when they were children, Alex has questions.

She decides it is time to find answers. With Sam's help and the support of her sisters, Alex begins to uncover answers that none of them expected... or wanted.

As events begin to unfold, Alex is threatened to stop asking questions or there will be trouble.

In the end, Alex comes face-to-face with the man who attacked her as a teenager. Is the man related to the mystery surrounding her parents deaths?

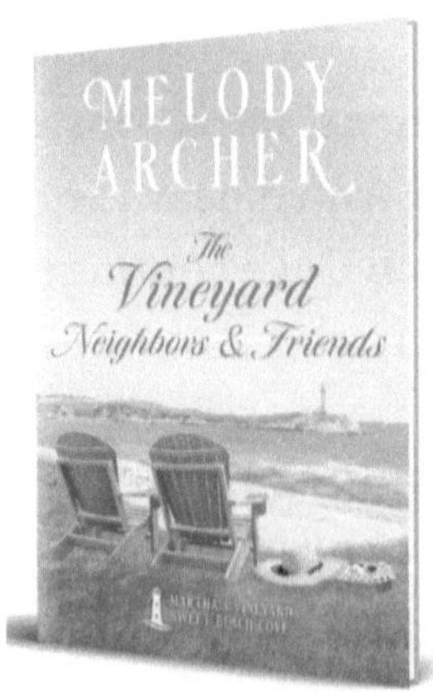

ALSO BY MELODY ARCHER

Clean Billionaire Fake Marriage Romance Series

Book 1: The Billionaire's Marriage Pact

Book 2: The Billionaire's Marriage Contract

Book 3: The Billionaire's Marriage Promise

Book 4: The Billionaire's Marriage Barter

Book 5: The Billionaire's Marriage Pledge

7 Brides for 7 Cowboys, Small Town Sweet Western Romance Series

Book 1: The Forgiven Cowboy's Best Friend

Book 2: The Redeemed Cowboy's Secret Baby

Book 3: The Honorable Cowboy's Convenient Marriage

Book 4: The Wounded Cowboy's Beauty Bride*(coming soon...)*

Books 5, 6 & 7 Still to Come...

Martha's Vineyard Sweet Beach Cove

Women's Fiction Clean Romance Mystery Series

Book 1: The Vineyard Inn

Book 2: The Vineyard Neighbors & Friends

Book 3: The Vineyard Mistletoe Christmas*(coming soon)*

Visit my website below:

www.MemorableFictionBooks.com

ABOUT THE AUTHOR

Melody Archer lives in Alberta with her husband and their four young adults.

Recently, her oldest son married his new wife from Brazil. Their family has been enjoying getting to know their new daughter-in-law.

She loves new and classic romantic movies, green smoothies and going on adventures with her family.

Melody would love to connect with you :)

facebook.com/memorablefictionbooks
instagram.com/memorablefictionbooks
pinterest.com/memorablefictionbooks
youtube.com/@memorablefictionbooks

ACKNOWLEDGMENTS

Thank you to all the wonderful people who helped me
with this book.

To my cover designer, Wilette from Red Leaf Book
Design, thank you for designing this gorgeous book cover.

Thank you also, to my very helpful proofreader Michaela
Hofer who patiently read through each chapter, helping
me make this story so much better.

A big thanks to all my wonderful Advanced Readers (my
ARC reading team), who faithfully read this book.

Lastly, a huge thanks to two of my young adult children
who read through the manuscript, giving me all kinds of
great suggestions on how to make this a better story.

Thank you everyone. I really appreciate you!:)

Copyright ©June 2024 by Lorna Faith Kopp

All rights reserved.

No part of this publication may be reproduced, distributed, or transmitted in any form or by any means, or stored in a database or retrieval system, without the written permission of the publisher.

The only exception is brief quotations in printed reviews. The reproduction or utilization of this work in whole or in part in any form whether electronic, mechanical or other means, known hereafter invented, including xerography, photocopying and recording, or in any information storage retrieval system, is forbidden without the written consent of the publisher and/or author.

Thank you for respecting the hard work of this author. This edition if published by Lorna Faith Kopp. First eBook Edition: ©June 2024.

This is a work of fiction. Names, characters, places, and incidents are either the creation of the author's imagination or are used fictitiously, and any resemblance to actual persons living or dead, business establishments, events or locales is entirely coincidental.

www.ingramcontent.com/pod-product-compliance
Lightning Source LLC
Chambersburg PA
CBHW032343310726
48973CB00007B/1836